I0564277

By Eldon Murphy

(Writing as Dean Murray)

Reflections

Broken

Torn

Splintered

Intrusion

Numb

Trapped

Forsaken

Riven

Driven

Lost

Marked

Dark Reflections

Bound

Hunted

Ambushed

Shattered

Burned

The Awakening

Reborn

Immortal

Endless

A Broken World

The Society

The Destroyer

The Warlord

The Founder

The Desolation

Reflections

(Dean Writing as Eldon)

The Greater Darkness

A Darkness Mirrored

The Compelled Chronicles

Stone Heart

The Guadel Chronicles

Frozen Prospects

Thawed Fortunes

I'rone

Brittle Bonds

Shattered Ties

The Greater Darkness

Eldon Murphy

The Greater Darkness is a work of fiction. Names, characters, places and incidents are the products of the author's imagination or are used fictitiously. Any resemblance to actual events, locales, or persons, living or dead, is entirely coincidental.

Copyright 2012 by Eldon Murphy

All rights reserved.

Published by Fir'shan Publishing

ISBN 978-1-9393630-8-4

www.FirshanPublishing.com

First Edition

The image used in the creation of the cover for this book is copyrighted by Kylee Ann Photography (www.kyleeann.com) and is used with permission.

For everyone who has risked everything to save someone else

Chapter 1

Geoffrey's legs were starting to cramp up from remaining motionless for so long. It was to the point now where the pain exceeded even the hunger that had been present for as long as he could remember. Still, he was reluctant to move. His memories were no longer able to guide him, so feelings had taken on greater importance. Remaining motionless *felt* important.

Finally the agony became too much, and Geoffrey steadied himself on the handrail as he slowly shifted positions. This fire escape, like most in the poor sections of the city, had long since started to rust in the humid New York summers. Some landlord, no doubt looking to cut costs, had ordered the metal painted over without first having it scoured clean. Of course the paint had continued to flake off over the years, requiring yet more coats. The latest coat had been applied fairly recently, resulting in something that felt smooth, despite an underlying texture of decay.

Geoffrey suppressed a shiver as he stroked the pitted metal and whispered silently to himself. "So you woke up in a bare room with no memories of your past. A knowledge of how to remain undetected while watching someone doesn't have to mean that you're a cold-blooded assassin. Just because Imastious says something is so, doesn't necessarily mean it's the truth."

It was a conversation he'd had with himself several times, but he couldn't escape the feeling that there was some truth to the other man's cold, casual allegations. If so, then his amnesia was nothing more than a thin finish that hid a corroded soul.

The longer Geoffrey sat pondering in the darkness, the more the night took on an oppressive, heavy feeling. Most of the streetlights in this section of town had long since stopped working, leaving only the harsh light of neon signs in the storefront shops below to wage a losing war against the darkness.

The feeling that he was somehow exposed, that someone was watching him as intently as he was watching the dark window before him, had grown so powerful that Geoffrey was having difficulty not looking over his shoulder. Finally a faint sound from the other side of the glass signaled the return of the apartment's tenant.

THE GREATER DARKNESS

Sliding carefully back out of sight, Geoffrey breathed a sigh of relief as the barely-visible front door swung open and the lights came on.

The twenty-something black man who swung the door shut behind him matched the picture that Imastious had given Geoffrey. Every detail was perfect, right down to the heavy gold jewelry and eyes that seemed to say that he no longer blinked at doing the kinds of things that would give most people nightmares.

A wave of something that felt like anticipation crept through Geoffrey, flushing his body with strength at the same time that it sickened him. The mind had forgotten, but apparently the body still remembered what to do in these types of circumstances.

Geoffrey's abrupt decision not to act, to put off the execution for at least a few more hours, calmed his mind but not his body. He was shaking as he quietly climbed down to the bottom of the fire escape, dropped to the ground and disappeared into the night.

Geoffrey covered several blocks in a slow walk before he realized why he kept looking reflexively over his shoulder. Apparently even the habit of looking for someone following him had become instinctive to whoever or whatever he had been. Suddenly the meandering routes he had picked over the last few days made more sense too. What better way could there be to tell whether or not someone was tailing you than to turn a corner and just see who followed?

Carefully steering clear of a large pile of garbage that left his nose burning, Geoffrey ended up a few inches from what had to be one of the cleaner windows in that part of the city. Pausing before the storefront, Geoffrey examined the reflection peering back at him through the protective bars.

The dark-haired young man who stared back was someone he would have called unremarkable other than the fact that he was hard-pressed to put an age to himself. It was a youthful face, but one that could have belonged to a late teen or even someone in their late twenties.

A casual perusal of the billboards and posters that seemed to populate every visually prominent piece of real estate in the city showed a male ideal that fluctuated between massively over-muscled and nearly effeminate. Given that, there was a chance that the high cheekbones and slender frame in the window's reflection would be considered handsome. The real question, though, was what exactly the troubled depths of his eyes concealed.

The seemingly ever-present hunger pulled Geoffrey's thoughts back to more mundane things. Most of the restaurants had closed hours ago. There was a chance one of the small corner stores would still be open, but he didn't hold out much hope. Even if he found someplace to buy food, so far eating hadn't actually done anything to calm the hunger.

Concentrating as he was on finding something to eat, Geoffrey almost ignored the faint sounds coming from the alley he was passing. Something tugged him towards the noise though, so he turned and crept into the near darkness of the alley. Geoffrey's heart sped up when he got far enough around the large dumpster to see two sloppily-dressed teens who had cornered a trembling, middle-aged Latina against a chain-link fence. Geoffrey was still trying to decide what to do next when one of the boys backhanded the woman, knocking her to the ground.

The other teen reached down and opened up the woman's purse only to start swearing as he found it nearly empty. Before either boy could contemplate further action, Geoffrey made up his mind and ghosted between them and their victim.

"Leave her." The words came out with such a cold indifference that a part of Geoffrey was startled, but the numbness actually matched perfectly with how he felt.

The two teenagers seemed startled by the inhuman feel to his voice. They stood motionless for several seconds and then sprang into action, as Geoffrey had somehow known they would.

The attacker behind Geoffrey lashed out with a wild-looking punch that, for all of its inelegance, still probably would have hurt whoever happened to be on the receiving end. Only it never landed. Geoffrey's body seemed almost to react on its own, throwing his right leg back and up, driving his heel into the teen's ribs with a grating crunch that flung the mugger backwards.

The second teenager threw a slightly more controlled punch a split second before his friend crashed into the building's brick wall. Again Geoffrey reacted without thinking, reaching up with his left hand to pluck the approaching fist out of the air.

A sharp tug on the captured wrist pulled the second youth off balance and brought him stumbling towards Geoffrey. Before the attacker could recover, Geoffrey's right hand darted out and clamped over the teen's throat, picking him up and slamming him into the wall opposite his fallen friend.

The force of the blow was sufficient to cause the boy's head to rebound off of the wall with a hollow thud. For a split second Geoffrey worried that he'd killed the would-be mugger, but the steady pulse surging through the carotid artery, just beneath his right index finger, said otherwise.

Geoffrey meant to turn and check on the woman. Instead he found himself unable to look away from the still figure pinned against the wall. The boy hung limply, motionless save for the rise and fall of his chest, and the almost imperceptible movement of the blood just beneath Geoffrey's finger.

Geoffrey was pretty sure he couldn't actually see the boy's pulse, but for all that it had to be nothing more than his imagination, he couldn't seem to see anything but that now-erratic motion.

The hunger felt like it was taking on a life of its own, causing Geoffrey's hand to tighten ever so slightly. The teen's pulse seemed to become more powerful as the pressure increased. The hunger seemed to demand more, to demand that Geoffrey clamp down harder. He squeezed harder and harder until suddenly he realized he had cut off the supply of blood to the kid's brain.

The pulse beneath Geoffrey's finger hammered away wildly as the heavily beating heart tried to force blood past his hand and up to the oxygen-starved brain. Geoffrey felt his trembling upper lip curl away from his teeth as he was nearly overcome by the desire to sink his canines into the teen's throat.

Nausea suddenly crashed through Geoffrey's body, leaving him feeling cold and filthy as he realized what he had wanted to do. What kind of person would do something so savage?

Shaking slightly, Geoffrey slowly lowered the teen until the unconscious body was resting motionless on the concrete.

Thoughts of running, of fleeing the scene, suddenly seemed distant as the physical effects of alternate waves of desire and disgust fully caught up with Geoffrey, and he collapsed to the ground. Even worse, the hunger, only slightly muted by Geoffrey's revulsion, had acquired a new eagerness.

The sudden urge to empty his stomach was too much. Shaking as badly as he was, he barely managed to lean over far enough to avoid soiling himself as heaves racked his body.

Geoffrey couldn't have said how long he sat there, all but kneeling in a pool of his own vomit, but a tentative touch on his shoulder pulled him back to the present.

Reflexes Geoffrey didn't remember training once again took over, causing him to pull the woman's hand downwards as his right hand swept up in what he would later realize was a killing blow to the throat.

A terrified voice pierced the haze surrounding his mind just soon enough for him to pull the blow.

"Lo siento, lo siento, nada mas queria saber si estaba bien."

Geoffrey looked into her eyes and saw the fear he'd been expecting, but not the revulsion. It seemed impossible. Surely she understood just how abhorrent his actions had nearly been.

A wave of dizziness crashed through Geoffrey's body. As he released the poor woman's hand, he collapsed onto the concrete again.

THE GREATER DARKNESS

The fear was still foremost on the Latina's face as she once again cautiously approached Geoffrey, but there was also something that looked like concern.

"Esta bien?"

When Geoffrey responded with nothing more than a blank look, the woman tried again.

"You are okay?"

Geoffrey opened his mouth to respond and realized his eyes were being drawn to the pleasantly dark skin of the woman's neck, skin that was stretched tautly over the muscles and veins to form the most delicate of protective barriers.

Geoffrey's gorge rose once again as he followed his thoughts to their logical conclusion, and he weakly waved the woman away. "I'm fine, please leave me alone."

The woman straightened up, but remained where she was. Suddenly Geoffrey was angry. Didn't she understand what he could do to her? It was all he could do to control himself, to ignore the hunger, and she just sat there like she actually wanted to be killed.

Swatting feebly at the woman, Geoffrey finally lost his temper. "Go away or I'll kill you!"

The concerned eyes that had been staring at Geoffrey widened; he realized he'd been shouting, but before he could decide whether or not to apologize, the woman turned and ran away.

The rest of the trip back to the apartment where he'd first awakened was little more than a blur. The hunger hadn't left, and Geoffrey sensed that it was somehow vital he get off of the streets as soon as possible.

After stumbling up the stairwell and finally arriving at his door, it took Geoffrey three tries to get his pair of locks open. Unfortunately, the place he'd hoped would serve as a kind of refuge was already occupied.

Imastious sat casually on the sofa, dressed as always in black, featureless clothes that sported a high, tight collar. Once again, Geoffrey wondered why Imastious' appearance made him think of churches and sermons. He still couldn't place the resemblance, but it almost felt like Imastious' clothing was the predecessor to something else that Geoffrey hadn't quite managed to place.

The gaunt face looking up at Geoffrey was relaxed. It combined with Imastious' bearing to convey the picture of a man at ease, but the illusion failed for anyone who looked closely enough at his eyes. The half-closed eyes examining Geoffrey seemed to be windows to a soul that was completely amoral, utterly willing to sacrifice anyone or anything in the pursuit of basic self-interest.

Try as he might, Geoffrey couldn't point to any one reason why Imastious seemed old, ancient even. Maybe it was the eyes. It seemed impossible for a young person to have lived long enough to sink to those kinds of levels. That required depraved experience almost beyond understanding.

Those cold eyes measured Geoffrey now, taking in both the slight shaking of his body and his vomit-stained clothes.

"You've not yet completed the task you were given."

Geoffrey thought about lying, claiming that he had indeed killed his target, but before he'd even had a chance to decide one way or another Imastious cut him off.

"Don't bother denying your failure, or rather, your lack of attempt. I already know that he's still alive."

For a split second Geoffrey wondered if Imastious was bluffing, but the emotionless eyes staring back at him seemed impossibly all-knowing. Instead of making the useless protest he'd been considering, he simply remained silent.

Imastious shook his head. "Like it or not, you will learn that I am to be obeyed. You have nowhere else to go, no one else who can protect you if your true nature is revealed."

Imastious struck without warning. Springing to his feet, he grabbed Geoffrey by the throat and slammed him against the wall, exactly as Geoffrey had done to the mugger a short time before.

Geoffrey tried to fight back, lashing out with a largely ineffectual kick, but Imastious' slender limbs and emaciated frame possessed such incredible strength it was like trying to fight back against a vise.

Still moving almost faster than Geoffrey could follow, Imastious grabbed Geoffrey's left wrist, snapping something closed over it Dand then spinning the younger man around violently and doing the same thing to his right wrist. By the time Geoffrey realized he'd been handcuffed, Imastious had thrown him to the floor and manacled his feet.

A strange sense of pressure was building inside Geoffrey's mind, clouding his thoughts, making it difficult to reason or respond to what was happening. As the pressure grew, it was as though Geoffrey lost time. One moment he was bound and gagged on the cold floor, the next thing he knew he was in excruciating pain, his back and arms seemingly on fire. It seemed now that a knife traced an erratic, bloody path down his body, starting at his cheek, near his right eye, and then moving in fits and starts down to his right hand.

When the knife started working its way around the thumb on Geoffrey's right hand he finally passed out.

Chapter 2

Sleep seemed reluctant to let Geoffrey flee its embrace. Even though he'd been dreaming of alternately being tortured and then being forced to drink blood again and again for hours, Geoffrey was equally reluctant to open his eyes. Having finally left his nightmares behind, he now floated in some kind of netherworld, not dreaming but unable to move or waken. When the transition to wakefulness finally arrived, it happened so slowly Geoffrey wasn't initially aware of it. It was actually the realization he wasn't alone that finally pushed him into full lucidity.

The sound of another person breathing was unmistakable, even when so quiet as to sound delicate. Equally telling was the smell of perfume, something incredibly pleasing, made more so by the fact that it bordered on the edge of being undetectable. Still, a woman could kill him just as easily as a man might.

An ethereal voice interrupted Geoffrey's thoughts. "As much as I would love to allow things to proceed at a more leisurely pace, I'm afraid our bloody time is somewhat limited today, so I'm going to have to interrupt your charade and ask that you open your eyes so we can be about the business of the day."

Somewhat hesitantly, Geoffrey opened his eyes and looked towards the corner of the apartment from where the voice had come. The most beautiful woman he had ever seen was currently sprawled across the room's only comfortable chair. Even dressed in worn blue jeans and a form-fitting button-up shirt, she still managed to look like a runway model who just happened to be slumming in his apartment. Even the dingy paint and broken light fixtures behind her only served to highlight her perfection.

Geoffrey started to sit up, only to wince as his muscles protested.

The blue eyes watching him from behind incredibly thick lashes briefly flashed with something that he wanted to call sympathy. Only the goddess before him made no effort to offer aid.

"You're no doubt feeling a bit rocky. Especially considering the fact that you were all but running on empty there at the end."

She tossed her stylishly-arranged platinum-blond hair and rose gracefully to her feet, the businesslike demeanor that she'd been displaying vanishing as she walked over to Geoffrey's bed.

"So how does it feel, love? I mean, do you really not remember anything?"

Geoffrey slowly shook his head. "How do you know that?"

A sly smile accompanied the woman's response. "I know everything about you. I'm honestly surprised you can't remember me. After what we shared I thought some little memory of your beloved Venice would remain. I guess that part wasn't meant to be."

Venice. Geoffrey rolled the name around his mind, half expecting some recollection to make its way up from the dark depths of his memory, but nothing appeared.

Venice was closer now, inching his direction as if worried that a sudden movement would frighten him. As he took in the delicate features and youthful, perfect body, Geoffrey felt a momentary sense of incredible fortune. It seemed impossible that someone so gorgeous would not only know his past, but also be interested in him.

The moment of perfection was ruined as Venice came within arm's reach of Geoffrey and he suddenly got a strong sense of wrongness. It was as if an errant breeze had wafted a subtle scent of decay past him.

The impression lasted only a split second. Once it had fled Geoffrey could detect nothing wrong with the picture of beauty that was moving ever so slowly closer to his lips, but he couldn't shake the sense of unease. It felt like the lovely exterior Venice presented to the world had been peeled back affording him a glimpse of the real person underneath.

Pulling back slightly, Geoffrey tried to sort out his thoughts, but Venice was sitting on the creaky bed now stroking his face.

"Come now, no need to be so shy. I know you better than you can possibly imagine."

When Geoffrey didn't respond Venice shrugged and then stood up. "Suit yourself, love."

Pointing at a long bundle Geoffrey hadn't noticed before, Venice smiled. "I did bring you a present though, something that should warm your cold-blooded little heart. At least in your present state you're controlled enough we can give you a weapon without worrying who you'll decide to chop into little pieces."

Geoffrey opened his mouth to snap back that he wasn't the killer Imastious was making him out to be, only to gasp as he got a strong impression that Venice was telling the truth. There was no way for him to know that she was telling the truth, but he somehow knew that she believed what she'd just told him. Who had he been that he'd thought nothing of killing random bystanders?

As preoccupied as he was about the ramifications of what Venice had just said,

Geoffrey was still able to catch the rest of her departing words.

"Imastious left strict instructions for me to tell you that a continued failure to kill your assigned target will be punished much more harshly than what you experienced last night."

Venice paused for a moment as if to let Geoffrey digest this latest piece of information. "I used to intervene with Imastious on your behalf, and I might be able to persuade him in your favor on some things still, but an attempt to do so puts me in no little risk of disfavor. That's a risk that I'm not willing to entertain for just anyone. You might give that some thought before you casually dismiss my affections again."

Geoffrey remained motionless on his bed for quite some time after Venice's shapely body had disappeared behind the closing door, but no amount of thought illuminated his path in the slightest.

The faintest stirrings of hunger finally pulled Geoffrey out of bed and into motion. The carton of leftover Chinese takeout did nothing to diminish the hunger. It didn't make sense, but it no longer surprised him. Once out of bed, it was only logical to shower and dress in one of the dark button-up shirts and the jeans that seemed to be the only things his closet contained.

Apparently even the damned tended to have a bit cheerier outlook once they were up and moving.

A short time later, Geoffrey found himself standing by the door holding the wrapped bundle that Venice had left. It seemed he had nothing to lose by opening it.

It really shouldn't have been a surprise that the bundle contained a sword, not after Venice's comment about cutting people into little pieces, but the katana inside the layers of cloth took Geoffrey's breath away regardless. It was that exquisite.

Without thinking Geoffrey whipped the blade through several strikes, and then stopped in amazement at how lively and perfect the weapon felt. Examining the sword, Geoffrey saw that the polish on the blade was superb, revealing the grain and hamon of the blade without becoming overly shiny. A hundred other signs, things that Geoffrey hadn't even realized he'd known about before that moment, all pointed towards this being a masterfully crafted weapon.

How did he know all of these things? How many hundreds of hours of practice went into being able to handle a sword as if it were a natural extension of one's arm?

Walking for several hours did little to calm Geoffrey's mind, possibly because the katana hanging at his side served as a constant reminder of exactly the things that were bothering him. He considered returning to the apartment and leaving the weapon there, but couldn't quite bring himself to do it, more because he didn't want to risk letting it out of his sight than because he expected to need it. Consequently, the katana accompanied him, hanging from the cleverly constructed harness that allowed him to hide the weapon under the dark trench coat that the weapon had been initially wrapped in.

The sword was only useful for killing people, but it was still a piece of what he'd been and he couldn't bear to part himself from anything-- even something this grisly--that might help put some of those pieces together.

The darkness didn't have the naked menace of the night before. Instead it had a cold, lonely feel to it that was every bit as bad in its own way. The steady drizzle of rain and the late hour had served to drive nearly all of the city's occupants indoors, while simultaneously muting the sounds of the few hardier souls still about. As a result, it was almost possible to believe Geoffrey was the only person living in the desolate ruins of a once-great city.

The cold had slowly seeped through the trench coat and now was becoming a pressing concern as Geoffrey started to shiver. How had his feet gotten so cold? The streams of water racing down each edge of the street were making steady progress on cleaning up some of the refuse that had been everywhere last night, but that seemed a poor trade for being so miserable.

The shifting curtain of rain almost completely hid the buildings on the other side of the street, but Geoffrey suddenly felt compelled to cross the road. Making his way in the direction of the tugging proved to strengthen the feeling, and Geoffrey was soon standing in front of what appeared to be a church—if the term could be applied to a building in such an obvious state of disrepair.

A pair of paper fliers, illegible after being exposed to the rain, hung from the doors, giving the impression that the church was open for business, as it were. A cautious touch revealed that the door was indeed unlocked, so Geoffrey quietly walked inside.

Once inside it was immediately obvious that a funeral was underway. From what Geoffrey was able to see of the casket, the deceased looked like he was approximately Geoffrey's age.

Other than hard wooden pews, the chapel didn't have many of the features Geoffrey expected from a house of worship. There wasn't any incense burning, the stained glass windows—if there had ever been any—had long since been boarded up, and there wasn't a cross or crucifix to be seen. The plain white plaster walls were clean, as was the dark, wooden floor, but that was about as much as could be said in its favor.

As he completed his survey of the room and its occupants, Geoffrey found his eyes drawn towards the man speaking from the heavily worn pulpit.

"James was, by all accounts, a fine example of a man in most all of the respects that truly matter. In the course of preparing to speak these few words tonight, I talked with many who knew and loved him. When he was sixteen, he drove off two other boys who seemed intent on victimizing a young girl he didn't even know."

Geoffrey spotted a vacant bench at the back of the room, one where he wouldn't have his back to any doors, and silently walked over and sat down.

The speaker continued. "I don't have to tell any of you the kind of risk that act entailed in our city. Offended gang members have shot people for less. But God protected James, and he suffered no harm as a result of his efforts."

Some tightly wound part of Geoffrey started to relax. The sound of rain falling on the roof wasn't loud enough to distract from the speaker, but the steady thrum seemed to echo around inside Geoffrey's head until it felt as if it came from all around him, especially from the people.

"In our city—where education has become a sorry attempt at validating even those students who refuse to put forth a minimal effort to learn—James applied himself and graduated with honors, securing a scholarship to Fordham University."

The thrum pulled Geoffrey's attention towards the front of the chapel where two women, one young, the other old, sat holding each other in a futile effort to calm their mutual grief, to quiet their sobs.

"…most young men in this town drift from one woman to another, fathering children and then taking no responsibility for their education and care. James is survived by his wife of three years, that same young girl he saved years ago."

The priest paused, seemingly gathering his thoughts. "Anytime someone is gunned down in a case of mistaken identity, it is a terrible day. James' death, the death of someone so essentially good, is nothing less than a tragedy."

The grief pouring from the two women was so obvious, so intense, that Geoffrey imagined he could almost feel it. It pounded at him in jagged waves, beating in time with the falling rain.

The words coming from the pulpit continued in the same measured, heartfelt tone that they had since Geoffrey entered the church, but he no longer heard them.

Some part of Geoffrey longed to comfort the women, so much so that he imagined reaching out and smoothing away the harsh, bitter edge of their sorrow. Only that wouldn't be fair or right. They needed their grief, needed to go through the mourning process. Instead of oblivion they needed shielded a little from the extreme pain, just enough for them to begin to heal.

The world spun away as Geoffrey focused on that one truth, the only thing that mattered in that instant.

THE GREATER DARKNESS

A gentle hand on Geoffrey's shoulder woke him some time later. Looking around in confusion, Geoffrey was surprised by his surroundings. What kind of hardened killer would allow himself to fall asleep in such an exposed place?

It seemed more than a little amazing that Geoffrey had managed to avoid hurting the poor priest when the other man had startled him awake, but if he could refrain from breaking a priest's arm in four separate places just for disturbing his sleep, maybe there was still some hope for him.

"Are you okay, my son?"

The kindly, old face that looked down at Geoffrey belonged to the priest who'd been speaking from the pulpit.

"Yes, I believe so; I just got very tired." As the words left Geoffrey's mouth, he realized it was true, or rather that he was very tired right *now*. He had been fine when he entered the chapel, but now felt exhausted.

"May I ask how you knew the deceased?"

Geoffrey wanted to bristle at the question, but something told him that the old man wasn't trying to pry.

"I'm sorry, I didn't know him. It was raining outside and something seemed to draw me here. It was so peaceful that I stayed. I never intended to fall asleep." Geoffrey was surprised as he realized that whatever half-formed lie he had been considering telling the priest had just been preempted by the truth.

A kindly smile rewarded Geoffrey, almost as if the man knew he'd spoken the truth rather than the lie that most people would have responded with. "I also find this building peaceful. It was abandoned by the Catholic Church many years ago, but has served this community for quite some time since. It hasn't always brought people the peace they were looking for though."

Geoffrey blinked slightly, wondering where the old man was headed.

"James' wife and mother were devastated by his death. They seemed to find no peace upon arriving here. In fact, they seemed to worsen as the night went on, until the last quarter of the service. Somehow in that last half an hour they began to accept their loss; it was like something was shielding them from the worst effects of their sorrow so that they could begin the process of becoming whole again."

The priest paused for a moment as if awaiting some response from Geoffrey, but the maelstrom of thoughts swirling through Geoffrey's mind precluded mere words.

"What do you think caused that change, my son?"

It wasn't possible. Geoffrey had just been pretending, imagining what he'd have done if he'd been able, but he hadn't actually done anything. Nobody could influence another's mind like that.

"I don't know, sir, I'm afraid I was asleep while all that happened."

A pair of weary brown eyes seemed to examine the depths of Geoffrey's soul. "I don't suppose I *know* either. However, you are welcome here whenever you feel inclined to come for a visit. It is always hardest for those who provide peace for others to find it themselves."

Chapter 3

Geoffrey tiredly wondered whether or not he should go home. He thought of the apartment as home now, but there wasn't any other place he'd rather avoid. The rooms had seemed to shrink as they'd come to symbolize just how little real freedom he had. He'd thought of leaving, of running away, or possibly of going to the police and reporting Imastious' attempts to have him kill the target. He had no resources with which to run away though and the police were likewise out as an option.

If even a fraction of what Venice and Imastious implied about his past was true, it was much more likely that he'd end up in prison rather than Imastious. Not only that, but even if Geoffrey did somehow manage to convince the police to believe him, he wouldn't be able to tell them where to find Imastious.

THE GREATER DARKNESS

With an exhausted shrug, Geoffrey turned and started back toward his apartment, which at least served as a refuge from the sunlight that increasingly seemed to be too much for his eyes.

A short time later, Geoffrey found himself standing before his door. As he pulled out his keys, he realized something was different. There wasn't any logical way for him to know that there was already someone inside his apartment, but he was somehow positive that there was someone waiting for him on the other side of the door. A flood of possible explanations flowed through Geoffrey's mind, but most of them didn't quite fit.

The only thing he could come up with that made any sense was that there were subtle physical signs that had tipped him off which he hadn't consciously noticed. Something that an experienced assassin would notice, but which he no longer even knew to check for.

Gripping the katana Venice had left him, Geoffrey debated whether or not to confront whoever was inside, only to hear a voice that had taken to haunting his dreams.

"Do come inside, Geoffrey; we've been waiting for you for quite some time now."

Carefully swinging the door open, Geoffrey saw Imastious sitting casually on the sofa once again. The empty, unblinking eyes watching Geoffrey made him feel somehow unclean.

"What do you want?"

For a second, Imastious didn't respond. Then, faster than Geoffrey's eyes could follow, the frail-looking man sprang from the sofa, grabbed him by the throat, and threw him into the wall next to the door with unbelievable strength. Geoffrey's ribs creaked from the impact. His head hit hard enough that he saw stars, but the more immediate concern was the fact that he couldn't manage to draw a breath, not with Imastious' hand closing off his windpipe.

"I have made some very unusual allowances for your behavior in light of your situation, in light of the fact that you have no memory of your true place in the world. Those allowances have been excessive. You *will* show me proper respect, or I *will* kill you."

The vise-like hand holding Geoffrey didn't move in the slightest despite his furious efforts to free himself. As Geoffrey's vision began to fade, his panic subsided long enough for him to remember the sword hanging at his side.

Releasing Imastious' wrist with his right hand, Geoffrey reached for his weapon. He drew it awkwardly, only to find his hand and arm somehow immobilized a split second later. Geoffrey directed the small tunnel of vision remaining him down towards his arm, expecting to find Imastious' free hand restraining him, but there was nothing visibly stopping him from completing the cut and chopping Imastious' right arm off.

THE GREATER DARKNESS

The last thing Geoffrey saw before passing out was Imastious' cold eyes staring at the katana with an intensity that was somehow surprising.

A sudden blow drew Geoffrey back from the abyss in which he had been floating. Apparently he was too slow regaining consciousness; Imastious cuffed him twice more before he was aware enough to croak out a protest.

"I hope you've been suitably chastised for your impertinence. Unfortunately for you, this still leaves the rather larger matter that brought me here in the first place."

The emotionless voice brought everything back to Geoffrey in a rush. He tried to flail, but silvery strands of duct tape cut into his wrists with each movement.

"I would be more than happy to leave you in the solitude you have always desired—that you no doubt still desire—if you would simply complete a few small tasks for me from time to time. For one of your skills and disposition these tasks are trivial, but for whatever reason, you find yourself reluctant to complete them in the desired manner and in the proper time frame."

Geoffrey turned his head enough to see Imastious once again sitting on the couch. Geoffrey's katana gleamed darkly on the floor where it had apparently fallen not too far away.

He shuddered at the memory of the way his weapon had refused to strike, but by the time he'd tried to use it he'd been pretty oxygen-deprived. The logical explanation was that he'd just been too far gone to lift it. Any other cause would border on the supernatural.

"Knowing you, and that obstinate streak you are sometimes possessed of, you're probably digging in, preparing to resist to the death because none of this was your idea. This simply won't do. I think it's time to show you that there are much worse things than simply dying."

Moving with a languid grace that seemed out of place on someone so emaciated, Imastious stood and walked over to Geoffrey with a look of cruel anticipation foremost on his face. A cold hand grasped the younger man's shoulder and pulled him around to where he could see the other side of the room.

"I trust you recognize her?"

Once again his mind rebelled at what he was seeing. It wasn't possible that Imastious had found the woman he'd saved just a few nights before. Imastious shouldn't even have known about the attempted mugging, let alone have had the ability to track one anonymous person down among the millions that lived on the island.

Try as he might to deny it, the terrified dark brown eyes staring at Geoffrey were the same ones he remembered. Underneath all of the terror, blood and bruises, the gentle face that had shown so much concern for Geoffrey was still very much the same.

"What, no protestations that you don't know her, that she should be freed? I'm favorably impressed, my son. That being the case, let's get started on the work at hand."

Geoffrey would have vocally denied knowing the woman, but his mind hadn't yet finished tracing down the chain of logic that would have led him to do so.

It wasn't until Imastious pulled a thin blade from his sleeve that Geoffrey realized the bound figure before him was bleeding in several places.

"You see, my son, not only do you live on my sufferance, but all those you would try to help out of some misguided sense of nobility will also die should I wish it."

The terror in the poor woman's eyes had reached heights that it seemed no sane mind could withstand. Geoffrey felt waves of fear clawing at him from the trembling woman, and it suddenly struck home fully that Imastious had been torturing her, probably for hours, while he waited for Geoffrey to return.

What followed had the blurry feeling of a dream, of something that had been dredged up out of the darkest corner of Geoffrey's subconscious. Yet at no point did he really believe it was anything other than real. The sense that the poor woman's emotions were tangible never went away. Instead it intensified to the point where, even when he closed his eyes in shame, Geoffrey was still able to feel the knife cutting into her dark skin.

Imastious paused whenever it seemed his subject could take no more, allowing her time to calm down slightly before returning to his grisly work. Every time Geoffrey became sure the woman's mind would shatter, Imastious interjected one of his breaks, stringing the spectacle on.

Geoffrey thought that nothing could be worse than what he was seeing, until Imastious bent down and licked the blood from the nearly lifeless body before him. As disgusting as that was, even more disgusting was the sudden spike of hunger that shot through Geoffrey. It had to be a sick byproduct of what Geoffrey had just gone through; he refused to believe he was as far gone as Imastious apparently was.

When the poor woman finally expired from blood loss a couple of hours later, Imastious had well and truly made his point.

"You see? There really are things worse than death. If you continue to fail, I won't hesitate to visit them on anyone who means even the slightest thing to you."

Geoffrey wasn't surprised when Imastious, blade in hand, turned toward him and began inflicting the same treatment on him that the old man had been inflicting, just moments before, on the Latina.

THE GREATER DARKNESS

The pain that followed was very real, but Geoffrey welcomed it, and fresh tears poured down his face once Imastious finally stopped. There truly were worse things than dying, and Geoffrey was pretty sure that living as the kind of sick monster that longed to kill innocents so he could lap up their blood was one of them.

Chapter 4

When Geoffrey next awoke, the setting sun provided just enough light to illuminate the pale, unbroken expanse of skin on Geoffrey's chest. It was nearly enough to convince him he'd somehow imagined being tortured for hours. Turning the lights on proved otherwise.

His sheets were drenched in unimaginable amounts of dried blood. Horrified, Geoffrey turned away only to find additional evidence that everything had happened just as he remembered it. The results of Imastious' handiwork left in the corner made him gag and bury his face in hands that were every bit as bloodstained as they had been the night before.

How long had he been asleep? Even if he'd somehow been asleep long enough to heal from the damage he'd remembered Imastious doing to him, there would have still been scars. He wanted to dismiss everything that had happened as some kind of vivid, extended nightmare, but the body in the corner was indisputable proof that at least some of it had been terribly real.

Geoffrey felt a rising sense of terror as he realized that he couldn't trust his mind. He didn't know how Imastious was doing it—maybe with some kind of memory-distorting drug—but he had to assume it had been at least partially staged.

The sound of voices in the hall sent Geoffrey into a near panic. He knew it would only be a matter of time until someone started looking for the Latina. If she were found in Geoffrey's apartment, they'd lock him up. The decision to leave the apartment brought with it a strange pocket of calm that allowed Geoffrey to start planning ahead. He needed a shower, new clothes, and a way out of the city.

During the trip to the bus stop, Geoffrey couldn't escape the feeling that everyone he passed was watching him. It seemed as if everyone who looked at him knew his guilt. The stress of trying to watch for people following him, without looking completely paranoid, sent him into shakes before he'd even made it halfway. He held on to what was left of his composure by remembering that he just needed to keep himself together for a few more blocks. After that, he would board a bus and disappear into some small town where nobody would ever link him to anything.

While still a block from the bus station, Geoffrey heard sirens and his already nauseated stomach dropped. There wasn't just one police car outside the bus station; there were three. A quartet of officers were watching each passenger board, obvious in their scrutiny of the buses and the would-be passengers.

A tiny rational part of Geoffrey's mind couldn't believe the police could possibly have discovered the corpse in his apartment so quickly, but the sensation that he was in great danger was so strong that his vision started to tunnel. Somehow they knew, and if he got close enough to them, they'd recognize him.

Geoffrey turned into a side street as calmly as he was able, and then as soon as he was out of sight broke into a stumbling run. People really were looking at him now, but it no longer mattered. Nothing mattered as much as getting away from the bus station, away from the cops who would surely shoot him on sight.

By the time rational thought returned, Geoffrey was in Spanish Harlem, and his obvious panic was starting to draw hostile stares from the few people still walking the streets at such a late hour. A half-glimpsed sign pointing to a nearby subway entrance represented his best hope of security. Down in the darkness there would be somewhere to hide. Maybe not indefinitely, but at least long enough for him to think of another way out of the city. One that the police wouldn't be watching.

THE GREATER DARKNESS

The subway platform was deserted, but Geoffrey still felt incredibly self-conscious as he climbed down onto the tracks, carefully avoiding the lethal third rail.

A few short steps brought Geoffrey into the welcoming darkness, calming him slightly as he realized that he'd made it to a form of safety. For the next half hour, Geoffrey's only companions were the rats he could barely hear scurrying across the tracks.

As acute as Geoffrey's night vision was, he still nearly missed the faint outline of the door to the service tunnels. The doorknob didn't turn, but someone had forced the lock so that the door swung freely open when pushed.

The area behind the door was even blacker than the subway tunnel. Geoffrey crept very cautiously, hands outstretched in an effort to detect any obstacles. Following the wall for thirty or forty paces brought Geoffrey around two corners. As he found a third, he noticed that it was getting brighter.

Walking more quickly as the visibility improved, Geoffrey realized that he'd found some kind of central hub from which a number of service corridors branched out to provide access for this portion of the subway tunnels. By the look of the trash all over the floor and the graffiti on the walls, he wasn't the first person to find his way down there, but it did have the benefit of still having lighting. It wasn't the classiest place, but part of him relaxed now that he'd found a relatively safe place to stay while he tried to figure out what to do next.

Geoffrey was shaking again, but more violently than before, violently enough that his feet were making noise against the floor. He needed to be quiet. He couldn't remember why, but he was pretty sure that was important.

The lights were still on, but for some reason Geoffrey was having a hard time seeing. Everything was inexplicably blurry, and he seemed unable to remember how long he'd been hiding in the near darkness. Hours? Days? He couldn't remember, but he knew he needed to stay down where it was safe until everyone stopped looking for him.

The sound of feet dragging somewhere nearby confirmed Geoffrey's worry that the noise he was making would draw unwelcome attention, but the thought was too listless to generate any force.

"Who the hell are you?"

The voice was strangely clear, the sound apparently unaffected by whatever was interfering with Geoffrey's other senses. He tried again, but couldn't decide where the voice was coming from.

"I asked you a question, man."

THE GREATER DARKNESS

The raw anger in the voice demanded a response. Geoffrey somehow managed to move his head slowly from side to side until a dark, fuzzy mass appeared in his field of vision.

Geoffrey opened his mouth to respond, but rough hands interrupted his train of thought as they pulled him to his feet. His efforts to help the hands were surprisingly ineffectual, and Geoffrey found himself slightly displeased by the weak way in which his legs flailed at the floor.

"How does a yuppie addict like you get down here?"

The hands shook Geoffrey, but he was oddly drawn to them. They gave off a warming heat, while at the same time singing a slow, two-note song.

Somehow the words penetrated the haze, and the slightest bit of anger kindled in the back of Geoffrey's mind. Who was this guy to accuse him like that? He'd never used any drugs...except he didn't really know that. He didn't *really* know anything. The anger started to fade, replaced by a growing sense that things weren't right.

Geoffrey pushed against the fuzziness surrounding his thoughts. He was thinking clearly enough now to try and free himself, but not clearly enough to actually succeed. Vague thoughts of breaking the man's arm floated through his mind, but he was too weak. He was hardly able to raise his arms let alone exert enough violent force to actually win free.

The rough grip suddenly pulled Geoffrey closer so that the dark form took up nearly his whole field of vision.

"It don't matter how you made it down here. What matters is that you, your wallet, and your fancy clothes won't be making it back up to the surface."

The hands holding Geoffrey shifted to his neck, and clamped down with incredible power.

Unable to breathe, Geoffrey tried to shake off the weights that seemed to be slowing his thoughts, but nearly his full attention was drawn to the hot breath that teased at his face as his attacker leaned in to better watch him die.

The throbbing was louder now, just beyond reach as it called to Geoffrey, resonating with a hunger that he hadn't noticed before that instant.

The blurry tunnel that was one of Geoffrey's last ties to the physical world was shrinking rapidly, but then his arms darted out with the strength that had been eluding him. A sharp pain flashed across Geoffrey's forehead, and then he was falling as if in slow motion, drawing his first breath in far too long.

That lone breath was forced out of Geoffrey's chest as he landed, crushing something lumpy beneath his weight. The drumming was still seductively calling for Geoffrey, now faster than before. Something warm splashed across his face before his mouth captured the flow, directing it down into his bruised body.

As blackness returned to claim Geoffrey, the drumming grew quieter and he felt an irrational anger that it would desert him.

Geoffrey looked up into a pair of soft brown eyes and a wave of pure contentment flowed through him. The eyes belonged to a gentle face that was smiling at him from behind a thin veil of long, dark hair.

Geoffrey smiled back, content with his full stomach and the heat of the wood fire reaching out from behind to envelop him in warmth.

Somehow, Geoffrey's point of view changed, leaving him standing in the other corner of the still-indistinct room. A sound, which Geoffrey knew existed even though he couldn't hear it, brought his head around enough to see a familiar figure setting places at a rough wooden table. Another silent sound, one that seemed to issue from Geoffrey, caused the lithe figure to turn, revealing the same beautiful face that Geoffrey had smiled at just moments before.

It wasn't until Geoffrey had taken a few steps toward the girl that he saw how she'd changed in those brief minutes, growing taller and losing the childish roundness that had graced her face previously.

With a mischievous grin, the girl walked across the small room to meet Geoffrey halfway, reaching into the pocket of her apron to fish out a small, dark object that he'd been wanting for hours.

The scene started to fade as the room trembled and shook. Geoffrey rolled over in an attempt to distance himself from the source of the noise pulling him away from the warm room, but an abrupt collision completed the unwanted transition into wakefulness.

It had felt too real to be nothing more than a dream. He'd almost expected to be able to open his eyes and see her standing there again.

For a brief moment, Geoffrey felt an intense hatred for Imastious. Anger over never being able to have a normal life momentarily peaked and then faded away. Geoffrey opened his eyes to surroundings much different than the modest apartment he'd been expecting.

Looking at the filth-covered room quickly brought back the vague, almost dreamlike memories of being attacked, as well as the spray of warmth that had splashed across his face. Geoffrey suddenly felt sick as he noticed the stiff, crusty feeling covering his face and neck.

A shaking hand came back dotted with a fine dusting of dried blood, and Geoffrey nearly vomited. He couldn't deny it anymore. He'd been drinking blood, just like he'd wanted to do for days. He didn't just kill people; he also got some kind of sick thrill from draining them dry.

THE GREATER DARKNESS

The knowledge that he was just as bad as Venice and Imastious had implied tore at Geoffrey's mind, leaving no room for rational thought, no room for anything more than the need to get away. Geoffrey stumbled back into the darkness, chased by the knowledge that this murder was undeniably his fault.

Geoffrey had been moving for hours, stopping only long enough to clean the worst of the blood off before quartering the city in an effort to find something. He didn't know what he was looking for, but this was the same kind of pull he'd experienced just before he'd walked into that church the night of the funeral.

Geoffrey briefly considered visiting the priest, but after what he'd done, shied away from the thought of trying to meet the gaze of someone so completely good.

It wasn't until after Geoffrey had traveled all the way to the tip of the island and back that he felt a distinct tug which gave him a definite direction in which to head. Some fifteen minutes later Geoffrey found himself before a large cathedral.

Walking up to the front doors, Geoffrey found a sign labeling the building the Cathedral of Saint John the Divine. It was hard to imagine a church more different than the last one he'd entered, but something was definitely drawing him to churches. Geoffrey already felt nearly as safe as he'd felt the night of the funeral.

Geoffrey was calmer now, but the thought of what he'd done just a few hours before was enough to stop him from talking to anyone, let alone seeking out a priest. Instead, he slipped around one of the velvet cordons meant to discourage visitors from exploring the less public areas of the church and quietly made his way down a set of stairs that led to the basement areas.

It felt right to be there in the church, but a corner of his mind kept telling him that the rightness was somehow unnatural. He shouldn't feel good about being in a church, not after what he'd done.

Wandering through the complex of infrequently used, but still richly furnished rooms, Geoffrey finally found a dark corner where he'd be safe, and the nagging voice telling him this wasn't right slowly faded away.

Exhaustion washed over Geoffrey almost as soon as he stopped moving, but even after sitting down with his back to the wall, sleep proved elusive. His mind, no longer fixated on pursuing the need that had brought him here, filled with an incredible array of thoughts.

What had happened to him in the subway? It was like time had stopped, and then he'd awakened weak, and unable to control himself.

No, that wasn't right. He could have controlled himself. He'd killed because he was weak, not because he'd really needed to satiate some unnatural hunger. Trying to believe anything else was just a lie designed to help him shirk his guilt.

As Geoffrey's eyes once again grew heavy, his thoughts settled down, returning to one series of questions. Why did everything else he'd just gone through somehow seem less important than his dream? How could a dream be so tangible, and if it was somehow real, who had the girl been?

Chapter 5

The pain that shocked Geoffrey awake shouldn't have come as such a surprise. Somehow he'd expected that falling asleep at a church would equate to waking in equally peaceful circumstances. Instead he was back in his apartment, stretched out on a metal frame with an incredibly strong electrical current running through him.

Imastious pulled the wires away from Geoffrey. "Very good, I'm happy to see that you've rejoined us on schedule."

Geoffrey tried to speak, but the gag stuffed into his mouth prevented anything recognizable from making it out of his throat.

"If only you were equally compliant and dependable in other things as well, we wouldn't be forced to continually experience these kinds of unpleasant episodes."

THE GREATER DARKNESS

Geoffrey thought that someone was standing at the head of the bed, but couldn't turn his head far enough to verify the fact.

"Now, now. Venice is indeed beautiful, but you should be contemplating your situation, pondering your sins if you will, rather than trying to sneak a peek."

Confident that he had Geoffrey's full attention, Imastious set down the wires, and then turned back to Geoffrey. "The first thing you need to understand is that trying to run or hide is futile. I've told you before that my resources are sufficient to know exactly what you do and where you go. We gave you several days in which to choose your hiding place, and then came and collected you."

Shaking his head at Geoffrey's lack of response, Imastious picked up the wires once again, and returned to the bed. "You will learn eventually. You'll learn to obey me and complete the simple tasks that you're given. Of that I have complete confidence. You learned during our last visit that there are things worse than dying. Today you learned that you cannot escape me. Before I leave you tonight you'll learn that you are not important enough to my plans to merit any further indulgence."

Before Geoffrey could fully process Imastious' words, the older man touched the wires to each of Geoffrey's wrists, causing him to convulse and scream as well as he could past the gag.

No matter how Geoffrey struggled and fought, he couldn't free himself. He was forced to endure shock after shock as punctuation of Imastious' determination to see his spirit broken.

Any thoughts that what he was experiencing was induced by drugs fled within the first few minutes. He still couldn't explain how he could have possibly recovered from earlier sessions so quickly, but he was finally sure that what he was experiencing was real.

At some point Geoffrey started expecting to pass into unconsciousness, but his body proved tougher than he'd expected. That toughness, combined with the careful breaks Imastious provided, kept him coherent for what must have been hours.

Geoffrey never felt the slickness of blood that would have indicated Imastious had started using his knife again, but Geoffrey eventually lost track of what was being done to his abused body. Pain simply moved from one part of his being to another at irregular intervals, leaving him shaking and ever weaker.

The torture had stopped for several minutes before Geoffrey finally felt Imastious pat his cheek to capture his attention. "I hope you are starting to understand just how badly you can be hurt. I stopped just now not because I couldn't continue hurting you. I have other ways of inflicting even greater pain than what you experienced tonight, but I think my point has finally been made."

Geoffrey wished that he could dispute the point, but Imastious had just shown him that things could always get worse, that there were levels of suffering that he hadn't even believed were possible. It had just been starkly illustrated in blood and pain that there would always be a greater punishment waiting in the wings if Geoffrey didn't behave.

"Do you understand, my son?"

A part of Geoffrey knew that answering Imastious represented the first step towards compliance and cooperation, but the thought of what Imastious could do to him drove a response from him almost before he was able to think, and he nodded violently in affirmation.

Imastious patted Geoffrey once more on the cheek. "You must understand and promise to do better. I do not wish to do this to you. I truly do care for you. It's only your disobedience that makes me treat you so."

As Imastious left the room, Geoffrey idly wondered what Venice was going to do now that her master had left, but the cumulative effects of the last few hours were just too much. He passed out before he could string any more lucid thoughts together.

Geoffrey woke to a fresh set of clothing and new sheets. The batteries and wires were all gone, and other than some slight soreness, there wasn't any real evidence that he'd been tortured for hours the night before.

The sound of someone shifting slightly should have made Geoffrey nervous, but he'd somehow known that Venice would still be there.

"Welcome back, love."

After everything that had happened, a certain amount of caution was probably called for, but Geoffrey opened his mouth and responded with the first thing he thought of. "Don't call me that."

Venice shook her head and flashed him a smile that seemed to invite him to laugh at some secret joke, one that was shared only between the two of them. "Angry I didn't interfere last night?"

Geoffrey nodded slowly. He knew she wasn't going to be honest with him, but he didn't see any reason not to tell her the truth. It wasn't like he knew anything valuable that she could trick out of him.

Venice smoothly rose from the chair where she'd sat both times she'd visited. Geoffrey absently realized that, consciously or not, Venice was staking out her territory, and not just with his furniture.

Smoothing the loose, black pants she was wearing, the blonde gave Geoffrey an appraising look. "I told you. I can't afford to incur too much of Imastious' displeasure. He is more powerful than you understand—maybe stronger than you can imagine in your current state—and my life is only of slightly more worth to him than yours."

Walking over to the bed, Venice continued. "At one point you had an incredibly logical and powerful mind, but apparently no more. The real question we should be examining is why you bloody well seem to want me to intercede on your behalf, while simultaneously denying the kind of attachments which would make me inclined to do so."

Taking in the smooth expanse of shoulder that Venice's tank top revealed, Geoffrey realized that he was more uncomfortable than the sight of so much perfect skin could account for.

What had happened to him? Had he really been the cold-blooded killer that she made him out to be? If so, why was he now so reluctant to kill again?

Venice seemed to mistake Geoffrey's silence for agreement. "That's what I thought. Honestly, you need to start thinking rationally before you force Imastious to kill you and save himself the aggravation you're causing him right now."

Geoffrey wanted to respond, but there were just too many things he didn't know. "What am I?"

Venice smiled, but it didn't reach her eyes. "I was wondering how long it would take you to ask that question. It was inevitable, unless you just decided that you were losing your mind."

Even though Geoffrey was aware that nothing Venice was about to tell him would necessarily be the truth, a tiny surge of hope washed through him at the prospect of finally understanding some of what was happening.

"Understand that there are a lot of subjects I can't talk about. Imastious would be very displeased to learn that I'd told you anything he didn't want you to know. There are a few things I *can* tell you though, things that I think will help you transition back to being a functional member of the team."

A cynical part of Geoffrey was pretty sure that the things she was about to tell him were the kinds of things that he would have figured out on his own eventually. She would be very careful to ensure that she could still throw him to the wolves later on if circumstances required it.

Venice sat down on the bed facing Geoffrey and leaned against his outstretched legs. "I'm kind of surprised that you haven't figured out some of it, especially with all the hints I've been dropping. The cravings for blood must have given you some idea that the myths and legends were based on something real."

She didn't have to actually say the word. If it hadn't been so impossible, he would have already admitted to himself that it was the only explanation for so many of the things he was going through. Vampires.

THE GREATER DARKNESS

"I'm told that our condition is caused by a virus of some kind, one so targeted that it can't survive in most hosts, and which hasn't mutated appreciably in the last several thousand years."

Geoffrey opened his mouth to protest that he didn't know anything about viruses, but as he thought about the subject he realized that he actually did know all kinds of things about various aspects of biology and pathogens.

"That rot really doesn't matter though. Most people die within a few hours of being exposed, which doesn't happen from just any bite. Those who survive, like us, enjoy a number of incredible benefits. Strength and speed surpassing that of most normal individuals, as well as a greatly slowed aging process. What do you think about eternal youth, love?"

Geoffrey suddenly had visions of unending life, of centuries passing slowly as he remained a slave to Imastious' whims. "You mean we're immortal?"

Venice shook her head with a pout. "Not quite. At least I don't think so. The older vampires like Imastious are obsessive about cloaking themselves in secrecy, so I don't know how old they really are. Probably thousands of years, but there are some indications that the aging process has other effects on the eldest of us that might eventually lead to death either effectively or actually. Not only that, but we can be killed through violence in much the same manner as a normal person."

Geoffrey's head was swimming, he could hear what Venice was saying, but another voice, one only inside his head, was telling him that she was leaving out information—important information.

"You said that we're the base from which the ancient legends sprang, but they aren't entirely accurate?"

Venice reached out and stoked Geoffrey's cheek. "There you go, that beautiful mind is working once again."

Geoffrey waited out the pause that followed, hoping that Venice would elaborate.

"Obviously we don't burst into flame once the sun comes up, but most of us sunburn easily and the older we get the harder it is for our eyes to adjust to full sunlight."

Venice paused again, as if trying to gauge the effect that her little tidbit of information was having on Geoffrey's thinking.

"As you've no doubt noticed, we crave blood. Most use normal food to fulfill their calorie requirements, but it still leaves some kind of dietary deficiency which blood is required to meet."

Geoffrey was desperately sure that she was lying. There had to be a way to survive without drinking blood.

Looking Geoffrey in the eye, Venice continued. "Based on how you've been acting lately, you're probably trying to think of some kind of alternate source for whatever it is we need. You should know that nobody has discovered one yet. Animal blood comes close, but still lacks something. If you go long enough without blood, you'll lose all ability to control yourself: you'll kill and feed again and again until the hunger has been satisfied and you finally regain your senses."

Venice seemed to expect a response, so Geoffrey shrugged.

"You probably don't believe me, but it's true. I'd much rather see you be selective in your choice of victim instead of suddenly snapping and killing the four or five people who happen to be handy. Also, you run the risk of killing yourself if you do that. We need blood, but too much blood at once will make you very sick. A binge like the one you'd probably go on if you were starving yourself could very easily kill you afterwards."

Geoffrey remembered the strange, disconnected way he'd felt in the subway tunnels, and felt the first glimmer of hope. Was it really possible that she was telling the truth? Had he really been unable to control himself? It would mean that the man's death would still be his fault, but it would be because of ignorance rather than an actual murder.

Venice interrupted Geoffrey's train of thought by reaching down to the floor and picking up not one, but two wooden swords. "Enough. Imastious left me with strict instructions and he's right; it's time for you to learn how to use one of these things again."

Despite all of the more weighty things worrying at the edge of Geoffrey's mind, a surge of anticipation swept through him as he accepted the practice katana and rose to his feet.

"You always did enjoy weapon work, but I suspect that it's going to be a while before you regain anything approaching your previous mastery. For now I get to be the teacher."

Geoffrey was still digesting Venice's statement when she drew her weapon and attacked him. It quickly became obvious she was just testing him, attempting to determine how much reflexive muscle memory had survived his amnesia. Despite that, it was all he could do to avoid or block her strikes in the limited space they had to work in. Venice finally cracked him across the chest with a casual blow, and then lowered her weapon.

"You're not very good anymore, obviously, but you seem to remember more than I would have expected. Your blocks and strikes are well executed still, you just don't know how or when to use them."

The next two hours were a bittersweet joy for Geoffrey. There was no denying that he derived great enjoyment from learning everything that Venice deemed him ready to know about fighting. Everything felt incredibly natural. Learning the correct way to hold the weapon, the various ways of executing a strike, it all felt right to him. It really was like he'd known it all before, like his body still remembered all of the things his mind had lost. The satisfaction was tainted by the thought that only a violent murderer would take such joy in learning how to kill and maim.

Once Venice felt that Geoffrey had received sufficient instruction with regards to the blade, she demonstrated a few unarmed techniques, one of which he recognized as the attack that he'd used on the person that had accosted him in the tunnels.

By the time Venice waved Geoffrey over to a chair, they were both soaked in sweat and breathing heavily. Venice waited until Geoffrey had set his practice weapon on the floor, and then sprawled out across his lap.

"You're doing well, love. All that remains is for you to make the kill. Once that happens, Imastious will be pleased enough to more or less leave you alone, except for those times when your special talents are needed."

Geoffrey stiffened, first because Venice had invaded his space, and then again as she calmly suggested that he take another life. The memory of his attacker in the subway dying beneath him terrified Geoffrey, but he knew that Imastious really would torture him if he didn't proceed with the hit. The torture had been bad enough when he'd thought it wasn't real. Now that he knew it wasn't a figment of his imagination he was realizing just what kind of things he was willing to contemplate to avoid having to go through it again.

For several seconds Geoffrey debated responding to Venice, but he had a strong suspicion that arguing with her wouldn't get him anywhere. He was better off just remaining silent.

"What, no denials? You are strangely compliant today, love. I suppose it is to be expected after a session like you had last night, but I must admit I'm surprised. Your general stubbornness should have seen you through another couple like that before you really started cracking."

Leaning her head slightly to the side, Venice looked into Geoffrey's eyes. "I don't suppose that your new attitude extends into other areas?"

Geoffrey felt his face turn to stone and, not trusting his voice, he shook his head.

"Very well. You probably have a few days before Imastious decides that you aren't going to comply with his wishes, and sets about arranging a suitable punishment for you. Since you're no doubt going to ignore my advice, at least enjoy the next couple of days. Whatever he plans for you will be much worse than what happened last night."

Venice rose from the chair and collected her things, leaving Geoffrey with nothing but his thoughts to torment him.

Chapter 6

Geoffrey had somehow hoped putting a night's rest behind him would provide the insights he needed. Unsurprisingly, his situation was no better upon waking.

Part of Geoffrey wanted to disbelieve Venice. He wanted to believe that she had been lying about the disease, about the absolute necessity of blood for his continued survival, but something told him that she was telling the truth. It had almost been as if he could read her thoughts. She'd been worried that he would disbelieve her, but amused that out of all of the lies she had told him, that this would be the thing he would choose to discount. Still, even over the amusement, Geoffrey had been able to tell that she'd been worried about the ramifications to her personally if he were to kill himself by overdosing on blood.

Getting himself out of bed and out the door was much harder than Geoffrey had expected.

Then again, given that all of his options for escape had been cut off, it made sense that he wouldn't feel particularly motivated. Trying to avoid torture might work as a motivation to do things, but he was pretty sure that wouldn't work long term. Human beings needed a purpose, something to live for, to work towards. The real question was whether or not he'd find a worthwhile purpose or if he'd become like Imastious and lose whatever small bits of humanity he still possessed.

As Geoffrey walked down the stairs and exited the building, a simple, even elegant, solution presented itself to him. He could always take himself out of the equation and just end everything.

Geoffrey dismissed the idea immediately, only to then pause and wonder why it was so repulsive to him. He thought it was because giving up ran counter to his nature, but he couldn't rule out the possibility that he was just too frightened to do it.

Once again, Geoffrey found himself aimlessly wandering the shadowed, crowded streets as the sun made its tired way down behind the skyline. Several miles later, he realized that he'd stumbled into an area that looked very familiar. He'd returned to the area where he'd attended the funeral.

As Geoffrey slipped through the dwindling crowds, he felt a sudden need to talk to the priest again. If anyone would understand what he was going through it would be the priest.

Arriving at the door, Geoffrey felt a premonition of doom. Everyone he'd had even the briefest of contact with had died. If Imastious was as all-knowing as he kept claiming, then Geoffrey was putting the priest in danger by going inside. The risk was just too great.

Geoffrey turned to walk away, but before he could complete the motion, the battered, black door before him opened to reveal a familiar, smiling face.

"Hello, my son. Please come in."

Geoffrey's mind spun for a second, looking for an excuse. "I don't want to keep you late. I can come back during your regular hours, if that would be better."

A pair of kindly eyes measured Geoffrey for a moment before the older man responded. "I was headed home, but you obviously need to talk, and nothing I have waiting for me there is more important than that."

Almost despite himself, Geoffrey followed the priest inside and joined him on one of the old wooden pews, which protested their presence with a tired creak.

"You have the look of someone who feels as though they have run out of options. Someone who feels that they've been forced into a very bad situation."

Geoffrey was startled by the priest's perceptiveness, but something about the man seemed to promise that he wouldn't betray a trust.

"I suppose that *is* how I feel."

Geoffrey waited, allowing the priest to interject a comment, but the other man seemed content to simply listen.

"I find myself among very bad company. How I got there isn't important, but I am unable to escape, they know too much about me for that to be a possibility."

The priest shifted slightly in his pew, almost as if he'd been about to interrupt but thought better of it.

"These people have done terrible things to me, and they will do worse things unless I kill a man for them."

When it became apparent that Geoffrey wasn't going to continue, the priest slowly nodded. "You do indeed find yourself in a difficult situation. A situation in which your courses of action are narrowed greatly from what most people experience."

Geoffrey felt a tiny flare of hope at the priest's words, not necessarily at their content, but rather the fact that he'd finally been able to tell even the slightest amount of the truth to someone.

"I obviously do not know the full situation in which you find yourself. Even if you were to tell me all that you know, your own beliefs and perceptions would naturally make you a less than completely objective witness. However, even if we accept for a time that your beliefs are correct, you still have choices to make."

Geoffrey felt as though he should take offense at the priest's words, but couldn't bring himself to do so.

"You could kill this man, possibly he is even a very bad man, but I think it's not for you or me to make that judgment. Alternatively, you could kill yourself. That is often something people consider when they feel like they have no other way out, but this also isn't a course I can condone. Finally, assuming you are correct in your assumption that you can't run, you could refuse to comply with the wishes of these evil people and endure whatever may happen next."

As Geoffrey finally opened his mouth to protest, the old man held up a hand. "You always have a choice, my son. Sometimes the choice is just not something that we are willing to do. I think *that* is what sets the truly righteous apart from the rest of us; they are so special exactly because they are willing to give anything for their beliefs, even their lives."

"Why should I be forced to endure torture? Where is the justice in that?"

The priest sighed, pausing for a moment before continuing. "Are you truly blameless with regards to the situation in which you now find yourself? It may be that you are, but I can think of few, if any, times in my own life where I didn't contribute, at least in some small way, to any bad situations in which I found myself."

Geoffrey wanted to protest, but there wasn't any way to know for sure what he might have done to merit Imastious' attention. His mind reaching wildly for a response that wasn't a lie, Geoffrey allowed the silence to stretch out for several seconds. "I don't know what I believe, and even if I did, I don't think I'm one of those special people."

The old man shrugged. "The question of what to believe is one that has caused more debate, confusion, and even bloodshed, than possibly any other thing in history. I can't tell you what to believe, but I can tell you that you'll find your beliefs piece by piece as you truly seek them with an open mind. They will fill you with light and warmth as you find them, one by one until you've constructed the whole, and suddenly realize that you know how you should respond in any given situation."

A quiver built inside of Geoffrey, and as tears started to fill his eyes. He was at a loss to explain how he knew what the old man was saying was true, but he couldn't argue with the statement.

The priest looked at Geoffrey out of shiny eyes and smiled once again. "As to the second part of your statement, that is why you are here. We are all here to determine for ourselves whether or not we're special enough to do God's will once we find it."

Geoffrey stood up, his desire not to appear rude overcome by his need to escape the church and return to the streets where he could think.

As he fled the church the priest called out one last time. "He already knows what we will do, and has provided a way for each of us to overcome our trials if we are willing; we're just here so we can find out for ourselves who we really are."

Exiting the church, Geoffrey took off at a fast walk to ensure that the priest wouldn't follow him and try to continue their conversation. How could letting Imastious torture him be just or good?

Geoffrey crossed the street and headed east. Ultimately there wasn't any way to know whether or not any of what he'd just heard was true.

It was odd that Geoffrey always seemed to seek refuge from his problems by walking the city when his exertions had yet to yield any kind of positive result. Possibly it was some kind of holdover from his previous life. It was hard to believe that anything would really bother the kind of soulless killer Venice kept telling him that he'd been. Maybe walking had been how he'd dealt with the few things that he couldn't immediately resolve by killing.

Geoffrey was nearing one of the more run-down, dirty parts of the city now. He nearly turned away in an effort to stay out of such an unpleasant area, but the garbage-filled streets matched his mood perfectly. The functioning lights were few and very far between, and there was an undeniable sense of movement in the dark corners between storefronts.

Several hours of wandering the area failed to lend any kind of clarity to his thoughts, and Geoffrey was nearly at the point of turning around and heading back to his apartment when a girl turned onto the street thirty or forty feet ahead of him.

Geoffrey was puzzled at first by the way his attention kept drifting back to the girl until he realized that she was giving off a tangible aura of fear and desperation. He couldn't help but wonder what could be driving her out onto the darkened streets at such a late hour. Anyone with any sense at all had gone to bed hours ago.

The streets were nearly deserted now, save for occasional groups of teenage toughs, who were watching the slim figure walking ahead of Geoffrey with an interest that made Geoffrey want to vomit.

Without really considering why he was doing so, Geoffrey quickened his step slightly so as not to fall any further behind the panic-stricken teenager.

Three blocks later the girl turned off into what was probably the only pharmacy still open for miles, and Geoffrey slowed to a stop, questioning for the first time what he was doing.

Boisterous laughter from the other side of the street pulled Geoffrey's thoughts back to the present, and anger rushed through him as it became clear what the three young men intended to do.

The trio separated, taking up positions far enough from the pharmacy door that nobody inside would be able to see them, but close enough that they were cutting off each of the girl's possible escape routes. It was obvious to Geoffrey that they were going to wait until the girl was far enough away from the store to ensure that she couldn't retreat back inside and then they'd jump her. As empty as the streets were, the odds of anyone passing by before they got her somewhere out of sight were near zero.

Geoffrey started to shake as he realized that he was the girl's only chance to avoid being raped. He wanted to intervene, but he didn't see any way that he could stop all three of her assailants. Even worse, if he somehow managed to save her then Imastious would know. She'd almost certainly die. Another bit of collateral damage in the next round of punishments that Imastious would visit on him.

The sound of a door opening brought Geoffrey's eyes back to the pharmacy just in time to see the girl exit. Astonishment flowed through Geoffrey like an electrical current as he took in her wavy, dark hair and innocent face. It seemed impossible that the anachronistic figure from his dreams would be made flesh and dropped into the middle of the slums, but he couldn't argue with his eyes.

The realization that he knew this girl, that some piece of his past hadn't completely been lost, made the decision for Geoffrey, and he moved forward as the teenagers closed in on their target.

As soon as the girl was far enough away from the tiny store, the closest gang member struck. He wrapped an arm around her while his free hand reached up to muffle any screams. A few seconds later he'd dragged her back into the dark side street behind them.

Geoffrey unconsciously moved with the effortless, gliding step that Venice had shown him such a short time before. As quiet as Geoffrey was, he was surprised that either of the two toughs just now making it to the alley heard him.

"Get lost, cracker, this ain't any of your business."

The words barely registered for Geoffrey. Words would be useless. The boy would fight for the thrill of it as much as for anything else.

As if on cue, the closest teen pulled out a switchblade and stepped towards Geoffrey. A split second later the other boy finally realized what was happening and started fumbling for a weapon of his own.

THE GREATER DARKNESS

Still acting on little more than instinct, Geoffrey raised his hands and realized he'd drawn his katana. Against all common sense, the teen with the knife continued his attack against a better armed foe, only to lose his hand to the edge of Geoffrey's weapon.

Another quick move and spray of blood, and the second teen went down, whatever weapon he'd been intent on drawing still concealed somewhere on his person.

A part of Geoffrey was horrified by what he had just done, but the cold, mechanical part of him that was currently calling the shots simply confirmed that the two gangers were too far into shock to pose any kind of threat, and moved him deeper into the alley.

The third boy couldn't have hurt her too badly; he hadn't had the time yet.

A scuffling sound up ahead warned Geoffrey a split second before the last teen stepped out from behind a dumpster, a revolver held to the girl's shaking temple.

"Get back, whitey, or I'll burn her down."

Geoffrey once again felt the urge to be sick as he thought about what a .357 hollow point would do to the unblemished face looking at him with terror that bordered on insanity. Only his understanding that the fear he was feeling came from the gang member, as much as from the girl, protected his fragile bubble of calm.

"You could do that. You have time for one shot no matter what I do. If you kill her, though, I promise you that you'll die. You'll never have time for a second shot before I remove your shaved head from your shoulders."

Watching the desperate face behind the gun, it was as if Geoffrey could read the youth's mind. The kid knew Geoffrey was right. There were only two options on the table, but the only thing he'd learned after twenty years in the hellhole of the projects was that backing down was a sign of weakness. Once you backed down, even just a little, those around you always used it as an excuse to try and kill you.

Geoffrey opened his mouth to try and reason with the teen, only to somehow sense that the younger man had come to a decision. Instincts took over, and Geoffrey found himself hurtling towards the ground without any clear reason why he was doing so.

A large crack destroyed the silence and further confused Geoffrey about the time his body converted the fall into some kind of roll. Fragments of brick rained down behind him as he regained his feet and struck out with his sword.

Once again blood sprayed through the air, covering Geoffrey and the girl in a sticky mist as the revolver hit the ground. By the time Geoffrey's mind caught up with what was happening, the gang member was on the ground, dead from a gaping hole in his neck, and

THE GREATER DARKNESS

Geoffrey was once again fighting the urge to be violently ill. He couldn't afford to be sick yet. He needed to make sure she was okay first.

The girl met Geoffrey's eyes when he looked at her, but she'd gone extremely pale. Even as he watched, she started to shake with an intensity that was as worrying as it was surreal. "The medicine. It fell when he grabbed me."

As Geoffrey started to ask what she meant, the girl's eyes abruptly fluttered, and she started to collapse. It was all that Geoffrey could do to catch her with his free arm without accidentally stabbing her with his sword.

Geoffrey carefully lowered the girl to the ground so that he could sheath his weapon only to stop as he realized he was forgetting something. He needed to clean it first. Then he needed to figure out what she was talking about.

Five minutes later Geoffrey found a small paper bag that looked too clean to have been in the trash-filled alley for long, and returned to where he'd left the girl.

His mind was still in a state of shock, but it was working well enough now for him to resume wondering what had driven her outside. She was wearing a tank top and faded cotton shorts. It wasn't the attire of someone who'd planned on going back outside. All he could figure was that she must have jumped out of bed, pulled on some tennis shoes and a jacket, and then run out to go to the pharmacy.

Staring at the bloody face before him, Geoffrey realized that the 'girl' was probably actually in her late teens. She was small enough, though, to pass for someone much younger. She also wasn't the girl from his dream. Her hair was shorter. The longer he stared, the more differences he started to see. Subtle differences between her and the girl from his dream: something in the shape of her mouth, and the positioning of her cheekbones.

He should have known that she couldn't really have been someone from his past life. It had likely been nothing more than a dream in the first place, but he'd latched onto it like it represented his only chance at salvation.

Slightly frustrated by the revelation that he wasn't any closer to unraveling the blank slate of his past, Geoffrey turned to the small package he'd been holding. The generic plastic containers had obviously been purchased at the drug store, but the unfamiliar names on the prescriptions didn't provide any further clues as to why she'd taken such risks to obtain them.

If the girl were some kind of addict it would explain the stupidity of her being outside alone at such a late hour, but he didn't see any of the physical evidence he would have expected from someone that far gone into an addiction. The address on the prescription was quite possibly a fake, but Geoffrey couldn't just leave her in the alley, so it seemed the next logical option.

THE GREATER DARKNESS

It wasn't until after Geoffrey had lifted the girl up onto his shoulder and started off that he realized how suspicious he looked. Even in New York, at such a late hour, people wouldn't just let someone walk around carrying an unconscious girl without doing something.

Geoffrey stuck to the shadows as much as possible, checking both ways before hurrying across lighted areas, but was still only halfway to his destination when the sound of approaching voices made his heart skip a beat. It was already too late to run, so Geoffrey decided to hide and hope for the best. Carefully lowering his passenger to the ground, Geoffrey knelt down next to her and did his best to disappear into the slice of shadow he'd found.

As the trio of individuals ahead got closer, Geoffrey's tightened up to the point where he had the beginnings of a headache. The trio who rounded the corner and stepped into Geoffrey's field of vision were all twenty-something males who'd obviously just finished a night of clubbing or some other form of entertainment involving plenty of alcohol. They joked and stumbled into each other with the kind of abandon only achieved by the truly drunk. The next few seconds, as first one then another of the partiers glanced in his direction without seeing him, stretched into hours.

As the last of the three started to turn onto another side street, the girl at Geoffrey's feet abruptly thrashed, as if in the throes of some nightmare, sending nearby garbage banging into the dumpster beside them.

The sound was so obviously artificial that even a drunk had to realize something was hiding behind the dumpster. Geoffrey's fears were confirmed when he looked up and saw a pair of bleary eyes staring directly at him with an intensity that had been missing from the casual glances aimed his way previously.

Geoffrey didn't want to be forced to silence the drunk; he mentally begged the other man to just turn and walk away, but he was already preparing himself to strike. The pressure inside Geoffrey's mind ratcheted higher in lockstep with his fear, and then the man inexplicably turned and staggered away humming something unrecognizable as he tried to catch up with his friends.

Geoffrey looked down to check on the girl, and felt an incredible sense of relief. She was unharmed, but still unconscious. The breath that Geoffrey hadn't realized he was holding escaped his lungs in a quiet burst that seemed to take all of his energy with it. It was several minutes before he was able to regain his feet and continue the journey to the address listed on the prescription.

The last few blocks of the trip passed uneventfully, and Geoffrey quickly found himself standing before one of the more run-down projects he'd yet seen. Amazingly enough, the lock on the front door still worked, and Geoffrey was momentarily worried until he found a set of keys in the girl's jacket. He took a surprising amount of solace in the fact that he wouldn't be forced to destroy the lock in what was probably the only project in the whole city with a front door that actually worked.

The thought of the look on some poor resident's face as the elevator doors opened to reveal a menacing, blood-covered man and an unconscious teen was humorous in a morbid sort of way, but not sufficiently so for Geoffrey to risk it, so he took the fifteen flights of stairs.

The door to apartment 15B was a graffiti-covered monstrosity with three deadbolts that didn't stand out at all from the rest of the doors in the hallway. As Geoffrey turned his borrowed keys in each of the locks, he suddenly became nervous that he'd open the door and be confronted by one or more angry parents. He paused for several seconds between each deadbolt, but heard nothing to make him think that anyone had awoken.

The apartment proved to be nearly as bad off as the exterior door. It wasn't that things weren't clean or tidy, but the peeling paint and shabby furniture bore silent testament to just how down on their luck her family was.

Geoffrey looked around, and then picked one of the two bedrooms at random and carried his charge over to it. The room obviously belonged to a teenage girl. A large picture collage, clearly from some of the more popular fashion magazines, took up most of one wall. The opposite wall had a needlepoint that was apparently done years ago with a little pink teddy bear, the text "seven pounds one ounce," and a date at the very bottom. The tiny desk and its contents drew Geoffrey's gaze next. The large diary stationed prominently in the center of the writing surface seemed to give the only other clue as to the girl's passions. Rather than the pink, frilly thing that Geoffrey would have half expected, it was a somber, hardbound affair with a dark blue binding.

Geoffrey was so tired that his first impulse was to lay the girl down on her bed. As bloody as she was though, all that would have succeeded in doing was staining her comforter.

The floor looked like it was finished with something that would clean up relatively easily, so Geoffrey gently set his charge down and then paused. He needed a plan to clean the girl, but was reluctant to proceed with the most obvious course of action.

The key thing was to make sure that she didn't wake up and find herself covered in blood. If he could put her back in her bed in a clean set of clothing there was a chance that she'd chalk everything up as having been nothing more than a nightmare. It was a small chance, but it represented the only course he could see that didn't end up with her being traumatized for life.

The thought of the girl waking up bloody and shaken from an attempted rape filled Geoffrey with sadness. The vampire wasn't sure how long he sat staring at the girl, but finally the pain in his head and his rapidly increasing exhaustion pulled him back to the present.

Geoffrey reached back down to the girl and then realized that his hands were still covered with blood. The nausea that had been suppressed by the need to get the girl home suddenly came back full force, and Geoffrey nearly ran to the tiny bathroom. He forced himself to not lose it. He couldn't afford to wake her family up.

Geoffrey cleaned his hands as best he could on one of the cleaner parts of his shirt and then decided to investigate the remaining bedroom. It was sound tactical thinking, but he knew it was driven more by his desire to delay what he needed to do next.

Padding over to the mostly-closed door, Geoffrey peered into the room and his heart dropped and tears started to well up in his eyes. Now he knew what would drive someone out into the night against all better judgment and common sense.

The shabby-but-orderly room was slightly larger than the girl's, but crowded as it was with medical equipment, it felt infinitely smaller. Most of the floor space was taken up by a large hospital-style bed. The little bit of room remaining had been divided out among a number of monitors that seemed to be keeping track of everything from blood pressure to heart rate and a number of things in between that Geoffrey had no idea how to interpret.

Lying in the bed, her tiny form nearly swallowed up in its white vastness, was the thinnest woman Geoffrey had ever seen.

As Geoffrey's gaze came to rest on the poor woman, he dropped to his knees. Pain. She was in an incredible amount of pain. There was no way he could know that, no reason he should feel it as his own, but he did. She was being kept heavily sedated, her mind slowly rotting away under the harsh tide of chemicals that were all that sustained her pale shadow life.

His hand held against his head, Geoffrey backed out of the room and pulled the door closed, unconsciously sighing in relief when the pain receded enough to begin thinking again. It had to be just the two of them there. There weren't beds for anyone else. It was possible that someone came by regularly to help care for the mother—the complexity of the machines she was hooked up to certainly would suggest as much—but still, he couldn't imagine the burden the girl must bear.

Secure in the knowledge that nobody was going to investigate any strange sounds, Geoffrey stopped off at the little bathroom and cleaned the blood from his hands and arms. There wasn't anything else left to do. It was time to stop stalling and give the girl back as much of a normal life as he was able.

Trying not to feel like a voyeur, Geoffrey returned to the bedroom and stripped off the girl's tank top and shorts. Keeping his eyes averted as much as possible from the pale skin he'd just uncovered, Geoffrey sponged her arms and legs clean, and then set about searching for replacement clothing that looked like it might pass for pajamas. The dresser in the corner finally provided another pair of shorts with the tattered remnants of some kind of logo, and another tank top that looked like it had seen better days.

Once the girl was properly covered, Geoffrey picked her back up and placed her under the covers of her bed, all the while trying not to think about how Venice, with her goddess-like beauty, hadn't kindled even a fraction of the desire he'd just felt.

Seeking some kind of distraction from his wildly spiraling thoughts, Geoffrey looked up at the needlepoint he'd spotted earlier and did the math around her birthday. He would have placed her at sixteen or seventeen, but apparently would have been wrong; she was older than she looked. Geoffrey cleaned the blood off of the floor and then just before turning to leave, he once again spied the girl's diary. Carefully penned on the first page were words that seemed to draw Geoffrey's eyes as if of their own volition.

Abhorred of fate
Forgotten by all
She falls unnoticed
And with her goes
My world

The room suddenly seemed to close in. Geoffrey fled from the apartment, only barely able to remember to lock the door behind him. He'd killed her. Her mother too. Imastious would find out and he'd kill them both to punish Geoffrey.

Chapter 7

Geoffrey knew he was dreaming, but that piece of knowledge faded into unimportance when faced by the power of his dreams.

The girl from the projects was back, dressed in dated clothes and smiling at him. No, he was wrong. This was the first girl, the one he'd thought he was saving.

Geoffrey tried to reach out to her, tried to go to her, but something was restraining him. The smile took on a teasing air that momentarily warmed the room, but Geoffrey's heart was beating so erratically in his chest that he knew something terrible was about to happen.

A tall, dark figure materialized out of thin air and loomed over the girl's shoulder. Unaware of the menacing presence behind her, the girl continued on with some trivial task, while every mote in Geoffrey's body cried out, begging her to run.

A black curtain rippled across the scene, leaving Geoffrey alone. Not just alone. Forsaken. Somehow Geoffrey knew the girl was dead. The sense of complete loss that entailed ripped something vibrant and living from his being, leaving him numb and hollow inside. He should have died with her.

The dream abruptly continued, and Geoffrey found himself staring at the girl he'd saved the night before. The smile she bestowed on Geoffrey was different than that of the first girl. There was too much pain and sorrow in it for anyone to fancy that it would light up a room, but it tugged at Geoffrey's heart in ways he hadn't anticipated.

How could someone who'd seen so little good still be able to smile? How did she continue on day after day?

As Geoffrey completed the thought, blood appeared out of nowhere and covered the girl's face, causing her to look down until she finally realized that it wasn't her own. The look of horror as the girl looked back up at Geoffrey, and then turned and ran away, filled him with such a profound sense of loss that he tried to follow her. He found himself unable to move, and when he looked down he found that his bloody hands were shackled to the floor.

"Wake up, love, the night is a-wasting."

Slightly disoriented, Geoffrey opened his eyes, half expecting to see the girl, but instead finding Venice poised inches above his face, so that her platinum hair walled them both off from the outside world.

Rusty reflexes that Geoffrey didn't remember ever training kicked in, and his palm shot up towards Venice's throat, only to be deftly blocked by her forearm as she dropped her slight weight down so that she was resting on him.

"Nice try, sweetie, but you're still too slow to pull off something like that."

Geoffrey pushed Venice off and rolled out of bed. "How do you keep getting in here?"

"Still not using that brain, huh?" Venice rolled her eyes while fidgeting with her outfit, as if to remove some imaginary flaw introduced by being flung to the side. "If you stopped to think about it, you would realize that there are any number of ways that I could get into your flat, but the truth of the matter is that you gave me a key before your unfortunate descent into amnesia."

She was lying.

"That is a nice story, but that's all it is. How did you really get in?"

Venice narrowed her eyes slightly, and then flashed a dazzling smile as she stretched out on the bed in a way that allowed her brown halter top to show off her tight stomach.

"Now you're guessing. I've played enough games, card and otherwise, with you over the years to know when you're bluffing."

Geoffrey shook his head again. "You're the one who's bluffing. You don't really believe that. In fact, you...fear something related to my knowing how you got in."

Venice smiled once again and then shrugged. "You are of course free to believe whatever you want, but we're wasting time. Why don't you join me back down here?"

Rage washed through Geoffrey as he realized once again just how easily he was being manipulated.

Without thinking, the angered young man scooped up his katana from where it was resting on the floor. Before Venice could move, he whipped it out of its sheath and down towards her so that it came to a stop with the point resting against her ribs.

"I'm through with your stupid games. You can tell me what you're hiding, or you can die."

Venice looked back at Geoffrey unconcernedly from beneath dark lashes. "Why, love, I do believe that I've finally managed to make you angry."

Geoffrey's hands started to tremble almost imperceptibly as Venice laughed slightly. "But do you really have it in you to just kill me in cold blood? You keep telling me you're not really a killer—that you've somehow magically changed to a kinder, gentler Geoffrey. Is this really how you want things to go down?"

Geoffrey responded by putting more weight behind his weapon, pushing it ever so slightly into Venice's skin, only to find it abruptly stop as if it had run up against a steel plate.

Venice smiled once again as confusion flashed across Geoffrey's face. "Nice trick, huh?"

Geoffrey pushed harder still, but the weapon remained motionless.

"Imastious is going to be so unhappy that you learned my little secret, but I can hardly be blamed for what happened. Even *he* expected you to go on whining about how you didn't want to kill anyone for another few weeks. Violence like this is quite unexpected."

Geoffrey tried to pull his katana back, but it moved only a fraction of an inch before a frown of concentration appeared on Venice's face. Once again the weapon felt like it had been encased in concrete.

Venice's countenance once again returned to its familiar, relaxed state as she looked at Geoffrey again. "I suppose I really should reward you for your progress, unexpected as it may be."

Something tore the weapon from Geoffrey's grasp, and then set it carefully on a chair across the room. "You see, we all have our little powers. Mine happens to be a form of telekinesis."

In response to Geoffrey's blank look, Venice gently laughed. "Your noggin shut down again, love? I can move things with my mind."

As Venice rubbed at the small spot of blood Geoffrey's blade had left on her, Geoffrey had a sudden epiphany. "Imastious can read minds, and…"

Venice smiled once again. "There you have it, love, but you didn't learn that from me. Of course Imastious has some telekinetic and pyromancer abilities as well, but he is primarily a mentalist."

Geoffrey almost didn't hear what Venice had just said due to the maelstrom of thoughts flying around his mind. He had to be a mentalist as well. It was the only thing that explained everything that had happened recently.

Venice watched him as he finally looked at her again. "Oh, I do love to see the gears turning away in that beautiful head of yours. In fact, I can almost feel the rebelliousness radiating off of you. Your next thought will no doubt be how you could possibly use this information to break Imastious' hold over you."

Rising from the bed, Venice walked over and ran her hands down Geoffrey's arms. "Since I'm feeling so generous today, I'll give you some freebies. Imastious can read your mind. You'll eventually figure out that you're a mentalist, but he is at least several hundred years older than you. As a result, his powers are much greater than yours. So, even though you're a tough nut to crack, he'll do it on any occasion where he feels there's a need to do so."

Geoffrey shifted, trying to maintain his distance from Venice as she edged ever closer. "Why are you helping me?"

"I told you, I'm feeling generous. That, and I want us to be together like we used to be. I'm doing what's required to show you I'm trustworthy."

Geoffrey nodded as though he believed her, but secretly wasn't convinced. So far Venice had just told him things that he would have eventually figured out on his own. He already knew there was more to his power than just reading minds. In the church he'd done more than just sense that the two women were sad. He'd cushioned them from their sorrow, just like the priest had hinted. Geoffrey wished that he could trust Venice. He needed to know the full range of what he might be capable of, but he knew that trusting her would be a mistake.

Venice continued while he was still thinking.

"As strong as Imastious is, he can only read your surface thoughts easily. As you become more disciplined, even that will become harder for him. That is part of the reason he tortured you the other night--it brought your mental defenses down to a point where he could penetrate them relatively easily."

Venice once again stepped closer, and this time there wasn't any room left for Geoffrey to back away. "This matters because as much effort as is involved in breaking into your mind, Imastious is only going to do so as long as he has reason not to trust you."

Geoffrey tried to ignore the warm breath that was caressing his neck. "Make the kill, toe the line, and you'll be able, for the most part, to keep your secrets."

The thought of killing again disturbed Geoffrey, more than he'd thought it would after having done so more than once already. This would be different though. It would be cold-blooded, with no excuses. No hunger, no imperiled teenager, just him taking a life prematurely.

With a mental effort that was so strong it almost pained him, Geoffrey turned away from Venice and pointed to the door. "If what you are telling me is true, I need some time to think."

Venice pouted as she stepped closer to Geoffrey. The pout turned to a frown as he pushed her away. "You have my thanks, now continue to earn my trust by respecting my wishes and letting me be for now."

Venice stood motionless for several seconds, and then shrugged and flashed him a smile that came very close to changing Geoffrey's mind. "That's the most reasonable you've been in ages, love. I'll comply with your desires for now."

Geoffrey had been fortunate. Imastious hadn't chosen to visit him in the two days since he'd talked to Venice, but more and more he worried that he'd return home and find the old vampire there waiting for him. If he hadn't killed the target by then, it was virtually certain that Imastious would invade his mind again and learn about the girl. Once that happened, it was only a matter of time until Imastious tracked her down and killed her.

Geoffrey had nearly come to peace with the idea until he realized that Imastious wouldn't offer the girl a quick, clean death. Imastious would torture her; he'd leave her broken and bleeding. More than likely she'd beg for death for hours, maybe even days before he'd finally allow her to die.

Killing, even once, for Imastious would set Geoffrey on a dark path. It was undeniable, but that fact seemed unable to drown out the profound sense of loss Geoffrey felt when he thought of the girl suffering as he'd suffered for so many hours. He'd seen the daily struggle the girl had to wage just to get by. In light of that, it was hard to argue that all lives were equally important. Could a life like hers really be said to be of no more value than that of the drug dealer Imastious wanted him to kill?

Geoffrey knew his logic was darkly seductive. A part of him knew his whirling, almost feverish mind wasn't thinking clearly—that the old priest would poke holes in his reasoning—but most of him didn't care. Geoffrey had already decided that the girl's life was more important than the lives of the three rapists that he'd cut down to save her. Even the priest wouldn't have been able to argue with that decision. If it had been okay to kill to save her life once, wouldn't the girl's life be more important than the life of Geoffrey's current target?

His mind still clouded with conflicting thoughts, Geoffrey turned down a side street and tried to avoid looking anyone in the eyes.

He must not have always been the monster Venice kept describing. Why had he taken that first step that ultimately led to him becoming a remorseless assassin? Had he once walked down a crowded street just before sundown as he was doing now, his mind full of the same kinds of justifications?

Would it be possible to do what would be necessary to save the girl and not lose whatever guttering pieces of his soul he still had left? Was he even doing this to save her, or was he just trying to save himself from another round of torture?

Geoffrey's feet, free from the interference of his conscious mind, had once again deposited him before the priest's church. For several moments Geoffrey debated the idea of going inside. He knew that the priest would disapprove of what Geoffrey wanted to do. Whatever counsel the priest was able to offer might make Geoffrey feel somewhat better, but the guilt would return quickly. Ultimately the advice he'd receive would offer nothing but pain in the short term and the slightest glimmer of hope in the long term. If Geoffrey was really destined to go through eternity suffering, at the very least he should be able to pick the pain on his own terms.

Still unsure why he was bothering, Geoffrey tugged on the door handle only to find that it hardly shifted. It surprised him that the doors were locked. The priest had been present later than this both of the other times that they'd spoken.

The tiny sign to the right of the door still declared that the church would be open for another hour, but Geoffrey's knocks on the battered wood failed to bring the sound of footsteps he'd been hoping for.

After a few minutes of waiting, Geoffrey realized that some of the people lounging in the fire escapes and doorways across the street were starting to watch him. Suddenly feeling as though his guilt was emblazoned on his forehead, the vampire turned and strode up the street at a faster pace than he normally used.

Geoffrey walked for another half hour and then realized he was in the area where Imastious' target lived. It would be a small matter to find another place from which to observe him, but Geoffrey didn't know if that was a good idea or a terrible one. Would knowing the target better than he already did make things easier or harder?

Geoffrey's heart rate went up as he tried to make the decision, but as he turned onto a side street the decision was made for him. His target was standing on the corner.

A host of possible actions went through Geoffrey's mind, paralyzing him as he once again felt that everyone looking at him knew what he was considering. Someone across the street exited a small store and the spell was broken. The gentle click as the door swung closed freed Geoffrey to walk over and enter the store.

From inside the store Geoffrey would be able to watch his target, and as long as it looked like he was shopping, nobody should suspect anything.

Slowly picking up a variety of fruit, Geoffrey pretended to be squeezing the individual pieces to test for ripeness, all the while watching his target through the window.

Before Geoffrey had picked up and discarded his fourth honeydew, a busty sixteen-year-old Armenian girl walked over to the target and handed him several bills. Geoffrey couldn't see what the girl received in return, but the expert way that the hand-off was performed left very little doubt in his mind. He'd just witnessed his first drug sale.

The drug dealer slapped the girl's butt as she turned to leave, and then ducked a slap, laughing as she stalked off.

For a moment, the vampire's rational side tried to assert itself, tried to stop his mind from replaying the assault again and again, but the scene refused to leave. By the third replay, the Armenian girl had been replaced by the girl from his dreams. The fourth replay featured the girl Geoffrey had saved, and a cold fury awoke inside the vampire with an intensity that would have scared him had he been entirely in control of himself.

The mounting pressure inside Geoffrey's head suddenly found a release as his thoughts pushed free of the physical shell where they normally resided and reached out towards the drug dealer.

As the first tendrils made contact, they seemed to stab into the other man's thoughts of their own accord. The torrent of fragmented, brittle memories and thoughts that raged down the connection and assailed Geoffrey's mind were incredibly vile.

Teenagers he'd given their first dose for free, living in a burnt-out shell of a building. Girls he'd taken everything from until they had only their bodies to offer in trade. Rivals gunned down from the shadows. It was all that the vampire could do to maintain his sense of self against the depravity that tried to wash away his identity. It took an incredible act of will, but he was somehow able to stay level-headed enough to force a simple thought back through the link.

Home, the man needed to go home.

The anger flooding through Geoffrey was only barely leashed. The metal table holding the fruit he'd just dropped groaned in distress, and he absentmindedly let go, releasing it before the sheet metal bent completely away from the frame.

Geoffrey's target flinched slightly as the vampire cut the connection. It was a piece of evidence that his efforts might have worked, but the information barely registered against his fight to steady his trembling legs. The fight to keep the fury raging through him from taking complete control took everything he had.

A few seconds later, the target exchanged words with a couple of the other dealers and then turned and headed into his apartment building.

Geoffrey took a deep breath and then walked out of the store, his anger pushing him to follow as soon as the drug dealer disappeared around the corner of the building.

Entering the building, with a casualness that felt forced, Geoffrey quickly found the stairs and headed up them trying to remember which floor he'd been on when he'd observed his target from the fire escape. He was pretty sure it was the fifth floor, but now wasn't the time to be wrong.

Once the vampire hit the fourth floor he slowed down and stopped taking the stairs three at a time. The doubts which had plagued him were gone now. This man needed to die. Geoffrey would be serving justice--no more, no less.

THE GREATER DARKNESS

Geoffrey reached the fifth floor and turned towards the footsteps approaching from the left. He'd do it nice and easy, just like Venice had taught him. A quick strike to the neck and it would all be over.

The vampire slipped the retaining strap off of his katana but held it with his left hand to ensure that it didn't fall to the floor. It sounded like the man had reached his door. He was just around the corner now.

Keys jingled just ahead, and then Geoffrey turned the corner to see his target opening the door. Before Geoffrey could take another step the drug dealer reached into his jacket and then Geoffrey was looking down the barrel of a handgun from just ten feet away. "Besides being stupid, what are you, cracker? Some kind of Goth detective? People don't come here unless they live here, want drugs, or belong to Five-O."

Geoffrey's mind was blank. The reflexes that took over when he'd saved the girl were shockingly absent. He teetered on the verge of hysteria as his rage evaporated, giving way to terror. He was going to die. How stupid could he have been?

Unsatisfied by Geoffrey's lack of response, the drug dealer walked a couple steps closer and yelled. "Answer me before I bust you, mother effer."

Geoffrey tried to answer. It was as if time had slowed down, but his oxygen needs hadn't altered. He couldn't get enough air, couldn't get the words out. Despite that, he felt himself come to a decision. If he was going to die, he would die fighting rather than just waiting to be executed.

Still seeming to move at half speed, the vampire drew his sword with his left hand and dropped to his knees as the katana slowly arced up towards the hand holding the nine-millimeter semiautomatic. A pressure wave tugged at Geoffrey's hair, and then his right hand joined his left on the long hilt of his sword. The lethal length of steel jerked slightly in his hands as it swept through the dealer's arm.

As the Glock fell to the ground, time seemed to speed back up to normal. Reflexes that went far beyond anything Venice had yet shown him took over and Geoffrey leaned forward, sweeping his weapon back around in a lightning strike to the man's neck.

Looking at the pieces that had seconds before been a living person, the vampire started shaking as the cushion of fear no longer shielded him from what he'd done. This hadn't been self-defense. Geoffrey had deliberately set out to kill this man. He was just as much of a murderer as his target had been.

The realization that his ear hurt, that the fluids trickling down his neck had to be blood, nearly drove Geoffrey over the edge to panic. An inch to the side and that bullet would have blown out the back of his head. What had he done? What had he gotten himself into?

With a mental effort that he hadn't believed himself capable of, Geoffrey pulled himself together. He had to get out of the building. People would have heard the gunshot; they would have already called the police.

Geoffrey looked around and then spying the open door to the drug dealer's apartment, quickly slipped inside, pushing the door shut with his foot as he went past.

Chapter 8

With darkness already closing in, fleeing the scene of the crime had been relatively easy. The fire escape had allowed Geoffrey to access the roof. From there it was just a matter of running from rooftop to rooftop until he reached the end of the block and climbed down another fire escape to the street.

Once the vampire had made it far enough that he wasn't in immediate danger of being apprehended by the police, he'd stumbled over to an alley and vomited. Shaking and weak, Geoffrey hadn't wanted to do anything more than head directly home, but instead he'd found a nearly deserted apartment building in which to hide for a couple hours while any search for him cooled down. After that, the route home had been long, circuitous, and filled with frequent stops to check for tails.

Geoffrey couldn't afford to have someone follow him home. If that happened he'd never even see them coming. Being gunned down in an ambush would be no more than he deserved but he was more concerned over the fact that he didn't feel more guilt. He did feel guilty, but it seemed like he should feel even worse. Maybe it was just that emotion on the scale that murder really deserved couldn't be maintained for very long.

Geoffrey breathed a sigh of relief as he finally entered his building and started up the stairs. He reached his door and unlocked it, but paused as he realized he wasn't alone. The vampire reached past his exhaustion, and clumsily tried to extend his thoughts as he'd done earlier against the man he'd murdered.

For several seconds, as he waited in the darkness, Geoffrey's efforts met without any success, and then suddenly, it was as if he'd pierced the surface tension on a bowl of water. A few tendrils of consciousness drifted free of his body, questing for another mind.

Geoffrey grabbed his head in pain and fell through the now-open door as something incredibly powerful lashed out, striking his thoughts hard enough to cause him to withdraw them.

"You've earned yourself some leniency by finally making that kill, but don't presume that it extends to allowing you to try and access my mind."

Imastious rose from the shadows that had hidden him in Geoffrey's chair, and walked towards the younger vampire, who'd fallen to the ground. The violence of the mental attack to which he'd been subjected left Geoffrey more than a little disoriented. As he looked up in confusion, Imastious shook his head.

"So your efforts were unconscious. That is unfortunate, as my response will no doubt lead you to discover your latent abilities sooner than you otherwise would have, but it's truly of little importance."

Imastious reached into one of the pockets on his suit coat and fished out a large stack of currency. "As I said, you've done well. You're free to do as you will for the foreseeable future. Here is sufficient money for your needs. Venice or I will let you know the next time you're needed."

After Imastious had left the apartment, Geoffrey locked his door and then collapsed onto his bed, steadfastly refusing to look at the stack of money on the dresser.

Geoffrey's dreams over the next few days and nights had been terrible blood-soaked things that left him shaking and cold each of the many times he'd awoken. The vampire had found that he could no longer keep a meal down. Each time he tried to eat, images of the drug dealer falling down in a spray of blood had invaded his mind, causing him to become physically ill at the way his body responded to the thought. It was bad enough that he was a killer, but craving blood like this surely was a foretaste of the hell that the priest had warned would await him.

The hunger was a curse, starting as a slight inconvenience about the time Imastious had left and then growing to a constant torment within a few days. In a way, Geoffrey welcomed the pain and discomfort. It did seem a fitting punishment, but it held within it the further seeds of his damnation. If he continued to go without, he would eventually lose control just as Venice had warned. Any doubt he might have had of that fact had been pre-empted by what had happened in the train tunnels. He'd already started losing track of time, so it couldn't be that much longer before he would find himself in unfamiliar surroundings, covered in blood.

Geoffrey finally pulled himself out of bed, showered, and left his apartment. After so many hours of torment, he'd thought he was resigned to the prospect of assaulting, and potentially killing, so that he could feed, but the vampire quickly found that the cold-blooded reality of stalking a target was more than he could handle.

He encountered four different girls. Each of them had seemed more than willing to go somewhere secluded with him, but he couldn't bring himself to go through with it. Once he'd spent a little while talking to them they'd become people to him. People with goals and fears. People with dreams, dreams that he couldn't risk extinguishing. There was just too much chance that the hunger would take over and push him into taking too much.

Instead of satisfying his craving, Geoffrey found himself once again walking the nearly deserted streets of the city as he looked for some kind of way out of the eternal hell in which he was trapped.

Realizing that he wasn't getting any closer to a solution, Geoffrey made a decision that he knew he'd eventually regret. The vampire looked up at the street signs to orient himself and then set off in the direction of the tiny church that had come to represent all the things he wished he was, at the same time that it condemned him for what he'd become.

Geoffrey already knew what the priest would tell him, but in a way he was looking forward to it. He deserved to suffer, and if nothing else, this would serve as one more way to achieve that end.

As he covered the three miles to the church, Geoffrey practiced reaching out with his mind. It might have been nothing more than his imagination, but he thought it was becoming easier to sense the thoughts of those around him. If he kept the mental touch light enough, then he didn't get bombarded with so much force. The surface thoughts he was able to read seemed like they would usually be more than enough for his purposes.

The vampire hadn't ever thought of the neighborhood he was approaching as being particularly bad, but the closer he got to it, the more the thoughts he sensed turned dark and fearful. It seemed impossible that people could really live like this, constantly worried about whether or not they'd survive to pay the next set of bills.

As Geoffrey got within a block of the church, he expected to find people more at peace, but instead he found the opposite. Something was obviously wrong. The tranquility that he'd felt before couldn't have been completely imagined, but that had changed. If anything, it seemed he was approaching the epicenter of the despair in the area.

The tiny building came into view, sandwiched between a pair of five-story apartment buildings, and Geoffrey's fears were confirmed by the sight of a pair of teenagers lounging next to the door. A cautious, sensible part of Geoffrey demanded that he turn and go back the way he came, but a strange sense of fury had started to bubble inside of him. How dare they take something sacred from him! It seemed only right to take something equally precious from them in return.

The bored gang members looked up disinterestedly as Geoffrey approached them, but they started exuding a sense of menace once they realized that he wasn't just going to pass by.

"Ain't gonna be no services tonight. Get lost."

Faking an easy, complacent smile to buy himself time, Geoffrey reached out with his thoughts. The amorality the vampire found before him was so sickening that if he hadn't been cushioned by his hatred, he probably would have once again been physically ill. These boys had killed, repeatedly. They'd killed for sport, for money, and even just to increase their reputation.

While he was digesting the implications of the gang members' thoughts, Geoffrey crossed the remaining distance to the church door. The closer, shorter gang member apparently decided that the vampire needed additional persuasion.

The hand that shot towards Geoffrey was probably just meant to grab him, but conscious thought never entered into his response. Geoffrey saw a flash of movement, and then found himself sliding backwards and to the left as his right hand reached up and plucked the shorter man's wrist out of the air.

About the time the vampire registered the fact that he had moved, his left hand came up in a knife-hand strike that crushed the other man's throat.

The second gang member's mouth had dropped open in surprise at the sudden explosion of violence that hadn't been accompanied by any of the posturing that he'd come to expect from his time on the streets. The teenager was still trying to understand what exactly was going on when a slightly curved, razor-sharp tanto that Geoffrey hadn't remembered drawing sliced through his neck.

Time was of the essence. Geoffrey needed to move quickly or the cops would arrive before he would be able to escape.

Geoffrey slipped through the door, and drew his katana, his thoughts reaching out for threats. The stink of sadism was strong throughout the building, seeming to justify the vampire's actions as he cut down one person after another all the while screaming. "Where is he, what did you do with him?"

Figures, all dressed in brown to some extent or another, charged towards Geoffrey, only to stumble and fall as the soulless edge of his sword took their flesh. The anger and hate burning inside Geoffrey shielded him from the illness he should have felt. The entire experience happened in a haze that obscured irrelevant details and reduced everyone to mere targets while simultaneously shielding him from the pain of the minor wounds he was receiving.

The vampire cleared the chapel and then moved to the tiny office and other attached rooms. The last gang member took refuge in a bathroom in a futile effort to hide, but Geoffrey pinpointed his thoughts, burst into the tiny room, and picked the teenager up by his throat.

"Where is he, what did you do to him?"

The eyes that stared back at Geoffrey were so fear-filled that for a moment the vampire thought the boy had retreated behind a shield of insanity. It didn't really matter though. He would take what he needed regardless.

Reaching deep into the gang member's mind, Geoffrey sifted through the chaotic thoughts, slicing through memories, hopes, and fears, until he found what he was looking for. The gang hadn't killed the priest, at least not as far as this kid knew. They'd just realized that the church was abandoned and thought that they probably had their turf so cowed that nobody would do anything about it if they moved in.

Geoffrey's anger, which had been on the decline, flared up again at the thought of all the terrorized people he'd felt brush his consciousness as he'd traveled to the church. Reaching his thoughts even deeper into the boys' mind, the vampire pushed his own feelings through the link, imprinting them on the quivering collection of memories before him.

What the boy had done to terrorize those around him was inexcusable. It was only just that he taste at least a small portion of the helplessness he'd inflicted on others.

The vampire pulled the boy down and spun him around so they were facing the same direction. The gangster had mastered his fear enough to want to resist, but Geoffrey intercepted the thoughts before they were able to fully coalesce and crushed them ruthlessly.

As the boy finally began to understand the futility of his efforts, Geoffrey sank his teeth into the tattooed skin before him. The pain that shot through the boy's thoughts should have revolted Geoffrey, but instead it gave him a sick sense of satisfaction.

He let his mind push a single additional message to the boy. "Yes, you are helpless."

The blood trickling down Geoffrey's throat sent little thrills of pleasure through him. For a moment he lost himself in the bliss of finally satisfying the hunger that had been stalking him for days. It wasn't until the trickle slowed, and the lattice of thoughts before him started to dim, that the vampire came back to himself and dropped the boy.

Geoffrey's hate and anger were suddenly extinguished as the magnitude of what he'd done swept through him. He'd killed them all. Most of them had been murderers, but he hadn't taken the time to be certain that they all were. The one he'd just fed from hadn't been a murderer. He'd been headed that direction, but he hadn't crossed that line yet. Geoffrey hadn't just fed on him, he'd enjoyed his terror.

Geoffrey had done exactly the thing he'd condemned the boy for. He'd tried to rationalize the deaths he'd caused up to this point as justice, but if this boy did die it would be something else, something darker.

Geoffrey reached down to pick the teenager up, only to pause at the sound of distant sirens. Reflexes took over and the vampire found himself running out the back door before his mind had fully processed what he was doing.

He was a coward. Not only that, Venice and Imastious were right. He was a killer. He should stay and let the police apprehend him, let them put him away like the animal he was. It was a tempting solution to his problems, but what if Imastious' reach was really as long as the older vampire kept implying it was?

If he could get to Geoffrey inside of prison he'd find out about the girl. He'd kill her as punishment. Geoffrey deserved to be punished, but the girl didn't.

Geoffrey couldn't change what he'd done, but he could at least protect her. He knew that he would hate himself later, but that didn't stop his headlong flight.

Chapter 9

Venice executed a blindingly fast overhead strike towards Geoffrey's head, but he caught her practice weapon on his own and turned the blow so that it slid past his shoulder.

"You're getting better, love. I'm still faster, but you're gaining ground on me."

Geoffrey launched an attack of his own, moving with speed he almost couldn't believe as he sliced his weapon towards Venice's stomach. She effortlessly parried the blow and riposted with an attack that hit his arm with bone-bruising force.

It was the kind of injury that should hurt for days, but his body seemed to heal faster than a normal person's. All of the wounds that he'd taken at the church had been gone within a day or so.

The thought of what he had done at the church brought a wave of sadness that must have made it to Geoffrey's face. Rather than telling him to defend himself again, Venice lowered her weapon and stepped back.

"There, there, love, don't fret. You're making real progress, especially considering how recently we started all of this."

Maybe Geoffrey would have felt a little better if the last kid had survived, but probably not. Even if the EMT's had arrived in time to save him it wouldn't have changed the fact that Geoffrey had tried to kill him. There wasn't any getting away from the seriousness of what he'd done.

Realizing that Venice was waiting for a response, Geoffrey faked a smile. "Oh, I'm fine."

Venice smiled back and then pulled her tank top over her head, leaving her dressed in just light cotton pants and a sports bra. "Well, I think we're pretty much done here, so it's time for a shower. I suppose that you're going to remain a prude and refuse to join me?"

Geoffrey had long since learned that the best course of action was to just ignore Venice when she started to flirt. "I'm going to go for a run while you're doing that. Lock up when you leave."

Venice's eyes tightened slightly, but then she shrugged in indifference. "I don't understand this sudden love of running, especially considering that you don't take any kind of weapon with you when you do it."

"You told me yourself that you run to maintain your conditioning. If what you tell me is true, no normal human could keep up with me, so it isn't like I have anything to worry about there."

"Yes, I do run, but I do so inside on a treadmill in the controlled environment of a very exclusive gym. That way, suitably overawed and appreciative males can watch me out of the corner of their eyes and wish for the kinds of offers from me that you so casually dismiss."

Despite his foul mood, a smile nearly made it to Geoffrey's lips. Venice really did have a way of growing on a person. He still didn't trust her, not by a long shot, but she was kind of nice to have around.

"Fine, continue with your uncivilized ways. I'll lock everything up when I leave, but in all seriousness, you need to stop thinking of humans as your only threat--there are other vampires out there who will kill you in a heartbeat if they realize who and what you are."

Geoffrey's mood further soured at the thought of someone like Imastious actively trying to kill him, but he just grabbed his keys and headed out the door.

Geoffrey had little if any real hope that running would help him sort anything out, but possibly it would at least serve as a distraction for a short time. The vampire settled into a natural pace that his body seemed willing to sustain, and absently wished that it was still light out so that he could see the vibrant green of the foliage as it slid past him.

No amount of exertion seemed able to tear Geoffrey's mind away from his problems, but he increased his speed with each mile in a vain attempt to force his thoughts into some semblance of order.

The last mile flew by in a near sprint, leaving Geoffrey feeling as crushed physically as he was emotionally, but it still didn't accomplish what he'd hoped it would. His mind still troubled, the vampire started walking in a random direction to allow his body to begin cooling down.

Venice had come over early enough that even after running for longer than normal, it still wasn't late enough for most of the city to have gone to bed. The first couple of panhandlers Geoffrey passed tried to accost the vampire, but halfway through their pitch something in his eyes caused them to begin stammering and back away.

Their business was one of making people feel guilt and loss, but when faced with real evil, actual suffering, apparently they'd turn and run lest it somehow prove contagious. None of them really knew what it meant to suffer.

Geoffrey's feelings boiled inside of him, seeking the catharsis that had been denied him during his run, and for a split second the vampire wanted to cry. Tears might be the only way to purge himself of everything he was feeling, but something refused to let Geoffrey break down. Instead the sorrow turned to anger, an anger that made him spiteful. He started reaching out with his thoughts to somehow punish them and then thought of the girl he'd saved.

She knew what it was to suffer. She knew what it was like to watch her only remaining family member slowly slip away from her, all the while wishing there was something she could do to halt their decline. She knew what it meant to slip out in the night, fearing for her life but still risking who knew what to try and bring relief to that last family member.

Geoffrey had avoided thinking about the girl for quite some time, as if doing so might somehow prevent Imastious from learning about her, but his worry for her now pushed its way to the forefront of his mind. Was she okay? How had the memory of what had happened affected her?

The vampire knew it was foolish to meddle any further than he had, but he nonetheless found his feet turning so that he was walking towards the projects where everything had happened.

He placated his conscience by telling himself that it didn't matter. He would get there, the door would be locked, and that would be that. It was too late for her to be out and about, so waiting to see whether or not she looked okay would be a pointless exercise. He would mope about and then, having safely gotten her out of his system, he'd go home and forget about her.

Geoffrey arrived at his destination, but his desire to see the girl had grown rather than fading as he'd expected. He looked up at one of the few windows still lit up in the building and tried to remember whether it was hers, or if hers had been the one just to the west. A memory bubbled to the surface of Geoffrey's mind, and he allowed himself to picture the way she'd looked lying peacefully in her bed, seemingly unspotted by all the violence she had just seen, unmarred by all the suffering she'd experienced.

Hesitantly trying the outside door, the vampire found that someone had destroyed the lock since his first visit. As he started inside, he told himself that he'd go to the top of the building, climb down to her window, and look in from the fire escape for just a few minutes. He'd be there just long enough to confirm she was okay and then he'd leave forever.

A few minutes later Geoffrey crept down the corroded metal until he reached her window. The lack of lights initially made it impossible to verify that he had the right apartment, until the vampire recognized the barely visible curtains resting against the window frame.

Trembling from emotions he couldn't identify, Geoffrey curled up in a shadow and closed his eyes. It was coming easier now, after so many hours of practice. Geoffrey filtered through the chaos of his thoughts and found the subtly alien part of his mind that allowed him to reach out with his thoughts.

The thinnest of tendrils drifted into the room, slowly questing for his target. When Geoffrey finally brushed up against the girl's thoughts, the contact was so light as to be practically imperceptible.

She was asleep, but not peacefully so. Geoffrey strengthened the connection between them until he was able to pick out more surface thoughts. As images started flowing through the link, Geoffrey found himself looking out of the girl's eyes as she stood in front of a mirror. He had just enough time to register he was in a public bathroom of some kind before his attention was captured by the figure staring back at him.

It was the girl, but she looked different. It was as if even the slightest of imperfections had been magnified and made more obvious. The lithe, almost perfect figure that Geoffrey remembered from the last time he'd seen her had been replaced with a heavier, average build that, if anything, was disproportionately small-chested and large through the hips. The shiny dark hair that had reminded Geoffrey so much of the girl from his dream was now dull, somehow changed to a decidedly less appealing shade of brown.

The only possible explanation for her altered appearance was that this was how the girl saw herself. Before Geoffrey could reflect on what would cause such a disconnect from reality, the bathroom doors swung open and a trio of emaciated teenage girls walked in and surrounded the sink where Geoffrey and his host were standing.

"What are you doing in here, loser?"

A wave of anger rose inside of Geoffrey at the hurt flowing through the link.

"Nice outfit, Melody, I think my grandma wore something like that back when dinosaurs roamed the earth."

The hurt increased, joined by spikes of inferiority and shame.

Once she stopped laughing, the blonde girl standing in the middle of the trio looked Geoffrey/Melody over and shook her head. "You so don't make the cut to be here, go use the bathroom down by the sophomore lockers."

As the scene dissolved into something else with the usual abruptness of a dream, Geoffrey withdrew his mental probe from the girl's thoughts. Melody, the girl's name was Melody. At least Geoffrey had that much now.

Chapter 10

Ever since Geoffrey had shared Melody's dream he hadn't been able to think of anything other than her plight with the three girls. Even his own situation hadn't made the vampire feel quite as helpless as what was happening to her. Geoffrey's plan to help had seemed much more reasonable before he'd spent several hours sitting out in the uncomfortable sunlight. He wished that he'd thought to pull the names of the three girls from Melody's mind when he'd followed her to school. Unfortunately, unless he was going to turn around now there was nothing to do but press on. If all else failed, he could always try again tomorrow.

Shrugging slightly, Geoffrey stood and walked towards the main entrance of the school. It had probably been a shiny marvel back twenty years ago but now just looked run-down and decayed. As the vampire stepped inside the building, a middle-aged man who managed to look stern despite a heavily-receding hairline intercepted him.

"Are you a parent?"

Geoffrey reached out with his mind, worming tendrils of thought into the man's subconscious as he pulled a leather wallet from his coat pocket.

"NYPD. I need to question some of your students about a sensitive matter."

Sight of the nickel badge initially garnered the incredulous response that Geoffrey had expected, but he ruthlessly suppressed the thoughts he didn't want before they made it to the forefront of the man's brain. It was the work of a couple of seconds to implant the belief that the badge was real and that there was nothing to do but just cooperate and hope that Geoffrey didn't cause too many problems before he left.

"I won't take up too much of your time, but I'll need to see your records to identify the students in question. If you'll point me towards the office and let them know I'm on my way, I'll be out of your hair before you know it."

The thoughts flowing through the link took on worries about student rights and possible repercussions, but Geoffrey rooted out the assistant principal's concerns and replaced them with the idea that it was really the principal's job to worry about that kind of stuff.

After a moment's hesitation, the other man reached down to his side and pulled out a walkie-talkie. "Beth, I'm sending a detective down to you guys. Please let Principal Sorensen know he's on his way and ask if he can go through the picture files we keep on the students."

Geoffrey suppressed the sigh of relief that tried to give him away, and instead gave the assistant principal a casual nod. "Thanks, and the office is...?"

After walking down the tiled halls in the direction he'd been pointed for a couple minutes, Geoffrey's senses picked up a gathering of minds that looked like it was probably what he was looking for.

Upon entering the office, Geoffrey was confronted by a number of giggling high school girls and three middle-aged ladies. The two casually dressed ladies had taken up positions behind the large counter that seemed to serve as a barricade to keep any irate students at arm's length, while the third lady was obviously waiting for Geoffrey to appear.

"Who the hell do..." The principal cleared her throat and then began again. "I mean why are you here, and why wasn't I notified you were coming?"

Geoffrey's thoughts had already reached out and threaded their way into the tightly organized mind before him. As a result, he knew exactly why the principal cleared her throat, and it was all he could do not to blush at the thoughts that were darting across the link. As he dove deeper into the principal's mind he wondered if Venice was thinking the same kinds of things while she was with him.

"Principal Sorensen, I presume?" Geoffrey flashed what he hoped was a winning smile, as he mentally reached to turn up the attraction flowing down the link towards him. The annoyance that had been predominant just a second ago was already melting away. A twinge of conscience reminded Geoffrey that he was very much interfering with the woman's free will at this point, but he ignored the inclination to back out. Something like this wasn't really all that wrong, not when weighed against the opportunity to make sure that Melody wasn't hassled so much.

Realizing that the principal was still waiting for him to answer her question, Geoffrey continued. "I'm Allen Smith, NYPD. I apologize for the unusual circumstances surrounding my visit, but the answers to your questions are somewhat confidential. Would it be possible for us to step into your office?"

Geoffrey had actually just been trying to stall for time to think of a reason he was here, but the sudden increase in desire he was feeling through the link told him he'd hit on one of the best possible suggestions he could have made.

Maintaining a slightly irritated exterior that was corresponding less and less with what she was actually feeling, the principal led Geoffrey to her office, invited him to sit down, and then instead of taking a position behind her desk, chose a seat only a few feet from him.

"Officer Smith, I'm sure you understand my position in all of this. We can hardly allow actions that could result in any kind of outcry that student rights had been violated."

Apparently the attraction she was feeling wasn't quite strong enough to do the trick. That, or maybe she was normally just such a bulldog that this was incredibly accommodating compared to how she usually would have treated an interloper.

Geoffrey braced himself and then dove deeper into her mind.

"Please, call me Allen. Of course I understand completely the situation you find yourself in. Trying to balance the rights of the students with their need for oversight and guidance is always going to be a very difficult path to walk."

As he continued talking, Geoffrey tried to fuzzy up her recollection of whatever laws might apply. Then he installed a solid belief that they'd adequately discussed the relevant points, and that she was completely covered from a liability standpoint.

"...so you see, Principal, although a case could be made for prosecuting the girls, we have much bigger fish to fry, and we'll forgo collecting any evidence that the DA's office could use against them. I just need to question them so that we can get a bead on who else is involved. We really need to trace this thing back to whoever is actually calling the shots."

The principal was nodding now as she tried to consider what Geoffrey had said through the artificial haze he'd placed over her thoughts.

"Please call me Julia, Allen."

Geoffrey headed off her inclination to ask for a signed statement outlining what he'd just said, and then had to stop her from getting caught up with the idea of just how pissed the girls' parents were going to be if any of this ever got out.

"That sounds entirely reasonable. I'll show you our records myself."

The search through the student records took longer than Geoffrey had hoped, but that was probably more a result of Julia standing over his shoulder sending affectionate thoughts his way than anything else. Then again, if Geoffrey hadn't all but disconnected her higher brain functions to get what he was after, she wouldn't have been in his way.

After searching through about half of the female students in the school, Geoffrey found one who looked familiar. If he idealized her face a little, imagined it as being even more attractive than it was, then it was a match for one of the girls from the dream. Geoffrey filed away the interesting tidbit that Melody had done the exact opposite with regards to her mental picture of herself as compared to the mental picture of this girl, and then looked up at Julia.

"Can you please pull up the pictures of all the females who have a class with this student, as well as the total number of classes they have in common?"

Only two other girls shared every class with the first girl, and they also bore more than a passing resemblance to the other girls from Melody's dream, so Geoffrey pointed them out to the principal.

"Would it be possible to have these three girls pulled out of class and isolated so that I can speak with them individually?"

Julia nodded slowly, and Geoffrey realized that she was having a hard time believing that these particular girls were guilty of anything that would require a visit from a NYPD detective.

"Are you sure these are the ones? They are some of my best students. I was really expecting one of these to be the one you were after." Julia pressed a few keys as she spoke, and eight other pictures popped up on the screen. Geoffrey scanned through them, more out of courtesy than because he had any real curiosity, but nearly did a double take when he realized that Melody was one of the 'trouble' girls.

"Why these?"

"These are all of the slackers and problem kids. Most of them have a list of infractions as long as your arm."

It seemed like she was really warming up to the idea of listing all of the things each of the girls had done wrong, but Geoffrey short-circuited the inclination and pointed at Melody's picture.

"This one hardly looks like a hardened criminal."

"Actually, you're right. She's only on this list because she was held back a year. It's kind of a sad story really. She'd have graduated by now except for the fact that her mom got sick and she missed a bunch of school. It was all approved, of course, but she bumped up against the state minimums and wasn't smart enough to appeal, so she's stuck here an extra year—I think she's been eighteen for most of this year."

Julia had said it was an unfortunate story, but he got a distinct impression that she actually found it quite funny. Geoffrey resisted the urge to probe deeper into her mind to confirm just how sadistic she was.

"That is too bad, but no, none of those girls are the ones that are involved with this particular bit of trouble. How soon can I talk to those first three?"

It took longer than Geoffrey had expected, but eventually he found himself alone in a dingy room with the girl who had been the ringleader in the dream. Things had been touch and go for a moment, but he'd managed to convince Julia that she didn't need to be present during the questioning. It had been worth the effort just to avoid the distraction she represented. Pretending to carry on a conversation with one person while messing with their thoughts was going to be hard enough. He was pretty sure he wouldn't have been able to manage two at once.

Cindy proved to be shallow and entirely self-centered—in short exactly what Geoffrey had been expecting from Melody's dream. As a plus, she seemed much less bright than he'd expected based on Julia's impression of her. That should make things a bit easier, but it was something Geoffrey noted only absently as he infiltrated in her mind. Mostly he was just astonished that this girl was only a year younger than Melody. She had none of the maturity he'd found in Melody's mind. She'd probably never had to worry about anything more traumatic than picking out an outfit for some school dance. It was going to be a long afternoon.

Chapter 11

Geoffrey crept across the clean, blue mat towards Venice. His left hand weaved slightly to screen the blunt practice knife in his right hand, thereby preventing it from being captured or trapped. Venice slowly circled, mirroring his movements—save for the fact that her right foot was forward in the 'short timer' stance commonly favored by smaller knife fighters who needed to try and negate some of the reach advantage of their opponents.

As Geoffrey realized that his left hand had shifted out of position, Venice struck at it with her practice knife, trying to make one of the many small cuts that, in a real fight, would be used to bleed him out until he was too weak to continue.

The reflexes that had saved him a number of times already took over and Geoffrey slapped Venice's wrist behind the knife. The blow sent the knife and the hand holding it wide. Geoffrey took advantage of the opening to step in and strike, choosing to reverse his knife and hit her in the head in the split second he had to choose his target.

Rather than trying to counterattack as Geoffrey expected, Venice took a quick step back and swore at him. "I've told you six or seven times now. If you are going to slash someone, do it somewhere that there are major blood vessels near the surface so you can do some damage. You pull that kind of crap in a real fight, and you'll probably end up dead."

Geoffrey recoiled slightly from the venom in Venice's voice. "I'm sorry, I was just thinking that maybe I could practice strikes that would incapacitate an opponent without killing them."

Rather than being calmed by Geoffrey's words, as he'd expected, Venice swore again and threw her practice knife at him. The dull pot metal made it through two complete revolutions before Geoffrey's hand reached up and plucked it from the air a few inches in front of his face. He wished it were that easy to deflect Venice's words.

"You don't fight to subdue. You've still got most of the reflexes you spent decades developing, but if you keep trying to override them you're going to end up dead. One stupid assassination where you almost got yourself killed doesn't even come close to making you qualified to start making up new tactics. If you get in a fight, one of two things happened. Either you started it or they did. If you decide to start something you bloody well better have decided that you're ready to go all the way and kill the sod. Otherwise you've got no business getting involved in the first place. If someone else starts something, you can bet that they'll be more than ready to kill you and leave your morally-superior butt dead on the curb."

Geoffrey opened his mouth to respond that he'd been in more than just the one confrontation, but changed his mind. Venice didn't need to know about that. Besides, even if he told her about that particular fight it wouldn't help his case. He'd fought to kill that time too, rather than trying to incapacitate his opponents.

The fact that Geoffrey didn't argue with her seemed to mollify Venice somewhat. She simply collected her stuff and headed towards the locker room instead of remaining to verbally flay him as she normally would have.

Shrugging resignedly, Geoffrey pulled his things together and walked the other direction towards the male dressing room and its shiny new facilities. At least most of the rest of the training session had gone well. Venice had been right to convince him to come here. Her gym was much nicer than his apartment. Not only that, the fact that the two of them kept such ungodly hours meant that they pretty much had the entire place to themselves.

The vampire showered and changed as quickly as he was able, but somehow Venice was still already done and waiting for him in the lobby when he finished. It boggled the mind that she was able to get ready so quickly and still look impeccable when she was done.

Geoffrey looked Venice over as he approached her and recognized some of the subtle clues he'd started to identify that indicated something was still bothering her. It wasn't like her to hold onto something for very long. Usually she would just ream him and then move on. He needed a way to try and defuse the situation. He cleared his throat and then said the first thing that came to his mind.

"Decided to stay and see if you could get a good night kiss?"

For maybe the first time that Geoffrey had ever seen, Venice looked momentarily confused, as if the sudden reversal in roles had completely thrown her. It only took a couple of heartbeats for Venice to regain her normal air of self-assurance.

"Please, like it would have mattered if I had. For whatever reason, you've decided that I'm nearly as much an enemy as Imastious."

Geoffrey shrugged, uncomfortable with how near Venice was to the truth. He didn't trust her, but he was actually finding it hard to preserve the kind of emotional distance he knew he should be maintaining between them. There were aspects of her character and personality that really bothered him, but he did enjoy their time together. It seemed to be one more symptom of just how broken he was. There wasn't any other explanation he could think of for why he'd ended up being friends with someone like her.

Venice shot him a sly smile. "Did I hit a little too close there for you, love? Or is it that I just sparked one of those internal debates you seem so fond of since you came back?"

Geoffrey did a quick scan of his thoughts, looking for something alien that might indicate Venice was using her very limited mentalist abilities to try and read his thoughts, but there wasn't anything that even hinted at a foreign presence inside his mind. He was still very inexperienced at using his own abilities, but when Imastious had tortured him he'd definitely been able to feel the older vampire pushing inside his mind.

All indications were that Imastious was much more powerful than Venice would be for several centuries yet to come, so it wasn't that she was reading his mind without him being able to detect her efforts. She just knew him well enough to read his expression much more easily than he would have liked.

He'd let the silence stretch out too long, but as he opened his mouth, Venice cut him off.

"Don't try to deny it now. You've still got a ton to relearn about lying. Half of what you're thinking may as well be written on your forehead in flashing neon letters, and the other half can usually be guessed by those of us who've known you for so long."

Geoffrey shrugged, but his mind keyed on to the last part of Venice's statement. Venice kept saying that he was a different person, but that didn't mesh with the idea that she'd known him for so long that she could predict his thoughts. It was a solitary straw in the wind, but it pointed towards the idea that maybe Geoffrey wasn't as changed as she and Imastious wanted him to believe he was.

Then again, she could just be playing head games with him. She was more than capable of doing that, or worse, if she thought it might gain her some kind of advantage.

Venice flashed a smile that was very nearly the picture of perfection she usually bestowed upon the world. "Don't worry about me. I've spent more years than you can imagine with people who would purposely say all kinds of things, true or otherwise, to try and throw me off my game so that they could take advantage of me in one way or another. Your current feelings about me are less than optimal, but they are also subject to change."

Venice stood up and turned to leave. "Oh, you should probably be warned. Things are starting to get a little tense out there. Not necessarily like something is going down right away, but like events are heading that way. You should watch yourself and be prepared."

Geoffrey's mind tried to switch gears and consider the implications of this new piece of information. "What do you mean?"

It was Venice's turn to shrug. "I'm not sure, it doesn't happen very often but occasionally one of the masters—individuals like Imastious, or someone even more dangerous—will make a play for more power. Usually their rivals are too strong to assault directly. After decades of planning, their strategies usually are too subtle to spill out into something you or I would see. Still, there are very real conflicts out there, ones in which pawns like you and I get assassinated as a way of trimming a rival back down to manageable size. That is pretty much par for the course, but this feels like something else—like maybe a real power in the city is getting ready to try and take a rival all the way out."

Geoffrey nodded. "Okay, I'll be careful."

"More likely you'll passively sit by and let them kill you, but I'll just have to hope none of them figure out that you work for Imastious."

Geoffrey stood at the door to the club, lost in thought for several minutes after Venice had left. Unsurprisingly, his thoughts once again returned to Melody.

THE GREATER DARKNESS

Implanting subliminal commands into the minds of the three girls had been extremely difficult, the more so because he wasn't really sure how to do what he'd wanted. In the end he'd worked out of instinct more than anything else. The process had taken nearly two hours and left Geoffrey shaking with exhaustion. Despite his inexperience, he thought his efforts would probably do the trick when it came to ensuring that Melody wouldn't be hassled so much at school. Not only that, he was optimistic that he'd even nudged the three girls in ways that might turn them into decent students eventually. Decent students and actual three-dimensional people.

Getting back out of the school without running into the principal had been a little tricky, but well worth it as the vampire hadn't wanted to deliver on the promises he'd let her read in his eyes. Of course leaving like that had the potential of making Julia feel spurned enough to try and make waves for 'Detective Allen Smith,' but hopefully the fact that the girls wouldn't be talking to their parents would help. It was less likely that she'd go ahead and make herself look like a fool for having given him access to the girls in the first place if she wasn't getting any kind of static from anyone.

It was all fine in theory, but Geoffrey couldn't quiet the tiny voice in the back of his head that kept pointing out that he didn't really know that she'd decide not to make a fuss.

Geoffrey pushed the door open and walked out into the light drizzle, but he already knew that he wasn't going to be able to distract himself. Part of what was bothering him felt very much like his conscience, but there was something else there too.

Melody was of legal age, but when you stacked her eighteen years up against the decades, or even centuries, that he'd probably lived, she really was little more than a child. There was plenty of reason for whatever was left of his conscience to be uneasy about his attraction for her, but what was bothering him most right now was the way he was mooning over her like a senseless animal. It was a level of obsession that he couldn't explain.

Actually, saying he was acting like an animal was a very appropriate choice of words. He'd killed people—and not just before he'd lost his memory. He lived on blood that he took from the unwilling, and he'd invaded their thoughts for whatever reason took his fancy.

Geoffrey pulled his trench coat tighter around his neck in an effort to keep out the rain, and adjusted his bag. It was going to be a long night full of internal arguments, but he already knew that before he went home he'd stop at Melody's. What he still didn't know was whether or not he should be happy about that.

THE GREATER DARKNESS

Geoffrey crept down the fire escape from the roof and, after verifying that there wasn't any movement inside Melody's darkened window, took a position as close to the window as he was able to get. He suspected that he was still just scratching the surface of what his abilities would allow him to do, but at least he was picking up on a few tricks. The key thing he'd learned so far was that distance mattered. The closer he was to someone, the easier it was to work with their thoughts.

Melody's thoughts were as bright and cheery as he remembered. They washed over Geoffrey with a refreshing tingle that temporarily swept away all of his doubts about the wisdom of visiting. As pleasant as her dreams were, they didn't reveal any of the things that he needed to know.

The vampire tried to probe deeper into Melody's psyche, but although he quickly got an overall impression of who she was, it was almost impossible to find one specific set of memories. Actually, maybe impossible wasn't the right word. It felt like it could be done, but that it would require much more time and effort than he could invest right then.

After a few more minutes of thought, Geoffrey hit upon a novel approach and directed his consciousness towards the area of Melody's thoughts that contained her dreaming mind. It was a simple matter to subtly manipulate the fabric of the mind around him so that Melody was dreaming about what he wanted to know. He pushed an image of the three girls into her dream and waited to see what happened.

It took several seconds, but then Melody's consciousness turned in the direction he'd prodded and he began to get a sense of her feelings towards the trio who had been persecuting her. Dislike was foremost, combined with an odd kind of guilt that she felt that way towards the three of them. Envy was there, but it was a clean envy, untainted by any kind of hate that they had so many things she didn't. There, right at the end was exactly the thing he'd been hoping for. Amazement that they'd begun treating her like a human being.

The rush of relief and gratitude that Geoffrey felt at knowing his efforts had succeeded was so strong that some of it leaked through the link, touching Melody's thoughts and diffusing through her mind like food coloring that somehow strengthened as it spread, rather than fading. The experience was truly incredible. Geoffrey wouldn't have believed that such simple, innocent joy existed if he hadn't been there to experience it himself.

As Geoffrey tried to carefully back out of Melody's thoughts, a subtle change coursed through them, a quickening that fascinated him.

THE GREATER DARKNESS

It was almost like she was waking up, but not quite. The link hadn't severed, so Geoffrey was still privy to her thoughts. Melody was just as amazed by the sudden happiness as he was. What was more, she somehow knew that the feelings had originated from outside her.

The thoughts, which up until now had been soft and yielding, took on a firmer, sticky nature, and the vampire suppressed panic as his efforts to disengage became largely futile. Melody's thoughts keyed in on his efforts, strengthening the force immobilizing him.

As Geoffrey gathered his energy for one final exertion to free himself, an incredible force reached out and ripped away the shadows that separated him from Melody. A brief flash of recognition flared through the girl's thoughts, followed by an astonishment that almost exactly mirrored his own.

Chapter 12

Geoffrey looked around the hospital waiting room and tried very hard not to be depressed. It helped a little that he was there to try and help, even if there ultimately wasn't much that he could do.

Although he'd been able to finally free himself from Melody's mind without waking her up, the experience had left him once more unsure of his abilities. Venice had deftly ignored his attempts to get her to teach him anything other than weapons play, so Geoffrey had been forced to strike out on his own.

Simply reading the thoughts of whatever random passerby happened across his path started feeling wrong after only a couple of hours. Not only that, he'd needed to practice more than just the ability to spy on those around him. Given that, there had been just one place that made logical sense for him to visit.

THE GREATER DARKNESS

New York-Presbyterian Hospital had been a tough nut to crack, but careful use of his abilities had eventually conditioned all of the orderlies and doctors not to notice his presence and Geoffrey soon had the run of several wings. Most importantly, he was able to sit for hours at a time in the sterile, inhospitable waiting room of the temporary psychiatric ward. It was a decidedly uncomfortable set of environs, but it situated him such that he could work on the one or two patients who happened to wander close enough that he could reach their thoughts through the wall.

His time wasn't always spent in the manner he intended. Sometimes the minds he was able to reach were too far gone to risk any kind of substantial contact, but even then the trip wasn't wasted. There was always a worried relative or two who could be calmed and reassured during the time that the vampire had allotted himself at the hospital.

Now wasn't one of those times. In fact, Tim seemed like one of the more normal people Geoffrey had so far met. Everything about this particular patient had been enviably normal until three men had kicked his door down. There hadn't been anything Tim could have done to save his wife or daughter. Geoffrey could easily see that from his perusal of Tim's memories, but Tim wasn't able to believe that himself.

Geoffrey hadn't spent much time inside those terrible memories. He'd learned just enough to determine where Tim's self-loathing came from, and then moved on. More time there wouldn't have helped. Instead, Geoffrey's focus was helping Tim understand that what had happened hadn't been anyone's fault.

Geoffrey smoothed over the most jagged edges of pain, leaving the sense of loss intact but speeding the natural healing process which would have slowly removed some of the immediacy and strength of the memories. It wasn't enough for Tim to notice the change, but it would hopefully be enough for the other man to finally start healing rather than continuing to damage his mind.

The next hour was tiring, if not nearly as much as it would have been a few weeks ago. By the time Geoffrey was done for the night, the quivering, pain-filled desolation that was Tim's mind had been subtly transformed into something endurable, if still not completely sane.

Geoffrey pulled himself to his feet and left, pleased that no one had interrupted his work with questions about why he was there or requests that he leave.

The vampire had been carefully avoiding thinking about Melody for a while now, but something in the way Tim had remembered his late family brought Geoffrey's thoughts back to the spunky eighteen year-old. He couldn't risk going back inside her mind, at least not until he had a better idea as to what had happened the last time he'd been there.

Given that, there wasn't any point in visiting her—or so he'd been trying to convince himself for the last several days. As he walked home, Geoffrey was so involved with trying to come up with reasons not to visit Melody that he didn't notice the muscular teenager walking towards him with all of the classic signs of someone looking for a fight.

By the time Geoffrey noticed someone ahead of him, it was too late to avoid the collision that the teen had engineered. Geoffrey was taller, but he hadn't been expecting the impact so it sent him stumbling backwards.

"What the hell are you doing here, whitey?"

Geoffrey's mind was still trying to catch up to events, but the words registered just in time for him to duck the punch headed toward his face.

The vampire's left hand caught the fist as it recoiled back through the space he'd just vacated, and followed it back to the teenager.

Geoffrey's opponent clearly hadn't been expecting the vampire to close with him, because his follow-up attack with his left hand was weak and off balance. Geoffrey easily deflected it too as he brought both hands up to the back of the teen's neck and tugged.

The technique worked exactly as Venice had promised, and a split second later the teen dropped to the ground unconscious and bloody as a result of his face impacting with Geoffrey's knee at high velocity.

A peculiar, muted metallic sound as the body hit the ground caused Geoffrey to pause and frisk his opponent rather than continuing as he had planned. A gun wasn't exactly a common thing to see in New York, but it shouldn't have surprised Geoffrey as much as it did. Maybe Venice had a point after all. If Geoffrey hadn't neutralized the teen so completely, he could have ended up being gunned down from behind as he'd walked away.

The sight of so much blood awakened even the jaded consciences of the few pedestrians near Geoffrey, and soon the vampire was sprinting down an alley trying to leave behind the screams of people calling for help.

Eluding whatever police response had been mustered proved ridiculously simple now that Geoffrey could implant suggestions in various people's minds; it was only a matter of making each of them call 911 and report seeing a suspicious individual in five or six different locations.

If only he could make his personal demons disappear so easily.

Just to be safe, Geoffrey found a relatively secluded park bench and waited for forty-five minutes before deciding he'd escaped unwanted attention. The wait proved too much, and by the end he'd convinced himself that if he were to pay a visit to Melody's, he might overhear something that would tell him how she was doing.

The trip to Melody's went surprisingly quickly and Geoffrey soon found himself in his usual position on the fire escape. The lights were on, but Melody didn't seem to be in her room.

Geoffrey debated his options for a few seconds, but he couldn't bear to leave without any kind of contact with Melody, so he finally, tentatively reached out with his thoughts.

There were two minds in the room next door. One was bright and vibrant, but yet oddly muted in comparison to what he'd expected. The other, however, really surprised Geoffrey. Melody's mother's mind was dim and guttered, like a candle nearing the end of its life.

Despite the voice inside his head that told him he was being extremely foolish, Geoffrey brushed the surface of Melody's thoughts. He found more worry and fear there than he remembered from the last time he'd been there. Worse, there was an almost overpowering sense of impending loss.

The glow from Melody's mom momentarily flickered, and he realized the cause of Melody's distress. Working quickly so as to deny himself time to reconsider, Geoffrey shifted his body to bring himself closer to Melody's mom and then threw himself into the sluggish current of her thoughts.

Sluggish wasn't quite the right word. The thoughts moved slowly, but were much more powerful than he'd expected. It was almost as though the medication she was on suppressed all but the most basic needs. That hadn't surprised him, but he hadn't expected the way that those suppressed thoughts were lending such strength and mass to the few things that she was still capable of feeling.

The surface thoughts were overwhelmingly focused on pain, so much so that Geoffrey had to penetrate deeper than normal just to learn Debbie's name. The vampire tried to soothe the edges of the pain, but his work was immediately carried away, even before he had a chance to finish constructing the suggestions.

Growing more and more frustrated, Geoffrey sent out additional whisker-thin probes looking for some kind of safe haven in which to work, driving them even deeper into the murky tides below when they failed to find what he needed.

A sudden jerk on one of the probes pulled Geoffrey mentally off-balance, dragging him deeper into Debbie's psyche than he'd ever been with anyone else.

Under normal circumstances, Geoffrey would have been working at the edge of his abilities and endurance, but the physical distance between he and Debbie pushed him far beyond the limits of what he would have believed himself capable. As he was sucked further and further under, Geoffrey simultaneously realized that he was capable of more than he'd thought, and that even so he was dangerously overextended.

Like a swimmer who had spent too long underwater, Geoffrey felt his strength bleeding away at an alarming rate as incredible forces tried to tear his mind completely away from the physical body that housed it. Some half-forgotten memory prodded at the vampire, and he stopped fighting for the surface of Debbie's mind and instead dove deeper.

Geoffrey's strength was disappearing at a slower rate now that he wasn't struggling, but he could still feel it fading and started to doubt his course of action. The vampire nearly turned around, but he somehow knew that doing so was as good as committing suicide. His strength pouring out of him like water, he rode the increasingly turbulent thoughts deeper, trying to shield himself as much as possible from the dark pain and helplessness that permeated Debbie's being.

As his mind began to disintegrate from the stresses it was being subjected to, he bumped up against something immobile that somehow still gave the sense of being yielding to the right sort of contact.

Working more out of a sense of instinct than anything else, Geoffrey matched himself to the barrier so that the next collision threw him through it and into an area of utter calm. It was like the perfect eye to the storm inside her mind. There were still thoughts there for him to read, but they were placid, semi-unformed...almost childlike.

Almost as soon as Geoffrey arrived, he realized that Debbie blamed herself for her illness. It wasn't rational, but that didn't stop her from feeling it, from believing it. In a way it had become who she was, even in her current state when she was incapable of feeling anything but pain.

The vampire felt the last bit of his strength slowly ebbing away. He realized that he only had a few minutes, or possibly even just seconds, before working from so far away, even in such complete calm, would be too much for him.

Working quickly, Geoffrey began spinning out a web of suggestions. He started with the statement that her illness wasn't her fault, moved onto the fact that she wasn't being punished for anything, and then focused on the pain. It wasn't easy to make her feel that the pain was something distant, not with having been immersed in it himself so recently, but he kept at it. He kept pushing and finally created the illusion that the pain belonged to someone else, far away.

The last message he tried to install was that there was a purpose to life and that she should have hope.

THE GREATER DARKNESS

Geoffrey worried about some of the thoughts he was implanting. The fact that they were being planted in such a calm area should mean that they would have more staying power than his usual work, but they were up against some powerful, deep-seated beliefs that would work very hard to erode these new, alien thoughts.

He'd already realized from some of his other work that the mind couldn't really hold two conflicting thoughts at the same time, not and believe them both with any kind of permanence over the long term. Either the pain and guilt would win, or his message would win. He just hoped that what he was doing wouldn't have unintended consequences.

Geoffrey's strength evaporated and something snapped him back to his body as he lost consciousness.

The pale glow in the eastern sky served to wake Geoffrey from his slumped position on the fire escape where he'd passed out. Counting himself lucky that he'd awakened when he did rather than later when someone would have seen him and called the police, Geoffrey pulled himself to his feet. As he turned to go, he looked into Melody's room one last time and was surprised to see a white rectangle taped to the window.

It was on his side of the glass and addressed to 'Mr. Dark.' Worryingly, Geoffrey couldn't remember whether it had been there when he arrived or if it meant that she'd seen him while he'd been sleeping.

Geoffrey stood motionless for several seconds before suddenly tearing the letter from the window and stuffing it into a pocket as he fled up the fire escape.

Hours later, Geoffrey found himself in the corner of a run-down, but surprisingly clean, diner at the other end of town. He was being irrational. If Imastious had been following him then Melody was already as good as dead, but Geoffrey's first worry had been making sure that Imastious wouldn't be able to follow him to wherever he read the letter.

Geoffrey took one last look around him to make sure he wasn't being watched and then carefully pulled the envelope from his pocket and smoothed it out, blinking as the glare from the sun on the white paper made his eyes water.

He felt a pang of sorrow at the state of the letter. It was wrinkled to the point of making some of the words hard to make out, but he hadn't been able to shake the worry that Melody's message was going to somehow disappear before he had a chance to read it. Its current state was the unavoidable consequence of his frequent checks over the last few hours to make sure that the letter had still been safely in his pocket.

As the vampire opened the letter, he couldn't force his hands to stop shaking.

Dear Mr. Dark,

I feel more than a little silly doing all of this. It is like when I was a child and would have a dream and be ever so convinced that it was real, that there were monsters under my bed, or that something terrible had happened to Daddy. Mom would always have to convince me that none of it was real.

Just when I'd finally believe her, and promise that I wouldn't be scared anymore, I'd have another oh-so-real dream, and the process would start over again.

As real as those dreams felt, this was a hundred times more vivid. Even after I woke up, I just couldn't quite shake the feeling that it all really happened.

Maybe it is just that I want to believe it so badly, but the dream that I was almost raped, the girls at school suddenly being nicer to me, that dream where you were somehow inside my head asking about those girls...all of those things happened in the last little while and they all seem to have some kind of common thread running through them.

With everything that's happened with my parents, I feel like an old person trapped inside a young person's body. Sometimes I'm not sure whether old me or young me will show up in a given situation.

Are you really out there watching over me? I hope you are. The child inside me still prays that you are.

Melody

Geoffrey read through the note several times and each time the number of thoughts running through his head increased. The possibilities and options before him had suddenly gone from nothing to almost limitless. Melody needed him, and he had the very real ability to make her life better.

As Geoffrey left the diner, he felt a new bounce in his step that he couldn't remember ever experiencing. He could only attribute it to the fact that, for the first time he could remember, he was actually feeling hope for the future.

Chapter 13

Venice had arrived unexpectedly at Geoffrey's apartment an hour ago and told him to get comfortable. "Imastious will be along sometime tonight, and he won't want to have to track you down, so just sit tight until he arrives."

Geoffrey had half-expected Venice to stay, but as soon as she'd delivered her message, she'd bid him goodbye and headed back out the door.

It wasn't the kind of announcement designed to make waiting an easy prospect. Imastious had left Geoffrey entirely alone since the hit on the drug dealer. The likely cause of the impending visit was that the older vampire simply had someone else he wanted killed, but Geoffrey couldn't escape the worry that Imastious had somehow found out about Melody.

Geoffrey knew that giving way to panic and fear was completely irrational, but the feelings kept bubbling up to the surface despite his best efforts to keep them under control. It was as if some gibbering part of his psyche, untouched by any sense or intellect, had taken over the reins to his mind.

Geoffrey suppressed thoughts of what would happen to Melody and her mother if Imastious had discovered them, and instead tried to practice his mental techniques. Just as the vampire calmed himself enough to regain the level of control required to cast his thoughts out, his probes ran into a mind surrounded by what he could only describe as a flawless wall.

His first thought was that it was a little like what Venice did to keep him out of his mind, but that was wrong. It was *exactly* like what she did, this was just the work of a master who understood what he was doing rather than a neophyte just doing by rote what she was told would protect her mind.

As soon as Geoffrey realized who must be behind that impenetrable shield, he attempted to pull his probes back. He was too late. Faster than he could follow, something grabbed the tendrils of thought, feeding just enough energy into them to make it impossible for Geoffrey to break contact, and then followed them back to Geoffrey's mind.

Before Geoffrey was fully aware of what was happening, Imastious was inside his mind, trying to sift through thoughts and memories. The older vampire was slower now that he was inside Geoffrey's mind, which offered the slightest bit of hope that they might be on more equal footing now than the speed of that first response might have suggested.

Doing his best to ignore the white-hot pain Imastious was causing, Geoffrey pushed back, isolating Imastious as best as he was able inside the limited part of his mind that had already been compromised.

Remembering the way that Melody had stifled his attempts to move around inside her mind, Geoffrey tried to do the same to Imastious, and was rewarded with a further decrease in the speed of Imastious' attacks.

The younger vampire started to try and push Imastious all the way out of his mind, only to realize, with alarm, that attempting to do so was draining his strength much more quickly. He would have to continue to confront Imastious at the slightly deeper level inside of Geoffrey's mind that had been their earlier battleground.

Settling back behind the defenses he had already constructed, Geoffrey watched as Imastious slowly made his way through the rest of the thoughts in the tiny portion of space that the younger vampire had surrendered.

Any question of what came next was answered a few seconds later as Geoffrey's thoughts began to take on a peculiar pattern. He'd never seen anything like it, but something was settling through the buffer he'd created. Whatever they were, they had to be created by Imastious. They were too ordered, too strong to be the kind of involuntary thoughts that he couldn't stop from passing back and forth across the barrier.

The only explanation was that Imastious had created some kind of suggestion and cloaked it as something that could bypass Geoffrey's defenses. Any questions as to what the construct was supposed to do were settled as Geoffrey felt his resolve to keep Imastious outside his mind start to weaken.

Maintaining his concentration as best as he was able, Geoffrey quickly found the construct scurrying from place to place—a spider weaving a web of apathy over everything it touched. A whip-like tendril of thought lashed out and splintered the construct just as another one tried to slide through his defenses.

Acting out of instinct, Geoffrey made his buffer more opaque and then disintegrated the second invader just as it exited the now more resilient barrier. Geoffrey knew he was running out of time. It seemed like Imastious had remade the section of Geoffrey's mind he'd been occupying into something that allowed him an easier time of working mischief.

Temporarily opening up a window into Imastious' territory, Geoffrey lashed out with another tendril of thought, aiming for the conduits of thought he could vaguely sense connecting Imastious' mind to his physical body.

THE GREATER DARKNESS

The attack severed the closest link before losing most of its energy and bouncing off of the second conduit. Imastious gathered himself and countered with a blow to the younger vampire's defenses that left his head ringing and brought the barrier to within a hairsbreadth of collapsing. It seemed impossible that Imastious was that strong, but there was no arguing the strength of the blow that he'd just dished out.

Geoffrey tried to pull himself back together and strengthen his defenses, but heartbeats after the first blow arrived, he was hit with a second, equally powerful attack. Imastious seized on the fact that his opponent was now virtually defenseless and expanded his area of influence inside Geoffrey's mind.

Suddenly, as quickly as the conflict had started, it was over. Imastious withdrew from Geoffrey's mind, and Geoffrey opened his eyes just in time to see Imastious kick his door open.

"You should have left the door open, my child. It would have eliminated the need for me to destroy the lock."

Imastious' gaze as he finished stepping into the apartment rested on Geoffrey's face in a satisfied manner, so much so that the younger vampire snuck a look in the mirror.

He felt a flash of surprise at what he saw there. His face was covered with blood.

Apparently the effort of trying to combat Imastious had triggered a nose-bleed.

Seemingly taking Geoffrey's silence for submission, Imastious shrugged and then took a seat. "Of greater worry is the fact that you tried to infiltrate my thoughts once again after already being warned not to do so."

Staring at Geoffrey with the dark, dead eyes that still gave the impression that they were able to see into his slave's thoughts, Imastious continued. "Luckily for you, I assumed that you simply acted out of ignorance and foolishness once again, rather than an actual desire to confront me. As you no doubt understand now, whatever tricks you've picked up in the last few weeks would do you no good in a true contest of wills. Had I thought otherwise, you'd now be a sobbing wreck with no sense of self, or ability to experience voluntary thought."

Geoffrey tried to remain silent again, but Imastious' eyes pried a response out of him. "Yes, I understand, it was a mistake."

The unblinking gaze regarding Geoffrey finally proved too much, causing him to drop his eyes rather than continue to look into the emotionless void that seemed to call his thoughts again and again to how tattered and black his own soul was becoming.

Geoffrey never even saw the blow coming; in fact the only hint he had of movement was a sudden rushing of air as Imastious lunged from his seat and knocked Geoffrey off of the bed where he'd been sitting.

"Yes, *master*. You will always address me as master. You've bought yourself some small amount of leniency because of your recent actions, but you're treading dangerously close to requiring disciplining once again."

The words caught at his throat like pins, but Geoffrey felt a presence building just outside his mind, and the thought of having Imastious inside his head again filled Geoffrey with an unexpected terror.

"Yes, master." The response was choked out of a throat so tight that the words caused an almost physical pain.

Imastious considered Geoffrey for a few moments longer before nodding. "Very good. You continue to show some small amount of promise. Enough to be spared destruction for the present at least."

The sense of menace just outside of Geoffrey's tightly-shuttered mind slowly dissipated as Imastious returned to his seat.

"I have another assignment for you."

Geoffrey eyed the packet that Imastious tossed on the bed for a heartbeat and then the fear started to rise inside him again, forcing him to reach over and open it.

"Her father nominally works for me, but he's become uncooperative as of late. It's time to remind him that although his services are really quite valuable, he isn't irreplaceable."

Geoffrey opened his mouth to voice some half-formed question, only to be preempted by Imastious, who continued with a grin that turned Geoffrey's stomach.

"Rather, he's completely replaceable, but his children are considerably less so."

After Imastious had finally left, Geoffrey found himself sitting motionless on his bed, staring at the photo of a smiling teenage girl which had slid out of the packet. Imastious hadn't found out about Melody yet, and would likely remain ignorant of her as long as Geoffrey continued to carry out missions for Imastious, but what would the ultimate price be for her safety? How could he kill someone so young, someone who hadn't committed any sin other than that of being born to the wrong parents?

Geoffrey's stomach had become more insistent over the last day. Enough that he knew he was running out of time before he started losing control.

Shifting his spotting glasses, the vampire scanned the cramped, one-way street, stiffening as his target came into sight.

She was right on schedule, just like always. He knew she'd go inside her building without any kind of delay. Her father was home now, but he'd be leaving in half an hour. She and her little brother would be spending the subsequent three hours alone until her mother returned home.

Geoffrey idly wondered if the fact that her father was always within three or four blocks of their home reassured the family that the children would be safe, even with no adults home to watch over them. After all, what could happen in the ten minutes it would take for him to get home?

A sharp pain shot through Geoffrey's stomach, but this time it wasn't the hunger, it was revulsion over what he was contemplating. Realistically, it was revulsion over what he'd eventually do. Geoffrey knew he would complain and resist, but he couldn't see any way out of the situation. The priest was wrong. It wasn't that Geoffrey was unwilling to pay the price to do what was right; the problem was that the price required wasn't his to pay.

Geoffrey forced himself to shrug with a nonchalance he didn't feel. He was really going to do it. He hadn't known until that instant, but there wasn't any other way to ensure that Imastious stayed satisfied enough not to invade Geoffrey's mind. Geoffrey had done terrible things, but he wouldn't be responsible for Melody being killed, which was the least that would happen if Imastious ever got inside his mind again.

Now that he was abandoning his surveillance, Geoffrey decided to go ahead and complete the two tasks he'd been avoiding. They needed to be done before the hit, and each day he waited to do them increased the odds that Imastious would become dissatisfied with how long it was taking him to complete the assassination.

Fingering the thick roll of cash that Imastious had given him, Geoffrey descended the stairs and headed off towards one of the more disreputable parts of the city.

It didn't take long, once the vampire arrived, to find exactly what he was looking for. Two women, little more than girls really, both obviously uncomfortable still with the idea of selling their bodies. They couldn't have been involved in their new profession for long yet.

Geoffrey wasn't any more comfortable with being propositioned than the girls were with making their pitch, so the next step didn't go all that smoothly. Eventually, however, sums were agreed upon, and Geoffrey was led by the pair of trembling blondes to a nearby hotel.

Once inside the tiny room, Geoffrey managed to ignore the near-terror the girls were exuding for just long enough to mentally push first one and then the other into unconsciousness. It was hard to believe that anything would drive someone into doing something they were so terrified of doing. It would have been one matter if they hadn't been so scared, but they were. It didn't make sense, why didn't they just do something else? Surely they had other options.

Looking at the unconscious forms on the sagging bed, Geoffrey realized that he was stalling. It was time to just get on with it.

Neither girl was big enough to provide a full meal, at least not without risking their death. Together though they represented enough sustenance to drive the hunger away for a week, maybe even two.

As Geoffrey bit into a vein on the first girl's arm, the hunger flared up with a power that strained the absolute limits of his control. Geoffrey had a split second in which to worry that he'd waited too long to feed, and then rational thought fled, leaving Geoffrey alone with the seductive beating of the poor girl's heart.

Hunger was no longer a suitable description of what the vampire felt. What had started out as nothing more than an easily disregarded message of his body's condition had become something almost tangible. The need beat down on him with the hatred of the noonday sun and he knew he wasn't going to be strong enough to resist it.

Time slowed in step with the absence of thought, allowing Geoffrey to bask in an incredible sense of satiation underlined by an odd connection to his victim. The euphoric feelings lasted until the steady call of her heart changed in a subtle way that Geoffrey somehow knew meant the poor girl's blood pressure was dropping to dangerous levels.

That tiny change opened the floodgates to Geoffrey's mind once again. Gathering strength he didn't know he had, he tore himself away from the arm that had taken on an alarming pallor. If he could get the bleeding stopped he was reasonably confident that she would be okay, but the experience had unnerved him more than he'd expected. He'd thought by feeding sooner he'd be able to control himself, but he'd still come dangerously close to leaving her a lifeless husk.

As Geoffrey applied direct pressure to the punctured vein, he tried to understand what had happened. The key question was whether or not he dared feed on the other girl. Would it be easier to control himself now, or would he still be risking adding another murder to the weight his soul was carrying?

The strength of the hunger had been unnerving. It had gone from a symptom, like pain in a broken wrist, to something even more basic like the fact that the broken wrist was no longer able to support the weight of a textbook.

Geoffrey sat staring at the first girl long past the amount of time required to ensure that the bleeding in her arm had stopped. As the vampire watched the rise and fall of her chest, his gaze fought to drift up and fix on the almost imperceptible throbbing of her carotid artery. It was a torment and a relief all at once. A sign that she was still alive at the same time that it reminded him just how easy it would have been to go too far.

A sudden sense of despair descended upon Geoffrey as he realized he was too much of a coward to do anything other than go ahead and try feeding from the second girl. He wasn't man enough to kill himself, and the only other option was to embrace, to some extent or another, the monster that he was.

Moving mechanically, Geoffrey stretched out the second girl's arm and bit down. The coppery flood of blood triggered a brief flare of hunger, but it was only a shadow of what he'd felt before. Instead, the sense of connection he'd felt with the first girl came to the fore, bonding him to this new victim in a bittersweet manner he wouldn't have believed possible.

As his breathing synchronized with the girl's, Geoffrey's despair was replaced by sorrow for his victim. She was doing so much for him, providing him with continued life, but she hadn't offered it to him freely and he was leaving her with nothing in return.

This time Geoffrey was listening for the change in the girl's heartbeat that signaled it was time to stop, and it was a much simpler matter to pull himself away and staunch the flow of blood.

Looking down at the two girls, Geoffrey found himself near tears. It had felt like he'd been part of them, but it had been wrong. It was something that should have been given rather than taken.

The money the vampire had planned on leaving the pair suddenly seemed inadequate, but he wasn't sure what else to give them. What else did he even have to offer someone?

Without meaning to, Geoffrey's thoughts reached out to first one girl, and then the other, probing their minds, attempting to distill chaotic thoughts down to a picture of each girl's true essence.

It seemed impossible that someone could come to believe that they had so little value, but each of them really did feel that they had no other option but to sell themselves. The two of them had each other, but it didn't help, not really, because neither was a whole enough person to lift the other up.

Geoffrey had thought he was sad before, but the picture of despair painted by the minds he was now touching made his earlier feelings seem pale and selfish. He couldn't help himself, he couldn't really help Melody either, but he could help Sara and Tami. An artist and a dancer. Neither had ever lost their dreams and hopes, but they'd let them become so weak that they couldn't touch them anymore.

Geoffrey's thoughts were moving faster now, faster than he'd realized they could, as they spun through the darkened mind before him. He needed to get to the center just as he'd done with Melody's mom.

The pressure surrounding Geoffrey grew as he tried to fight his way deeper into Sara's mind. Unlike the last time, there wasn't any whirlpool in Sara's mind, no drawing of everything down to a place of twisted destruction. Instead all of Sara's energy was directed to keeping others out of her most secret, personal parts.

Suddenly Geoffrey bumped up against something simultaneously hard and yielding, and he reflexively matched himself to the barrier and felt the pressure disappear as if it were water parting before a surfacing swimmer.

Inside the perfect calm of Sara's center, Geoffrey began cutting away the belief that she was worthless, and building a new set of beliefs that would hopefully radiate out and wash away the darkness that constantly tore at her self-image. He started with the message that she was an important, valuable person despite what anyone else might say or believe.

Next Geoffrey weakened the cynical pessimism that seemed to be eating away like a cancer at her center. He couldn't get rid of it altogether, not all at once, but he removed the supports that gave it shape and form so that one or two tastes of success would be able to cause it to shatter and decay away into nothing.

Looking around at the tiny ball of light that was now positioned to take over Sara's center, Geoffrey felt as though something was still missing, and for some reason he thought of the priest. The priest had always been so calm, only calm wasn't quite the right word. It was more a sense of peace that had seemed to define him above anything else. Peace was good, but peace without some kind of motivating force would be nothing more than a different kind of slavery. A slavery of the mind that she wouldn't even know to resist.

Mindful of the fact that his strength was slowly being depleted, and that he still needed to do the same kind of work with Tami, Geoffrey worked quickly, expanding the ball of light out so that it was a pool of peace and calm that was too good for the tawdry world in which the girls lived their life.

As soon as the pool was satisfactory, Geoffrey reached out and created another construct, one that reached out to touch Sara's dreams. This construct would return her dreams to things of beauty that she would be compelled to try and recreate with canvas and paints. Hopefully in so doing, she would find something to continue to strive for.

Geoffrey paused for only a second to examine his work before diving into Tami's mind. The work was somewhat easier, as he now had an idea what he was trying to accomplish, but his strength was fading so quickly that he nearly didn't finish in time.

With the last of his strength, Geoffrey pulled back to examine the lattice of pink strands he had just finished. Watching the calm white light reflect off of the warmth of the lattice made Geoffrey's eyes tear up again. Perfect contentment opposed against exquisite anguish and an angst for perfection that would never really be achieved.

Suddenly, the rising sense of hope and contentment that Geoffrey had been feeling reversed with incredible speed. It was replaced with a despair as deep as anything he'd ever felt. Was he really helping or had he just doomed both girls to a tormented existence, one in which they'd never know the reason for their persistent dissatisfaction? Geoffrey didn't know the true limits of his abilities, or the possible, unintended consequences that could come of him playing God in such a manner.

Overcome by self-doubt, Geoffrey pulled several thousand dollars from his pocket, threw it down on the bed, and stumbled out of the room. The sense of connection was gone, replaced by foggy memories with no real weight to them. How could he have felt like what he was doing was right? How could money or a few mental parlor tricks possibly compensate for having almost killed them? He really was nothing more than a self-aware parasite.

A decision that Geoffrey hadn't even realized he still had to make was suddenly crystal clear in his mind. His hand was shaking as he pulled a carefully-sealed envelope from his jacket pocket. It had been foolish to spend so much time composing a response. It had been even more foolish to risk Imastious finding it between when it was composed and now. A risk which turned out to be all for naught. The letter he'd planned on delivering was of no more substance than what he'd just accomplished. It was time to write another letter, an honest one.

A few hours later, Geoffrey found himself standing outside Melody's window staring at both letters, the words of the newest burnt into his memory.

Melody,

There is a very real possibility that I shouldn't respond to your letter, both because it puts you in danger, and because I am not the kind of person that you should be talking to, but I find myself doing it nevertheless.

All of those things really did happen. You were nearly raped, but I stopped your attackers. I persuaded those girls to be somewhat less self-centered, but I wasn't sure that my efforts would work, so I entered your mind in an attempt to find out if I was successful.

Despite my efforts to help you, you should know that I am in no way an answer to your prayers, as no god known of man deals with demons. You are so pure and innocent though, that even one as fallen as I couldn't help but try to aid you in your difficulties.

That hasn't changed—I still want to help you but it isn't safe. Everything I touch goes wrong, and I wouldn't wish that on you. On anyone really, but you least of all. My presence would corrupt and ruin you.

My thoughts will remain with you,
Geoffrey

As the sky started to lighten, Geoffrey affixed the second letter to Melody's window and turned away, thoughts of fire flitting through his mind. He needed to destroy any physical evidence and stop thinking about her. Otherwise everything he'd done to help would just be wasted.

Chapter 14

Geoffrey tried to calm his breathing once again, but only just managed to bring himself back from the edge of hyperventilation. He hadn't expected it to be so much harder this time around, but all of the time he'd had to think about what he was about to do wasn't helping things.

This girl was an innocent, or at least innocent enough that she didn't deserve to die. She hadn't killed anyone, wasn't selling crack to school kids or any of the other things he could have rationalized as being deserving of the fate he was about to deliver.

Geoffrey was acting now with the full understanding that what he was about to do was wrong, but he couldn't see any other way to protect Melody. He had to keep Imastious happy so that the other vampire wouldn't try and invade his mind again.

Geoffrey looked around at the dirty subway platform with its yellow-tiled walls and fought a bout of queasiness as he thought about the end result of what he was about to do. Once he was done, it would probably take the authorities hours to confirm the girl's identity.

The sound of hundreds of approaching footsteps signaled that it was almost time. Geoffrey's hands started to tremble as the first set of teenagers made their way down the stairs. Kids from high school, kids from junior high. There were tens of thousands of them all over the city right now getting out of school and heading home. Many of them lived close enough to school to walk home, but an incredible number of them would take the buses or the subway. It stressed the public transportation system every day at this time, and it wouldn't have surprised Geoffrey to find out that more bodies would be transported over the next hour than would be transported in the subsequent two hours when some of their parents got off of work.

Kids being kids, they took up less space; but that was only half of the equation. Kids also seemed to need less personal space, so they tended to pack themselves in incredibly tight. They would squeeze themselves into the buses, they'd cram themselves into the trains, and they would dangerously overload the platforms.

Geoffrey had watched it happen several times now. They seemed utterly without fear, sometimes standing within inches of the edge of the platform, never really understanding how inadequate those inches were to protect them from harm.

They probably read the headlines, the ones about the accidents where a crowd surged at the wrong time, or the senseless revenge carried out via a hard shove, but the fact that those inches weren't enough just didn't seem to sink in.

The girl finally appeared on the steps leading down to the platform. She was all but indistinguishable from her friends, all of whom were dressed in matching uniforms, but something pulled Geoffrey's attention past the skirt and white blouse. There was no doubt but that she was the one he was looking for. His worries vanished. Things would go just like he'd rehearsed. As long as he followed the plan, this would all be over in a few minutes.

As much as Geoffrey had hoped his target would walk right up to the edge, he'd known that the odds were against it. As a result, the vampire had prepared for the possibility that he might have to compel her. The fact that he was using his abilities to kill her somehow made the crime worse, but that couldn't be allowed to stand in the way.

Opening his mind, Geoffrey was nearly swept away by the maelstrom of thoughts surrounding him. There were so many of them, and they were so energetic and undisciplined. It was like everything happening right then was of life-altering importance for each kid.

THE GREATER DARKNESS

Geoffrey tried to build an island of calm around his mind, and succeeded just enough to find the girl's thoughts. "This is boring," he told her. "Boring just like every other day. You can feel it building inside of you, demanding you do something exciting and adventuresome. Your friends are boring, those boys are boring, none of it is interesting."

It took longer than the vampire had expected, almost as if his efforts were less effective than normal, but soon Geoffrey saw the girl's thoughts begin to shift. She was tapping her foot now, flipping her long, dark hair. She wasn't even listening to her friends now.

Once the girl started moving towards the edge, her fate was essentially sealed. A quick pull on her trendy black backpack was all it took to send the poor thing onto the tracks a heartbeat before the train came barreling up to the platform.

The ensuing pandemonium was more than enough to cover Geoffrey's exit from the area. By the time the police arrived and decided that the girl's death was nothing more than a tragic accident, the vampire was several miles away.

The whole operation had gone so smoothly that an hour passed before what Geoffrey had done fully sank in. He didn't even know what her name was. Tami? Tallie? Tanya? It had started with a 'T', but he couldn't remember quite what it had been. Was that just happenstance, or was he already dehumanizing her?

"Come on, gorgeous. I'm not letting you miss weapons instruction two times in a row. You should know better by now than to stand up a beautiful woman."

Geoffrey didn't open his eyes. He'd expected that Venice would probably show up next to his bed tonight despite his having changed all of the locks on the apartment, but hadn't been able to bring himself to really care.

"I'm not feeling well. I can't train today."

A springy weight settled onto the bed next to Geoffrey. "Listen, I understand that killing the little girl had to be hard for you. I don't really know why, not considering the fact that not too long ago you wouldn't have even batted an eye over something like that, but I've come to accept that things have changed. We're no longer together, and those things bother you now."

Unexpected emotion welled up inside of Geoffrey, and he fought the desire to curl up next to Venice and sob. It wasn't real; she wasn't being genuine. She was just telling him what she thought he wanted to hear.

"Based on all of that, and the fact that you're barely functional now, I imagine there must have been something pretty important to make you go through with the hit. I don't know what it was, but you have to focus on that reason. That's why you did it. You have to cling to that reason, or you'll lose your sanity."

The unexpected emotion in Venice's voice pulled at Geoffrey's heart, and he found himself opening his eyes so that he could meet her gaze. Try as he might, he couldn't tell whether her concerned expression was just a facade, or if she was really feeling the things she seemed to be feeling. It seemed hard to believe that she could be that concerned about his sanity. Maybe something about the situation brought back ghosts from her past.

Venice stared into Geoffrey's eyes, but seemed to be looking past him for several seconds before blinking and then attempting a smile.

"Careful there, love, next you'll decide I have a soul after all, and then where would you be?"

Geoffrey opened his mouth to respond, but he was torn between an honest response and the flippant sarcasm so normal between the two of them. Before the vampire could decide between the two options, Venice shrugged. "It was just a joke."

The blonde paused on her way out the door to adjust her hair. "I won't bring all of this up to Imastious, but I'm no mentalist. If he decides I'm trying to hide something, there isn't anything I can do to stop him from invading my mind; he won't even have to starve and torture me like he does to you. I just thought you should know. There's more than just you riding on you behaving and keeping him happy."

Geoffrey stayed in bed for quite some time after Venice left before forcing himself to get up and head outside. It would have been easier in some ways to just stay in his hole of an apartment, but that would have just resulted in him starving. Even assuming that he managed not to lose control and kill someone, it would only be a matter of time before Imastious eventually stopped by, and Geoffrey couldn't afford to be weak when that happened. It was all he could do to fight off Imastious when he was at full strength. If Imastious found him half starved, it would require next to no effort on his part to overwhelm Geoffrey's defenses.

The idea of going for a run to try and clear his mind was briefly considered, but discarded in the end because the hunger had Geoffrey feeling so weak. He knew he'd probably just collapse at about mile three if he tried.

Instead, the vampire found himself wandering through the sparsely-populated financial district in an attempt to avoid the kinds of places where it would be all too easy to find someone to feed from. Geoffrey tried to distract himself by examining his surroundings, the proud metal and glass buildings that still looked new and unblemished. In time they'd enter the state of semi-disrepair so common elsewhere in the city, the same kind of near ruin he'd seen at the school. The inevitability was depressing, but didn't manage to truly distract him from the things really bothering him.

Feeding from those two girls had been intoxicating. The satiation of the hunger had combined with a very real danger that he'd take too much blood and kill them. The feeling of being connected to them might have been an illusion, but it hadn't been like that the first two times he'd fed. This had felt real, and it pulled at him with a strength nearly as powerful as the hunger had been. It would be very easy to become addicted to the sensation. Truth be told, he wasn't positive that he wasn't already addicted. He couldn't get his mind away from the idea of getting another fix.

A low growling, almost too faint to hear, brought Geoffrey's attention fully back to his surroundings. Underneath the concealment of his coat, the vampire gripped the handle of his katana while scanning the darkness. It was obviously some kind of animal, maybe a large dog, but that didn't seem quite right to him.

A chill crept up the back of Geoffrey's neck as something operating on the level of instinct told him he was in the presence of extreme danger.

There hadn't been very many people out and about this late into the night, but what few there had been seemed to have disappeared. It was like they'd sensed something bad was coming and sought refuge indoors where they had a chance of avoiding whatever was stalking him.

Looking around, Geoffrey saw that the one other person on the street, a middle-aged woman in a dress suit that marked her as some kind of business executive, looked frightened. She was actually moving towards Geoffrey at a quick pace, as if hoping to find some kind of safety in numbers.

Venice's warning that he shouldn't become too secure in his superiority over the humans around him flashed through Geoffrey's mind, and suddenly he wondered if there wasn't some kind of predator out there that preyed on vampires the way that Venice sometimes insinuated he should prey upon humans.

The thought of something faster, stronger and even more deadly than him made Geoffrey's blood run cold. It was ludicrous to think that something was actively hunting him, but he found himself hurrying towards the woman with a smile on his face that he hoped looked reassuring, but which he suspected looked more forced than anything else.

Maintaining an awareness of his surroundings while extending his mental senses was a trick that the vampire hadn't fully mastered yet, but the need to know what was out there stalking him drove him to try.

He could feel the woman's presence ahead and to the left of him. He skimmed her thoughts enough to register that her name was Alice and that she was even more terrified than he was. Now that he was oriented, he reached out further, looking for whatever was out there prowling in the darkness.

At first there was nothing, but then Geoffrey reached a little further afield and brushed against a presence unlike anything he'd ever imagined. It was ferocious...and tortured, and it felt somehow fuller than it should be. The only parallel he could draw was a glass that someone had poured memories and knowledge into until it started to overflow.

The brief contact was all Geoffrey was able to manage before his mental probes were torn away by a huge, mostly unformed, presence, leaving him with an incredible headache.

The vampire stumbled in pain, reflexively grabbing Alice to avoid falling to the ground.

Alice's gasp of surprise, brought about by the unexpected contact, nearly drowned out the sound of many feet padding through the darkness, but Geoffrey retained just enough composure to duck as he sensed something leap towards him from out of the night.

A dark form sailed over the vampire and crashed into Alice as something else latched onto Geoffrey's left arm and bore him to the ground.

Venice's training largely deserted Geoffrey. None of the reflexes he'd spent so many hours retraining were appropriate for a close-quarters struggle.

The crushing pressure on the vampire's forearm was so great that he wasn't really surprised when first one and then the other bone broke, crushed despite the protection of his heavy trench coat.

The next few seconds were a nightmare of fur and pain, but Geoffrey somehow managed to get to the knife he'd secreted in his boot. Once that happened, the fight was quickly over.

Rolling to his feet, Geoffrey was just in time to see a large Rottweiler release Alice's arms and turn towards him. The vampire took a step back, and dropping his knife onto the corpse of the first dog, drew his katana. It was obvious that the beast would rush him, but its hind legs didn't seem to be working quite right. It was a small thing, but it might buy him a split second or two in which to respond, and he was quickly realizing that fights were won and lost on smaller things than that.

With a weapon in hand, Geoffrey was once again on familiar ground, and his training, both the parts he remembered and the parts that were now nothing more than reflex, took over. The dog's leap became a slow, predictable arc that his blade intercepted, neatly beheading the animal as he spun out of the way to avoid being carried to the ground again.

Not surprisingly, considering the extent of injuries to her arms, Alice was in shock.

THE GREATER DARKNESS

Geoffrey started to apply pressure to the wounds, but when he heard sirens in the distance he realized that someone must have called the police.

He deserved jail, or worse, for his crimes, but he wasn't ready for that. He whispered an apology as he turned away from Alice and faded into the night. He wanted to stay and help her, but the police would ask too many questions that he'd be hard-pressed to answer.

It had been all that Geoffrey could do to roll out of bed once the sun went down the next day, but he didn't dare miss another training session with Venice. It had the feel of the kind of thing that spun out of control quickly. One missed training session had become two, and unless he got back into the right routine things would snowball. The last thing he could afford would be for Imastious to kick his door down again.

It wasn't until Geoffrey got out of the shower and accidentally bumped into a doorway with his left arm that he remembered the events of the night before, remembered how badly his arm had been damaged. He was suddenly less surprised that he was tired and more astonished that he'd managed to sleep at all, considering how much pain he should have been in.

Geoffrey probed his arm, but aside from some tenderness it seemed perfectly normal. It should have been impossible. He remembered the bones breaking. He tried to remember whether or not Venice had mentioned anything with regards to abnormally fast healing. As unlikely as the idea was, the only other explanation would be that his memory couldn't be trusted.

The speed with which he had healed continued to worry at the edge of Geoffrey's mind, so much so that he asked Venice about it within a couple minutes of arriving at her club.

"Increased regenerative abilities are part of the package that comes with being turned. A vampire will basically fully recover from anything that doesn't kill him outright...but the speed with which we heal correlates with our age."

The hesitation with which Venice made the last statement would have gone unnoticed a few weeks previous, but Geoffrey had come to realize that he had as much to learn from how Venice said things as what she said.

"So I just gave you a hint as to how old I really am then?"

Venice paused, maybe more startled by the fact that she was about to answer honestly than that he'd caught the misstep.

"Basically yes. It isn't a perfect science, obviously, but to regenerate from something like you described in the space of eight or nine hours is pretty impressive. It isn't as fast as someone like Imastious would do it, but it makes you older than I expected. Older than your speed would seem to indicate too."

Geoffrey shrugged. "So we get faster as we get older too?" At Venice's nod, he continued. "I guess I'm a freak even among vampires then. I just must heal quickly, because I'm obviously not much, if any, faster than you are."

Venice returned Geoffrey's shrug. "I suppose." Stripping off her warm-ups to reveal loose cotton pants and a white tank top, the blonde continued. "I'm actually more interested in the dogs that attacked you; do you have any idea why they did so?"

Geoffrey shook his head. "I don't know that much about mutts, but it wasn't like I was doing anything to provoke them. They seemed entirely normal other than the fact that they were so aggressive, and that the one had some kind of injury to his back legs."

Venice paused mid-stretch. "When you say injury, do you mean he was bleeding?"

"No, there wasn't anything wrong that I could see, it just looked like they didn't work quite right."

Venice went even whiter than usual. "Rabies, it has to have been rabies. You're absolutely sure that you killed them both?"

Geoffrey nodded slowly. "Yes, they were both quite dead when I left. Why are you so concerned?"

Venice put both of her hands behind her, as if to ensure that they weren't trembling, and then started to pace back and forth. "I don't know, not completely at least. There are rumors of course, stories about things that prey upon us like we prey upon the humans. Things that own the night, that can appear out of the darkness and kill you before you know that they're there. I always assumed that they were just stories, kind of like the ones about us descending from something else thousands of years ago, things that won't be happy with what we've become when they return to check up on us. I dismissed them all until I found out that once something is infected with rabies it can sense vampires. Not only that, they always become abnormally aggressive in our presence."

Venice looked up, and Geoffrey realized he'd never seen Venice scared before. "You wouldn't believe the way Imastious reacted the last time there was a case of rabies in the city. He all but disappeared until the humans were positive that they'd contained the incident. He kept muttering about a massive outbreak."

Geoffrey's blood ran cold as he realized he'd been exposed to whatever Imastious was scared of. "Are we exceptionally vulnerable to contracting rabies?"

Venice shook her head. "No, as nearly as I can tell there hasn't ever been a case where a vampire picked up the disease, it just boiled down to Imastious worrying something would hunt him down."

"So if somehow there was a big enough outbreak, it is conceivable that the city's population of vampires could be decimated?"

Venice nodded in response to the question. "The humans don't realize how ill-prepared their medical establishment is to deal with something like that in a city this size. Imastious went on and on at the time about population density's effect on transmission rates, and a bunch of other stuff I understood even less well, but he sounded worried, and he told me it was more than my life was worth if I ever withheld information like that from him."

Geoffrey still felt like someone had injected ice water into his veins, but he tried to inject a little levity into the situation as Venice began packing up her things again. "He doesn't seem like one who would be all that worried about the good of vampire-kind."

"He isn't, he's worried about his own skin. That, and he'll no doubt be looking for ways to profit from an early warning if things really get as bad as he seems to think they may."

It wasn't until Venice had been gone for half an hour that Geoffrey realized the matter-of-fact way she'd described Imastious' desire to profit from the pain and suffering of others bothered him more than the thought of packs of rabid dogs cornering him in dark alleys.

Chapter 15

Geoffrey had been hoping that over time he'd manage to get used to what he was. He'd been prepared to deal with things remaining just as bad as they'd been, but he hadn't even considered that they might get worse. It seemed like everyone who looked at him now could see his guilt.

Geoffrey self-consciously looked around, but even if anyone had been nearby, the odds of them noticing him, positioned as he was in the shadows, were pretty remote. It was all he could do to stop himself from compulsively scanning his surroundings.

The sudden appearance of heavy clouds early the day before had caused the temperature to drop significantly, and Geoffrey pulled his trench coat tighter around him as he examined the course of events that had led him back to Melody's building.

THE GREATER DARKNESS

Venice had told him that the only way to keep his sanity was to focus on his cause for performing the hit. He felt like he was holding onto reason with the weakest of grips, so maybe she was right. Maybe seeing Melody again would be enough to keep the shards of his being together long enough for the nightmares to go away. There were countless reasons not to go, not to put Melody in any further danger, but Geoffrey couldn't seem to get past his own need to see her.

His decision made, Geoffrey stood and headed towards Melody's building. A short time later, he was once again crouched outside her window.

Questing fingers quickly found and removed the letter that Geoffrey had half-hoped to find. After securing the note in a pocket, the vampire's eyes turned to the pale, blanket-covered form just visible in the darkness. His night vision seemed to have improved now that he wasn't spending quite as much time outside in the sun, but it still wasn't quite good enough for him to see the details that he'd come hoping to see.

Tearing his eyes away from Melody, Geoffrey looked past an unusually familiar-looking backpack to her diary sitting closed on the desk. He couldn't seem to shake the worry that the letter wasn't going to tell him how she was really doing. The obvious solution was to go inside her mind again. He was stronger than he'd been last time when she'd nearly trapped him, but it felt wrong. She hadn't invited him in, and he'd be doing so out of selfish reasons rather than because he was trying to help her.

The vampire closed his eyes, fighting the temptation to let his thoughts slip out and touch Melody's mind and then shook himself and climbed back up the fire escape.

The earliness of the hour meant there were still a large number of establishments open, and it didn't take Geoffrey long to find a bar that was well-lit enough for him to read the letter Melody had left.

Dear Geoffrey,

You don't know how much it means to me to know your name. I find it's the small, even insignificant things that give me the strength to go on. You call yourself a demon, and I don't dispute that you may have done terrible things in the past, or that you may even now be involved in such things, but anyone who would intercede on my behalf as you have without looking for some form of payment has elements of good in them.

Knowing you're there, that you cared enough to come back and help cushion me from the cruelties of those girls, means more than you will ever know. Even if you are never able to help in any way again, I think that should count for something.

It really is the little things in life that set us apart from those around us. For Anna, it is the fact that she comes and checks on Mom far more often than she is paid to, and sometimes brings a little surprise like the backpack she brought last week. For you, it's simply that you exist, that maybe once again in a time of great need you'll be there to help protect me.

Melody

Despite still waking up nightly with nightmares from killing the girl, Geoffrey had started to think of himself as the soulless, hardened killer Venice and Imastious insisted he used to be. It surprised him when he once again found himself fighting back tears over something so trivial.

Melody didn't really know. Despite his efforts to tell her, she still didn't understand how bad he really was. Still, she knew he was bad and cared for him regardless. If only he were actually worthy of her.

Geoffrey was down on the subway platform again. A cold wind pulled at him as he watched his target. It was all chillingly familiar, but this time he didn't have to touch the girl's thoughts to get her to the edge. She was already standing there, her back to him, patiently waiting for the train.

Something seemed to nag at Geoffrey, telling him it was impossible to kill the same girl again;

but as had happened so many nights before, the vivid reality of his dream drowned out thoughts that anything might be amiss.

Geoffrey was shaking again as he tried to steel himself against what he was about to do. Children filled the area between him and the girl, but they melted away, giving him a clear path to his mark. It was as if they were offering her up to satiate his blood lust.

Geoffrey could hear the train now, charging through the darkness towards the platform, as he strode over the rough, filthy concrete that separated him from the girl. As the vampire reached his target, the rush of air that pushed out of the tunnel blew her short brown hair about. Once again, Geoffrey reached up to the stylish black backpack before him and gave it a sharp tug.

The poor girl stumbled over the edge a split second before the train arrived. She turned as she fell, revealing her face for a split second before the train hid her with a squeal of brakes and a cascade of sparks.

Geoffrey awoke panting and drenched in a cold sweat. This time it had been Melody he'd pushed off of the platform. He'd found himself back in that station countless times now, but this was the first time that it had been Melody he'd killed. It made no sense, but something had happened to change the dream.

The vampire wanted nothing more than to wall the dream away in a portion of his subconscious where he wouldn't ever have to think about it again, but instead he forced himself to examine it, noting each difference from previous dreams in an effort to understand why his nightmares had become even more disturbing.

He shouldn't have had to see her face to realize it was a different person. Her hair had been different. The girl he'd killed had had long hair. The clothes seemed like they'd been a little different, and he was pretty sure the two of them had slightly different builds. He couldn't see any reason why he would have been so sure it was the same girl despite all of the clues that indicated otherwise.

Geoffrey replayed the approach in his mind again and again until he suddenly realized what had remained the same. It was the backpack. The backpack he had pulled on to send the first girl to her death was the same backpack that he'd glimpsed through the darkness the night before. It was the backpack that Anna had given Melody, the one that had helped tell her that someone cared about her.

Geoffrey had hoped that the passage of a few additional days would lessen some of the vividness of the dreams, or that at least he'd stop seeing Melody's face when he pushed the girl off of the platform. Instead he was now sometimes having them more than once in a given night.

The vampire had stumbled his way through weapons practice twice already this week, and each time he'd been slower and less skilled. Venice had scored more touches on him during the last session than she had the first time they'd sparred.

Finally disgusted, and apparently sure that Geoffrey wasn't even trying, Venice had ended the practice session and sent him home.

Geoffrey was half an hour late already tonight for the last session of the week, but between the hunger and sheer exhaustion he couldn't seem to muster enough energy to care. He couldn't keep going like this, but he was having a hard time coming up with alternatives. Maybe he could anger Imastious enough for the older vampire to just kill him outright rather than invading his mind and then hunting Melody and her mother down.

Time skipped forward, as it often did when the hunger started to take a life of its own, and Geoffrey lost an hour or so dreamily contemplating the death he'd receive when Imastious finally found out that he wasn't training anymore. In Geoffrey's fantasy, Imastious kicked the door down again and then swooped in and broke Geoffrey's neck with his bare hands.

A persistent knocking at Geoffrey's door finally penetrated the hunger haze, and he absently wondered why Imastious had decided to knock instead of just killing him.

"Geoffrey, I know you are in there, please come open the door."

Venice's voice was full of the usual self-confidence and exasperation that Geoffrey had come to associate with the gorgeous vampire, but there was something else there as well that he couldn't quite place.

"Please, Geoffrey. We have to talk. I'll come in like I usually do if you won't open the door."

Unsure why he was doing so, Geoffrey tried to rise, only to find that he was too weak to get out of bed.

His vision had started to become blurry due to the hunger, but Geoffrey was just able to see the locks as they turned one by one, seemingly of their own accord.

"By the blood, you look terrible."

Geoffrey tried to tell Venice he was fine, but his thoughts never made it down to his mouth, instead wandering off to wonder if what he'd heard was genuine concern.

Venice pulled off her black leather jacket as she crossed the room, but Geoffrey's vision began to fade out again, barely allowing him to see that she was wearing a white tube top and leather pants that matched her jacket.

"How long has it been since you fed?" demanded Venice as she knelt on the bed next to Geoffrey.

Apparently alarmed by Geoffrey's inability to communicate, the beautiful vampire used her fingernails to open up a vein in her arm and pressed the wound against his mouth.

The hot flow of sustenance awakened the hunger tenfold inside of Geoffrey, and he found himself sucking greedily as rational thought began to return. A split second later that was all swept away by a pale shadow of the sense of connection that seemed to be such a part of feeding.

For a few moments, nothing existed save the few, incomplete thoughts that trickled through the connection, and Geoffrey's need for more blood. Venice suddenly tore her arm away from his grasp, stanching the flow of blood as best she was able while trying to fight off Geoffrey.

"It's me, Geoffrey. Stop or I'll be forced to hurt you."

The words, repeated again and again, finally penetrated the hunger and Geoffrey opened his eyes to find Venice trapped under him, a dagger held to his throat.

The imminent threat of violence was somehow made worse when viewed against even the weak bond the pair had just shared. Realizing what he had almost forced Venice to do, Geoffrey recoiled and tried to flee into the bathroom, only to stumble and crash weakly onto the ancient hardwood floor after only a few feet.

THE GREATER DARKNESS

When the vampire regained consciousness, he found himself cradled in Venice's arms as hot tears splashed onto his neck.

"Why are you doing this to yourself? I lied for you last night to Imastious, I'm doing what I can to protect you, but you don't care. All you seem to want is death, and there's only so much I can do to keep you from finding it."

A wave of guilt and sadness crashed through Geoffrey as Venice's worry caused tears to flow down his face as well.

For a time, nothing else was said, and Geoffrey felt nearly the same closeness that he'd experienced while feeding.

"I see her when I dream, every night." It was hard, but Geoffrey forced the words out past the sobs. "At first it was the girl I killed, but now it is the one that I dreamed about before this all happened."

Even now, being held by Venice, Geoffrey didn't completely trust her not to convey what he said to Imastious. The lack of trust tore at him almost like a physical wound, but he just couldn't quite believe her tears were completely real.

Venice made shushing sounds and held him, rocking back and forth for what seemed like hours. "She must have been the reason that you finally went through with the hit."

Geoffrey nodded, not trusting his voice.

"And now the very reason you killed the girl is the thing that's eating at you."

Venice had spent hours holding Geoffrey before gently telling him she had tasks from Imastious that had to be taken care of before sunrise. Geoffrey had reluctantly promised to feed as soon as it got dark again, and then watched as the other vampire flirtatiously blew him a kiss and left the apartment.

Despite feeling more physically and emotionally drained than at any other time he could remember, sleep had proven elusive for Geoffrey. There was too much risk that he'd still have nightmares and he wasn't sure he could handle another bout this soon.

Geoffrey had dropped into a light sleep a few times, only to start awake before he could begin dreaming. When night finally came, the vampire slipped out into the darkness.

Venice was right. Melody was the reason that he'd killed that girl, but now the thought that it could have been her he'd killed instead was slowly eating away at him. He'd promised Venice that he'd feed, and it was a promise that he'd keep, but first he needed to visit Melody.

The clouds from earlier in the week were finally fulfilling on the rain that they had been promising for days, alternating between a constant drizzle and torrential downpours. The conditions were miserable now that things had cooled off so much, but it was probably the cleanest the city would be for weeks. Maybe a little misery was always exacted as a price for washing away the filth.

After slogging through what seemed like hundreds of foot-deep puddles, Geoffrey finally reached Melody's building. Making his way down the fire escape from the top of the building was more difficult than normal, but at least he didn't have to worry about anyone seeing him through the gloom.

Settling down in his usual place against the window, Geoffrey carefully let his thoughts reach into the room before him, lightly brushing the surface of Melody's mind.

She was dreaming of pleasant things and places. He could only assume that her mom was having a good day. Geoffrey was overcome by a wave of regret and sadness. What right did he have to come here and ruin her innocence? Once again he was pursuing the course that protected him regardless of the cost to others.

Wiping away the traces of something that could have almost been tears, Geoffrey strengthened the contact enough for him to begin to affect Melody's dreams. Within moments, he was able to pipe his thoughts directly into her mind. She wouldn't have the ability to focus her thoughts enough to respond to him, but he was reasonably confident that she'd be able to remember what he was about to tell her once she woke up.

Melody, it's Geoffrey. I know I shouldn't be here, but I felt like I had to tell you the truth. You think that I'm good, that whatever I've done is outweighed by the good I've tried to do, but it isn't true. I've killed people. Some of them were murderers themselves, sometimes it was in defense of myself or others. I guess I don't feel as bad about those times as maybe I should, but I knew beyond a shadow of a doubt that they had done terrible things.

Regret and sadness tried to well up out of his center, but he was just too exhausted for the feelings to gain a real foothold.

Others were innocent. A little while ago I killed a girl about your age. I didn't want to, her only sin was being born to parents who were involved with the wrong people, but if I didn't, there was a chance that you and your mom would have been killed to punish me. I wasn't ever going to tell you about that, but the backpack Anna gave you is just like the one that my latest victim was wearing when I killed her.

The tears were back now despite the exhaustion, ripping at the remnants of Geoffrey's soul, and he almost couldn't go on.

I've been having nightmares where your face replaces hers. I'm beyond redemption, but I wanted you to know. I've never lied to you, but I didn't want to conceal something like this from you. That would be another kind of lie. You need to know what I'm really like before you try to turn me into one of your heroes.

THE GREATER DARKNESS

The vampire disengaged his probes and headed back into the rain, having been very careful to ensure that none of Melody's emotions or thoughts had been able to flow back up the link to him.

Chapter 16

The nightmares hadn't left completely, but they were less intense. It was less often Melody's face that looked back at him as she was pushed off of the platform, and when it was her she seemed somehow less condemning.

As a result, Geoffrey had been sleeping slightly better. He was still slower than he should be, but training with Venice was going much better, and that wasn't just because he was getting more sleep.

The vampire mentally shied away from examining the changes that were happening to his relationship with Venice. Actually that wasn't quite true. He'd examined them; he just wasn't comfortable with the direction they were going. He was sure that it was a bad thing, but it felt very much like he was starting to care for Venice.

The other thing that Geoffrey had been avoiding thinking about was the fact that he'd fulfilled his promise to Venice and fed. Even having just fed from Venice, it was hard to avoid taking too much. Afterwards he'd thought about trying to engineer some constructs in the poor girl's mind, but it had seemed like doing so would just mock what he'd taken from her. She deserved more than a few mental tricks that might or might not work, and if he couldn't really help her it seemed a sad thing to salve his conscience like that.

Geoffrey finished stretching on the blue mats as Venice came out of the dressing room. "I stretched out before leaving home, love, so I'm ready to go whenever you are."

"I think I'm pretty much there, too."

Venice nodded, but Geoffrey snagged her arm before she could turn away. "Thanks for this. Not just teaching me, but for helping, for being understanding."

"I told you, love. We used to be close. You've forgotten, but I haven't."

The moment could have grown awkward, but Venice smiled and turned back to her duffle bag.

After putting on some minimal padding and face protection, the pair squared off without weapons and Geoffrey was surprised to find that for the first time he seemed to be faster than Venice. He'd managed to press the lithe vampire on more than one occasion, due mostly to his superior reach, but today Venice was on the defensive from the start.

Geoffrey's right fist flicked out again and again, and if Venice was able to dodge or block most of the jabs, there were still a significant percentage of them getting through. The pretty face behind the headgear was getting more and more frustrated as Venice proved unable to close to a range where she could punish Geoffrey with the body blows that were her usual response to his attempts to stand back and wear her down.

Geoffrey began to relax as the fight continued in a rapid exchange of blows and counters that required no conscious thought on his part. Gradually Geoffrey realized that his blocks were being executed as soon as Venice began her strikes. It was almost as if she was telegraphing everything, but he couldn't point to anything having changed on her side.

Venice launched a punch towards Geoffrey's face, but he inexplicably knew it was nothing more than a feint and he brought his right foot up and lashed out to the side, catching Venice in the ribs as she charged in.

The blow picked the smaller vampire up and knocked her to the ground several feet back from where she'd started. Geoffrey ran over, worried that he'd hurt her.

Venice stripped off her head gear, obviously mad until she saw the concern on Geoffrey's face. "I'm more or less okay. You probably broke some of my bloody ribs, but it's nothing that shouldn't heal in a couple of days."

Geoffrey sighed in relief and then watched as Venice's eyes momentarily became distant.

"You sneaky jerk. At first I just thought you'd finally started to speed up to where you used to be, but I just realized that you were using your abilities to predict my actions."

Geoffrey rolled away from a weak punch as he considered Venice's words and realized that she was right. "I didn't mean to..."

Venice shrugged and then grimaced and grabbed her side. "It's okay; I should have realized that this was bound to happen sooner or later." The younger vampire waved Geoffrey off again. "I'll be fine, but we'll have to wait for a bit. It will be a day or two before I'll be up for a full-scale practice again."

The rest of the training session consisted of Geoffrey performing a wide variety of techniques while Venice watched and critiqued his form.

When the beautiful blonde finally allowed Geoffrey to collapse to the floor, tired and sweaty, he found he was exhausted enough that he couldn't seem to achieve his usual level of self-condemnation. At least he hoped that was the cause. The alternative was that he was getting to the point where what he'd done didn't bother him anymore.

Even as tired as he was, Geoffrey managed to beat Venice to the lobby after showering and changing. It was more proof of how badly he'd hurt her. Until those ribs healed she would be moving more slowly than normal.

When Venice finally came out of the locker room she flashed Geoffrey a smile that had only the smallest shadow of pain attached to it. "So, oh chivalrous one, you decided to wait and make sure that the damsel you beat up wasn't going to need help getting dressed, huh?"

Geoffrey blushed, but managed to shrug. "It seemed like the thing to do at the time."

Venice paused, and for a second looked as if she would apologize for making Geoffrey feel uncomfortable. "Listen, I told you a while ago that things are starting to get a little hairy out there, but there's been a development that nobody was expecting. A vampire named Slasher was found dead a couple of days ago."

Once she was satisfied that she had Geoffrey's full attention, Venice continued. "We've kept you pretty much isolated from the rest of vampire society, but it probably won't be any surprise that vampires are killed on a pretty regular basis. One or two a month isn't that uncommon if a given Elder is making some kind of subtle power play. Venice hugged herself as if chilled. "What was different about this was that he wasn't just killed, he was torn apart."

Geoffrey's stomach rebelled at the image Venice's statement conjured up. When he'd killed the three kids who had been about to rape

Melody there had been an obscene amount of blood spilled. If someone was really ripped to shreds blood would be splattered everywhere, almost like some kind of grotesque paint.

"I don't know what could have done something like that. Slasher wasn't a neophyte. He was stronger than either of us, and his primary ability was telekinesis. Some people are claiming that one of the masters like DeRys, or maybe Bajuel, used their telekinetic abilities to do him in. More worrying is the fact that there's another group, mostly made up of telekinetics who are in a pretty good position to know what's legitimately possible with mind power, who think that something else is responsible--that something he was hunting reversed roles on him and made him the prey."

In light of Venice's warning, and the fact that she was obviously worried about the implications of Slasher's death, it would have probably been prudent for Geoffrey to remain inside as much as possible. Instead he found himself walking the streets once again as he tried to make sense of all the thoughts screaming for attention inside his head.

He'd really needed to get out. Running would have left him weaponless, so he compromised and went out fully armed even though it limited him to a walk. It wasn't as good as a run, but it was better than nothing.

The sidewalks and streets were already dirty again, and Geoffrey soon found himself spending as much time watching the sidewalk for gum, and other less-desirable things as he did observing his surroundings. It wasn't until he'd been walking for half an hour that the vampire realized that he'd been wandering the same general area for quite a while, and that it was an area of the city that he recognized. His mind spun for a second as he tried to remember when he'd last been there.

A wave of uneasiness washed through Geoffrey as he realized that he was very nearly to the hospital, less than a block from where he'd been attacked by the teenager weeks before. He instinctively knew he needed to get out of the area so he turned up his collar and changed directions, hoping he'd be able to go unnoticed for the few minutes it would take him to make it somewhere less dangerous.

Geoffrey made it a block before three sloppily-dressed teenagers, whose pants seemed ready to finish their downward slide past their boxers, detached themselves from a wall and moved as if to intercept him. The vampire turned his head with the intention of retreating back to a more public area, only to see the teenager who'd attacked him approaching from behind with two other men.

THE GREATER DARKNESS

Geoffrey backed up to a wall to avoid another pile of garbage and ensure that nobody could circle around behind him while he tried to prepare himself for what was about to come.

"You've got my gun, dog." The rest of the toughs all laughed, but Geoffrey hardly noticed as he concentrated on sending out tendrils of thought to brush the surface of each man's mind.

This group wasn't going to back down. He could sense a desire for pain and suffering coming off of them, and it was strong enough that even his death might not satisfy them. A couple were uneasy at his failure to respond to their barbs, but most seemed to be taking it as a sign of weakness.

As Geoffrey established the intent of the gang members, a variety of improvised weapons from knives to chains appeared in every hand.

A single concern that he'd regret what he was about to do spidered across the calm that enveloped Geoffrey, but then the first ganger prepared to strike, and conscious thought fled.

Able as he was to read the thoughts of each attacker, Geoffrey started countering their actions before any of them physically moved.

The first attacker ran into Geoffrey's heel as he launched a back thrust kick even more powerful than the blow that had fractured Venice's ribs. Geoffrey then stepped inside the chain that came sweeping towards him and threw another attacker into two of his fellows.

The next two attackers tried to spread out and trap Geoffrey between them, but he had his katana drawn, and it licked out in short, brutal arcs that left bloody corpses at his feet.

By the time the last two gang members made it back to their feet, Geoffrey was already upon them, crushing the throat of one with a snap kick, and trapping the knife-wielding hand of the second just long enough to pull him in close and spin him around.

When the teen that had started it all tried to escape Geoffrey's hold by stomping down on the vampire's instep, Geoffrey simply slid the foot out of the way and broke his opponent's neck.

Not waiting for witnesses to call the police, Geoffrey cleaned his weapon on one of the fallen, and disappeared into the night.

Chapter 17

Geoffrey couldn't shake the feeling he was being watched. The vampire had doubled back several times in an effort to catch whatever was following him, but hadn't been successful in finding anyone.

It was possible that he was just being paranoid because of last week's ambush, but he still took a degree of comfort in the fact that he hadn't gone anywhere that would have given anything important away. Even if someone was stalking him, it hadn't gained them anything yet.

Still, the feeling was out of the ordinary, and he was finding that anything outside of the norm practically made his skin crawl. Venice hadn't come by yet to tell him her ribs were healed enough to resume training either, so his mind kept trying to link the two events. If Venice hadn't finally contacted him earlier in the day and told him to meet her, his paranoia probably would have made it to record levels.

Geoffrey finally arrived at the designated meeting point in Central Park, arranged his trench coat, and sat down to wait. Venice arrived a few moments later.

The gorgeous vampire looked around to ensure they were alone, and then sat down next to Geoffrey, leaning into him slightly. "It is good to see you, love. I was half afraid you wouldn't get the note."

Geoffrey nodded absently, wondering if Venice had really been a party to the decision on where to meet, or if Imastious had just dictated to her the same way he called all of the shots with Geoffrey.

"How are your ribs?"

Venice shrugged. "They've been fine for a few days now, but Imastious had a number of chores that he wanted taken care of, so I've been too busy of late to stop by and let you know that you could try and beat me senseless again."

Geoffrey was on the verge of apologizing again for hurting Venice, but he knew that it would only goad her into giving him a worse time, so he remained silent.

"Six men were killed or seriously injured last week, the same night as we trained. Descriptions of the one who did it to them had him using some kind of curved sword, and wearing a black trench coat."

Realizing that Geoffrey wasn't going to respond, Venice shrugged. "Suit yourself, but

Imastious has hundreds of years of practice at reading people; if I know about your little tussle, he'll know about it too. You may want to have a response prepared for when he asks why you're getting involved in fights that make you higher profile, and consequently less useful to him."

Geoffrey opened his mouth to respond but a chill ran up and down his spine as a voice interrupted him.

"Indeed, Imastious does know about the altercation, and I very much would like to know the reason for the conflict."

Venice rapidly stood, pulling Geoffrey to his feet with her.

"Master, I'm sorry, we didn't know you were there."

Imastious waved away the apology. "I'm waiting."

Geoffrey felt light, probing touches against his mental defenses and fought down panic at the thought of another confrontation with the older, more powerful vampire.

"Sir, I wasn't looking for a fight. One of them had attacked me days before. I dealt with him, but hadn't realized that I'd wandered back into the area. Once I realized where I was I tried to leave, but they jumped me before I could get out of the neighborhood."

Imastious stared at Geoffrey with cold, dead eyes for several seconds, and then nodded. "You are fortunate that the accounts of the few witnesses back up your story. I'm satisfied that you are telling the truth, and that discipline will not be required."

Geoffrey clamped down on the sigh of relief that tried to escape him.

"Still, in the future you will report all such encounters to me or Venice immediately. You are insufficiently skilled at this point to determine when these types of attacks are the result of happenstance, and when they represent an attack by a vampire Elder attempting to weaken my base of power."

Venice took a breath, and for a second Geoffrey thought she was going to apologize to Imastious for not having already conveyed those instructions to Geoffrey, but Imastious' gaze had already turned to her, preempting speech.

"And you, my daughter, you should be mindful of where your true loyalties lie. I know that you have some infatuation with Geoffrey, but if you ever let that lead you to crossing me in the slightest, we'll undergo another session similar to the one after the high rise incident, and I don't think you want that."

Venice's breath caught for a moment, and she shook her head violently. Imastious smiled for the first time that night. "On the other hand, even allowing for the exaggerations to which witnesses are prone, it appears that you have done an excellent job returning our

Geoffrey to a state of readiness, so if your feelings lead to superior performance, they are not entirely unacceptable."

Imastious gazed off in the distance for several seconds before looking back at the pair and handing Geoffrey a packet of papers. "Your next assignment is in there. Although you shouldn't face any of our kind, this target is of much greater importance than your previous two, so don't be surprised if you find him guarded by some humans."

Geoffrey had noticed that all of Imastious' words came out in such a manner as to leave the hearer with the impression that the older vampire despised whatever he was talking about, but the emphasis placed on the last word conveyed a special brand of disgust.

It had become apparent to Geoffrey that Imastious viewed his underlings as nothing more than slightly useful tools. It only followed that he'd view humans as nothing more than perpetual nuisances to be dealt with whenever or however he pleased.

Just before he turned to vanish into the night Imastious looked once more at Venice. "The nature of this assignment is such that you should probably be involved in the planning of it. Although Geoffrey's capabilities are steadily improving, it bears remembering that he is still far from what he once was. Failure this time could be significant for all of us."

Geoffrey tried as much as possible to maintain a facade of calm as he watched the various VIPs leave city hall at the end of the day. Venice had indeed been involved in the planning stages of the hit, but it hadn't ended up making much of a difference when all was said and done. Mostly it had just made her extremely frustrated at Geoffrey's refusal to do things 'by the book.'

As Geoffrey's target came out and waited for his car to pull around, the vampire extended his thoughts. His range was steadily improving and it took only a heartbeat to locate and touch the councilman's thoughts. Forcing down the impulse to retch at what he found was more difficult. The sophistication that the man exuded from the outside covered up a rot the like of which Geoffrey hadn't ever seen previously. Greed was the primary motivator, touching nearly every thought or memory Geoffrey rifled through. It didn't look like the man had ever killed someone with his own hands, but Geoffrey had already found a number of instances where decisions had been agreed to which the man had known would result in potential pain and death for the residents of the city. Each decision had been purely to line the man's pockets with even more money than he had already.

THE GREATER DARKNESS

As contemptible as what he had found was, Geoffrey wasn't sure that there was anything in there that would cause a court of law to deliver a death sentence. He was just about to pull back out when he saw a different memory. There was a woman involved, a wife, or maybe a mistress, and the memory was tinged with jealousy and rage. As Geoffrey followed the memory trail he realized that the man had put out a contract on the woman's lover.

As the vehicle pulled away, Geoffrey broke the contact and tried to settle his stomach, relieved that he would be spared the decision of whether or not to kill an innocent again.

Venice paced back and forth across the room. "I'm glad that you aren't hedging about whether or not you'll do the hit anymore, but I don't understand why you are insisting on doing this by yourself. I should be along to help out in case things don't go as planned."

Geoffrey shrugged. "Imastious gave the assignment to me. There isn't any reason for you to get involved now that we are done with the planning stage. At least look at the bright side, you finally convinced me that it would be foolish to try and use a gun on the hit."

The slender vampire already looked like she was about to throw something at Geoffrey. It was better not to let on that the alarm likely to be raised by gunshots had been the real deterrent. To Geoffrey, the idea that a passing pyromancer might realize he was carrying a gun and ignite the gunpowder seemed too impossible to him to merit the kind of fear that she was demonstrating.

Venice appeared to be expecting some kind of additional explanation, so Geoffrey continued on. "From everything you've indicated, this hit is dangerous primarily due to what will happen afterwards. If this guy really does have a powerful vampire patron, it makes sense to ensure that only one of us is on the chopping block in the event he manages to track me down."

What Geoffrey didn't want to admit was that he didn't want to watch Venice kill someone. He couldn't stop her from killing anyone else Imastious might assign her to terminate, but he could at least make sure that this particular hit didn't add to the number of murders currently damning her soul.

Venice shook her head. "We don't know that he has a vampire patron, and if he does, this guy is highly placed enough that it won't matter how the hit is accomplished, or who is involved. Any Elder with an interest is going to investigate things as thoroughly as he's able. If he does track you down, it's guaranteed that he'll find our connection and come after me as well."

Geoffrey reached up and gently stopped Venice from pacing. "This isn't like you. What's really wrong?"

Venice looked for a second like she would cry, and then she collapsed into Geoffrey's arms clinging to him with all of her considerable strength. "I don't think you understand how big of a step this is. Imastious hasn't ever used one of us to go after another Elder's assets. At least not one who was this highly placed. I think he's had a few people killed here and there before, but he's always used humans to do it, humans who were completely deniable."

Geoffrey smoothed Venice's hair as she continued. "If he's really gearing up for some kind of bid to dramatically increase his power, we are both probably going to die. It just doesn't seem right that he can use us up like that, discard us without a second thought, not after all that we've done for him."

For a second it seemed that sobs would overcome the slender vampire, but she fought them down with visible effort and continued on. "It isn't just that either. For all this to happen now, just as things seemed to finally be going the way that I'd hoped, is so typical."

Geoffrey cocked his head to the side and then gently pulled Venice's face around to where he could look into her eyes. "Are things really going where you think they are? I don't know if I could have killed again if this guy wasn't so deserving of punishment. What would you have done then?"

The brilliant blue eyes looking back at Geoffrey seemed confused for a moment and then became filled with frustration. "Is that all this is about? Every time I think maybe this isn't all just an act, you pull something like this and prove that you are the same cold, manipulative jerk you were before. I won't disobey Imastious, not in any way that will result in any kind of punishment. Both of us together, even when you were more powerful than you are now, wouldn't have been enough to defeat him. I'm not about to risk death or worse at this point."

Venice let go of Geoffrey and stood. "You can't stop Imastious, and pretending that you've become worried with the right or wrong of a given assignment won't shelter you in the least from his displeasure if you fail."

After Venice left, Geoffrey mulled over her parting shot for quite a while. "And I won't be taken down with you. If that is how you want to play things, you're on your own."

Geoffrey had spent hours worried about what to do with Venice. It was possible that she'd let more slip than she'd meant to. Was he really a different person than he was before? He clung to the slim hope that he might become something other than he was. If that did happen, would Venice come to understand him, or would his morality continue to baffle her?

Part of him wished Venice had Melody's innocence. Then again, if Venice were that clean and pure she wouldn't want him, wouldn't be able to get past all of the things he'd done.

Thinking about Melody awoke a different kind of worry. He shouldn't have gone there earlier that night, not right before a hit, especially not when he still felt like he was being watched half of the time. He'd done everything he could to make sure he wasn't followed, but it had still been stupidly risky.

Geoffrey looked away from the residential building for a second to check his watch. It was slightly past the time when he expected the councilman's car to pull up to the stately, timeless building, but he wasn't too concerned by the delay. It likely meant that the council session had just run a little longer than normal.

The vampire's hand brushed against a letter in his pocket, confirming its existence. That letter had been the real reason he shouldn't have gone by her house. Just seeing Melody from afar would have been distraction enough. He hadn't expected to find another letter, this one carefully taped inside a plastic bag to protect it from the weather. He'd known she would be horrified by what he'd told her, but he'd expected her to just cease communicating with him rather than writing something to rebuke him or tell him to stay away.

As despair tried to wash over him again, Geoffrey wondered again just how scathing Melody's reply was going to be, but once again held to his resolve not to open it before the hit was successfully completed. It would be better to deal with the uncertainty than to know exactly how much she hated him.

A brand-new limo pulled up to the parking garage entrance. Geoffrey did a quick check to verify that the license plate matched the one on the limo in which the councilman always departed City Hall. It did so he took a deep breath and then he started towards the front door.

Geoffrey had scouted the building a few days previously to verify that there weren't any security cameras, but he still pulled on a mask to ensure he couldn't be identified later. It made sense that these particular residents wouldn't want any record of the comings and goings of their mistresses, but if Geoffrey was wrong then he didn't want the mistake to result in his death.

Stopping just out of sight of the doorman and leaning against a richly finished wall, Geoffrey freed his thoughts from their physical moorings and touched the unsuspecting man's mind. He quickly led the doorman's thoughts down the desired path, calming the man to the point that even the appearance of a host of heavily-armed men wouldn't cause him to do anything other than just sit there quietly as they stormed past.

A few minutes later Geoffrey entered the building and climbed the sterile-looking metal stairs to the top floor. Pausing for a moment at the last landing, the vampire reached out and scanned the minds on the floor. On this floor there was a guard present.

Even just touching surface thoughts at this range was tiring, but Geoffrey managed to infuse the guard with a slight sense of drowsiness. There was nothing left to do but just rush him.

His previous explorations had revealed that the doorway to the stairs was hidden by a bend in the hall, so Geoffrey exited the landing as quietly as possible and crept as close as he could without being seen.

A few seconds later the guard was unconscious from a blow to the head and Geoffrey was breathing heavily from his sprint down the hall. The poor sucker hadn't even had a chance to yell. Now it was time to deal with the Councilman.

The condominium was large enough that Geoffrey might have been in trouble if his target had been on the far side of the unit, but luckily the councilman was close enough for the vampire to gradually build an impulse to go check the door.

As soon as Geoffrey heard the chirp of the security system disengaging, he launched a powerful side-thrust kick that tore the door from its frame and knocked the councilman to the floor. Before the dazed man could fully register what was happening Geoffrey had drawn one of the many knives he now kept secreted about his person, and the hit was finished.

A minute later, the guard had been dragged into the apartment, the door had been pulled closed, and Geoffrey was on his way back down the stairs.

Chapter 18

Geoffrey had slept well, surprisingly so, considering all of the things still preying upon the edges of his mind. After waking, the vampire found that he was oddly reluctant to get out of bed, so he stayed there for the better part of an hour watching the orange and pink highlights from the sunset dance across his ceiling and wall.

He didn't actually feel any guilt over having killed the councilman. He'd done what society couldn't and he'd known that the man he'd executed was absolutely guilty. Even better, Melody's letter hadn't been at all what he'd expected.

Once again, tranquility settled upon him as he mentally reviewed what the letter had said.

Geoffrey,

It isn't my place to condemn you for what you've done. It seems you already know you shouldn't have killed innocent people. Still, from what little I know of you I have to wonder if there isn't more to the story than you've told me. It seems impossible for the goodness I know to reside inside you to coexist voluntarily with the other. I wonder if you're fully in control of your destiny? I suppose that wouldn't justify murder, but it might explain the conflict.

You may of course wonder how I know you are essentially good, but that is a secret I'll have to keep for now. If we ever meet face to face again, I'll tell you what I saw when you were inside my mind.

If that never happens, if you can't continue to stop by, I understand, but please don't refrain from doing so because of me. I...Mom's going through another bad time, and I could use a visit from a friend.

Melody

Thinking about Melody's letter finally broke the spell holding Geoffrey in his bed. Almost before he'd realized he'd moved, he found himself at Venice's gym squaring off against her for unarmed combat training.

"Remember, love, this time I'll be using my powers as well, so no free ride today."

The snap kick Venice launched at his stomach lashed out with no warning. Geoffrey tried to slide back out of range, but moving required more effort than it should have. The air had hardened around him.

The kick caught Geoffrey, knocking the wind out of him, and he frantically extended his thoughts towards Venice in an effort to counteract her telekinetic abilities.

The slender vampire's mind was guarded against just such a contact, but it appeared that maintaining that mental barrier made it harder for her to effectively use her talents. Geoffrey's speed returned to something more like what he was accustomed. The advantage initially residing with Venice now tilted back slightly Geoffrey's way, and the fight continued on with Venice ruthlessly trying to exploit her now-superior speed to defeat his occasional ability to pick up exactly what she was going to do.

Geoffrey blocked a reverse punch and then launched a hook kick at Venice which she easily dodged. Panting heavily from the combined mental and physical exertions, Geoffrey realized he was fighting a defensive battle. He wasn't fast enough to catch her anymore. He was managing to block most of her attacks, but he was tiring out quickly. If he didn't come up with a new trick quickly something was going to get through and then he'd be the one on the ground with cracked ribs.

Venice seemed to realize she had Geoffrey on the run. She stepped up her assault, committing herself to a greater degree in an effort to make sure that whatever got through would end the fight.

Sweat rolling down him in streams, Geoffrey suddenly had an idea, and without thinking of the possible consequences he acted on it. As soon as he was sure that Venice was about to launch an attack, Geoffrey threw out a side-thrust kick, catching her as she came in.

His reduced speed meant Geoffrey wasn't quite able to generate the kind of bone-breaking power that he usually did, but the kick still picked Venice up and knocked her backwards. Geoffrey was moving in to continue the onslaught when he picked up the hint of something in Venice's thoughts that made him try to jump back. Before he could reverse direction, an invisible force struck him across the face with enough power to make him see stars.

When Geoffrey managed to blink his vision clear Venice was panting heavily and rubbing her newly-healed ribs.

"Now that was fun, love. Not only was it fun, but it's the first time I've beaten you like that in ages."

Geoffrey shook his head again and then returned the smile. "It looks like I still have a lot to learn."

Venice shrugged. "I wouldn't worry too much about it, you're actually doing really well with the combat side of things. I never expected you'd catch me with a stop hit like that. Now that you know a telekinetic is more dangerous when she's not engaged, you'll remember for next time and press the attack sooner so I don't get a chance to hit you like that again."

THE GREATER DARKNESS

It was a valid point, but Geoffrey also made a mental note that executing a blow like that took more out of Venice than she probably would have been willing to admit. The way that she was shaking left no doubt of that.

The rest of the training session revolved around purely physical skills, which Geoffrey figured was probably due to the fact that Venice was as exhausted as he was. By the time they'd both showered and met back up in the lobby three hours later, Geoffrey was seriously considering returning home for a nap.

His refusal to include Venice in the hit had introduced a new element of strain in their relationship, so Geoffrey was surprised when Venice greeted him with a smile and suggested that they stop at a cafe somewhere for a quick drink.

Once they'd been seated in a secluded corner, Venice got down to business. "Imastious wants you to know he's generally pleased with how the hit went down. There are a couple of wrinkles though that you should know about."

Geoffrey sat forward, abandoning the hot chocolate he hadn't really wanted in the first place.

"First, least important in my mind, although it seems to weigh fairly heavily with Imastious, there is a definite uptick in the number of rabies cases here in the city."

Thinking back to the dogs that had attacked him, Geoffrey shuddered.

Venice nodded. "I agree, love. It creeps me out but I don't know that there is much we can do at this point. The humans will do a pretty good job handling the dogs that are bitten, but Imastious seems to be worried that the disease will make its way into the city's rat population. If that happens, he thinks we'll see an explosion of rabid rats because the poison the humans use to control the vermin won't work."

Geoffrey raised an eyebrow and Venice shrugged. "According to Imastious they seem to be able to detect the poison and won't eat it after they're infected."

It was another fact to file away and examine later. To Geoffrey's mind rats were rats. It shouldn't matter whether or not they had a disease. If they couldn't detect the poison in the food when they were healthy, they shouldn't be able to detect it once they were sick.

"Well, considering the fact that being eaten alive by thousands of abnormally aggressive rats is a pretty unappetizing prospect, I assume that the other item is a real winner?"

Venice smiled at the joke, but her heart wasn't in it this time. "It is. The word on the street is that the guy you clipped did have a pretty powerful patron, and he is out for blood."

Geoffrey's insides turned cold and he had to force himself to pay attention to the rest of what Venice was saying.

"I don't know how they can possibly connect you to the hit. Even if there's video footage of your entrance, you wore a mask. Still, Eculdes is one of the most powerful mentalists out there. He can pull memories from people that they don't know they still have, so if anyone is able to track you down, it will be him."

Geoffrey nodded slowly. "Does it look like he'll get involved personally in the hunt?"

Venice shook her head. "No, that isn't how this usually works. He'll assign one of his people to do most of the footwork. Eculdes is even older than Imastious, so he tends to spend even more time fighting with the time funk than Imastious does."

Geoffrey realized she was talking about the altered time perceptions he dealt with when he went too long without blood. The thought awoke the hunger inside Geoffrey, reminding him it had been too long since he'd fed.

Seeing that Geoffrey understood, Venice continued. "Depending on how much he has on his plate, and the amount of time he's cognizant of his surroundings, he may get involved if the subordinate doesn't seem able to handle things. It's more likely, though, that the subordinate will just take you out himself."

Geoffrey shrugged. "So maybe I have a chance then, even assuming they figure out it was me."

Venice shook her head. "No, if they figure out it was you, Imastious will probably have you eliminated before they can get to you. He's not the kind to leave a trail that can be traced back to him."

Chapter 19

The hunger was starting to get bad, but Geoffrey was worried about what would happen if he went outside to find someone to feed on. He should have moved, should have changed apartments right after or right before the hit. It would have at least reduced the chance that whoever was after him would stumble into someone in his neighborhood who might recognize him.

The thought had crossed the vampire's mind at one point, but he'd dismissed it as overreacting. Honestly though, it might have been because he'd become so used to his little apartment. It was the only home he remembered ever having known. These walls were the closest thing he had to a refuge, but now they were closing in a little more each day.

Geoffrey struggled with the hunger for another couple of hours before deciding that he could probably slip outside, find someone, feed, and be back inside in less than a couple of hours. It was a risk, but it should be a minimal one, and it would buy him another couple of weeks. If he did that, he could make it until the next time Venice stopped by. She'd be able to advise him on whether or not to move. It seemed impossible that anyone could have tracked him back to this neighborhood, or any other. There were millions of people just in Manhattan, which made him smaller than a needle in a haystack, but Venice would know for sure what he was up against.

His decision made, Geoffrey exited the apartment and headed in a random direction. Once again the vampire couldn't shake the feeling of being watched, but he chalked it up to being nothing more than nerves. Nobody he passed seemed to be taking any kind of special notice of him.

An hour of haphazard searching didn't provide any likely prospects, and Geoffrey was becoming more and more uneasy the longer he was outside, so he finally decided to swing by an area close to Melody's where he knew a large number of prostitutes gathered. It increased his chances of being recognized, but he should be in and out in a couple of minutes, so it still seemed like an acceptable risk.

Geoffrey was in the process of cutting through an alley when two figures stepped out of the shadows in front of him. Mental alarms started going off immediately. It had become almost second nature now to skim off the surface thoughts of those around him, and these guys were extremely uneasy. Uneasy, but giving off a definite sense of being ready for a confrontation. Geoffrey reached deeper, trying to establish why they were so uneasy, and then found a fragment of a thought in one of them. They knew they were up against a vampire.

Geoffrey's questing thoughts brushed up against a solid surface and he threw himself to the side as a bolt of fire streaked past him, near enough for the heat to make his clothes smoke.

Rolling to his feet, Geoffrey furiously beat against the mental wall separating him from the other vampire's thoughts. Sensing that the two humans were in striking distance, Geoffrey ran past them, slashing twice with the katana that he didn't remember drawing. The pair went down in a spray of blood, and Geoffrey ducked behind a dumpster as another ball of fire nearly clipped him.

Frantic efforts to worm probes into the pyromancer's mind were meeting with almost no success, but the sudden increase in the air temperature around Geoffrey was enough to tell him it was time to move. He was overmatched. He couldn't break the other vampire's mental shield and it was only a matter of time before the other guy lit him up and the fight would be all over.

Acting on little more than instinct, Geoffrey suddenly realized he was once again fighting defensively. Instead of running away as he left the cover of the dumpster, he ran towards the other vampire, launching a mental attack that consisted of nothing more than a crude blow of pure force.

Geoffrey's clothes had just started to heat up when the mental hammer hit the other vampire. Rather than failing as he'd half feared it would, the attack destroyed the other vampire's concentration sufficiently to save Geoffrey from bursting into flames.

There was the briefest of instants to savor the success, and then the pair clashed together in a whirling storm of steel.

Now that he was inside his opponent's mind, Geoffrey found it only slightly better protected than that of a human. Unfortunately, ensuring that the pyromancer was too off-balance mentally to roast him left Geoffrey with insufficient resources to get any sense of what physical attacks to expect.

A pale, freckled face pulled back in an expression of rage and hate as the other vampire launched a series of strikes with his sword, an ancient-looking straight-bladed thing about four feet long.

Geoffrey wasn't as used to countering stabs, but he managed to dodge each attack, and his katana licked out twice to score minor wounds on the other vampire.

THE GREATER DARKNESS

His opponent was probably a little stronger and faster than Geoffrey, but his weapon was heavier than Geoffrey's katana. As long as Geoffrey managed to avoid having his weapon damaged, they were on nearly even terms.

As the fight ground on, Geoffrey seemed to be slowing faster than his opponent. He was into the other man's mind too far. If he didn't pull out further he'd get worn down all the way.

Panting, Geoffrey tried to retreat slightly from the depths of the other vampire's mind, but that triggered a sudden spate of mental attacks designed to push him far enough out that the other could access his pyromancer abilities again.

One of the mental blows nearly succeeded and Geoffrey momentarily slowed as the mental battle took up his full concentration. That was all the other vampire needed, and one of his thrusts went home, piercing Geoffrey's stomach.

The pain shattered Geoffrey's probes, and he suddenly found himself confined to his own mind with a certainty that his opponent was about to finish him with conjured fire.

Reflex once again took over and Geoffrey grabbed his enemy's hand to trap the long sword before it could be withdrawn. A split second later, Geoffrey's katana found its mark and the other vampire collapsed like a puppet whose strings had been cut.

Geoffrey managed to sheath his sword before collapsing to the ground in agony. His organs didn't feel right, and he had a nagging feeling that he'd almost been too late. His opponent had been a split second from cooking him from the inside out.

He had to get somewhere safe and hope that he wasn't injured too severely to heal on his own.

Venice came to mind first, but Geoffrey had no idea where she lived. Maybe that was for the best. She'd indicated that Imastious would have him eliminated if anyone managed to pin the hit on him. He couldn't afford to place himself in Venice's hands right now.

Geoffrey had been insulated from the pain of his wounds by the adrenaline coursing through his system, but now that the immediate emergency was over, he could feel shock setting in. He couldn't go back to his apartment; it might already be compromised. Plus he was going to need help if he was going to survive.

The next few minutes were a haze. Tapping into reserves he hadn't known he had, Geoffrey levered himself back upright and plugged the hole in his stomach enough that he didn't immediately bleed out. The vampire hadn't had an actual destination in mind when he'd started out, but he shortly found himself in front of Melody's building. Without thinking of the possible repercussions, he made his way up to her door and feebly knocked on it until he heard movement inside.

The peephole in the door darkened, and then Melody called out. "Who...Geoffrey, is that you?"

The vampire mumbled an affirmative and then all but collapsed into Melody's arms once she got the door open.

"I'm sorry. I shouldn't have come, but I didn't have anywhere else to go."

Melody shushed Geoffrey as she guided him into her room and parked him on her bed. "I'll call an ambulance."

"No. They might be watching the hospitals. Even if they aren't, the police will ask questions about how I was stabbed."

Melody looked at Geoffrey with a trembling lip and then nodded. "Okay then, we'll just have to do the best we can here. Daddy made Mom and me learn some basic first aid. He said he didn't want us panicking and being useless in an emergency, but I don't know if it will be enough."

Geoffrey was having a hard time focusing on what Melody was saying, but he understood enough to nod and mumble. "If I can make it the next few hours I'll probably be okay. I heal faster than humans."

Melody might have said something in response, might have had a question, but if so Geoffrey missed it. The exertions he'd made both before and after being wounded had finally caught up with him, and unconsciousness claimed him.

Chapter 20

The darkness was usually a friend that concealed and protected Geoffrey, but this darkness was different, it seemed determined to envelop him. The vampire somehow knew that if the darkness was successful in capturing him it wouldn't free him ever again. Geoffrey tried to fight, but his efforts seemed ineffective.

It was like he didn't have any strength. How could he fight without strength?

That question awakened the hunger, and Geoffrey realized that he hadn't eaten in far too long. Was that right? It seemed like he'd fed just a little while ago. How could he be so hungry already? Maybe his weakness wasn't caused by the hunger, maybe something else had burned up his strength and in the process left him hungry sooner than normal.

The darkness gradually lost its hold on Geoffrey, and he finally opened his eyes, squinting against the burning light.

THE GREATER DARKNESS

Something stirred next to him. "Geoffrey, are you awake?"

The vampire tried to nod, managing a jerky motion that seemed to satisfy his questioner. He tried to take stock of his surroundings despite the hunger tearing at his mind. He was in a bed. The room he was in was tidy and worn. There was something wrapped around his stomach...bandages possibly.

A face slowly came into focus before Geoffrey and he pushed the hunger back a little farther, clearing his thoughts enough to recognize the girl.

"Melody." Speech hurt, almost as if his throat had been rubbed raw from screaming, or maybe burned.

"Shh, you don't have to say anything." Melody pulled the comforter away and untied the string holding the makeshift bandages in place. "Your stomach wound looks like it's about healed. I never would have thought something like that could happen in less than twenty-four hours, but there it is. It doesn't look like you're fevered or have any signs of infection either, but something is still wrong, isn't it?"

Nearly exhausted by the effort of listening to Melody, it took Geoffrey a few seconds to realize she'd asked him a question. Panting, the vampire tried to understand what she'd asked. His insides and throat hurt, but that didn't seem quite like what she was asking.

When Geoffrey didn't respond immediately Melody seemed to think he needed a little prodding. "You called out for blood while you were fevered, and you said that you healed faster than a human...what are you?"

Geoffrey's mind seemed unable to process the questions as fast as they were being asked. Now that his vision was starting to clear up, he found his eyes returning again and again to the expanse of white skin revealed by Melody's faded blue top.

The hunger. How much longer did he have before it took over and he hurt her without meaning to?

The thought of Melody lying dead on the floor, drained of blood, finally penetrated the vampire's mind and he struggled feebly to get up. "Must go."

Melody put her hands on Geoffrey's chest and held him down. "No, you're still hurt; you wouldn't even make it down the stairs right now. Don't be silly."

Geoffrey's world started to darken as he realized he wasn't strong enough to escape Melody, at least not without seriously hurting her. Desperation gave him the energy to push at least some of his words past the pain in his throat. "No, I have to go now before the hunger gets too bad and I hurt you."

Melody looked at Geoffrey without understanding, and tears started to form in his eyes. "You don't understand. I won't be able to stop myself. I won't have control. The hunger will take over and then you'll be dead just like the others."

For a second it seemed that Melody was going to let him up out of shock, but then understanding flared in her eyes. "You're really not human, are you?"

Geoffrey shook his head weakly, expecting Melody to turn from him in disgust as she realized what he was. "No. Vampire."

Melody began trembling, but she didn't turn away. "You don't want to hurt me though?"

Geoffrey's negative was more emphatic now as he tried to sit up again, but he was too weak. He collapsed back to the bed and the tears that had been building broke free and coursed down his face.

Seeing the tears, Melody was unable to restrain tears of her own, and she gingerly hugged Geoffrey while whispering in his ear. "Then we'll just have to make sure that you get the blood you need so you don't hurt anyone by accident."

Melody's tears joined with Geoffrey's, but he was too far gone with exhaustion and hunger to remain coherent. Instead he slipped back into unconsciousness despite his best efforts.

The smell of blood pulled him back to a state of awareness sometime later. Opening his eyes to lengthening shadows, Geoffrey found Melody next to him holding a razor blade and looking paler than usual.

Tears once again filled brown eyes as Melody tried not to laugh hysterically. "I guess I should have thought to make sure you were awake before I cut myself. I wasn't sure if you'd drown on the blood if I started to feed you while you were unconscious."

Still having a hard time thinking past the hunger, Geoffrey opened his mouth to ask what she meant, and Melody placed her arm against his mouth.

For a second Geoffrey tried to force the arm away, but he'd grown weaker, and the hunger was even more compelling than before. Bracing himself against the rush of satiation, Geoffrey fought it with all of his will.

Once again, time stopped as the hunger swelled and tried to take over. Geoffrey found a surprising ally in the sense of connection that bloomed between the two of them.

Without meaning to, Geoffrey sent his thoughts out and touched Melody's mind. Amazed by the lack of resistance and the fact that she felt the connection as much as he did, the vampire strengthened the probes and allowed thoughts to flow back and forth between the two of them.

For a few moments Geoffrey explored Melody's innermost fears and hopes at the same time that she did the same inside his mind. All too soon, he felt her growing weaker, felt the flow of blood lessening.

Tearing himself away from the trickle of life making its way down his throat was one of the hardest things Geoffrey had ever done, but Melody had realized her danger as well. She pulled her arm away from his weak grasp even as he forced himself to let go.

The vampire fought the darkness long enough to make sure Melody got her arm bandaged, and then let the black claim him.

Geoffrey awoke slowly, once again more than a little confused by his surroundings. He was awake now but it was still black everywhere. The only explanation was that it must be dark outside. Not just dark like the sun had gone down; dark like there weren't any lights anywhere. No clocks, no signs, a complete lack of artificial light that could only be explained by a power outage.

Suddenly the vampire's unfamiliar surroundings became recognizable and everything that had happened came back in a flood.

Geoffrey rolled over, frantically searching for Melody, and his heart skipped a beat when he saw her motionless and pale in what little light filtered through the blinds. Geoffrey reached out a trembling hand and touched the delicate neck before him. His insides relaxed when he finally found a pulse—weak but steady. She'd probably be okay if he could get some food into her.

It wasn't until Geoffrey had climbed out of bed and made his way through the darkness into the kitchen that he remembered his wounds. They didn't hurt anymore. The accelerated healing must have really kicked in to take care of both the stab wound and the cooked organs.

The cupboards were nearly bare, but Geoffrey's search finally turned up some bread, which was better than nothing.

Returning to Melody's bedroom, Geoffrey gently shook her awake and tried to get her to eat.

"What time is it, Geoffrey? How long has the power been out?"

"I don't know, I just woke up and got you something to eat."

Melody shook her head in the dim light. "I have to check on my mom first. Her equipment has batteries, but if it goes too long without power I'll have to call an ambulance."

Geoffrey was half afraid that Melody would fall. Probably due to weakness, but he wasn't prepared to rule out the possibility of her tripping over something in the dark. Instead of arguing a point he was sure to lose, he just picked her slender form up and carried her into the other room.

THE GREATER DARKNESS

The vampire was momentarily worried Melody's mother would be alarmed by his presence, but any fears to that effect were laid to rest as soon as they entered her bedroom. She was obviously still too heavily sedated to awake. He was struck again by just how frail she looked. It was like the drugs and disease had eaten away all of her substance. All that was left was bits and pieces in the shape of the woman she was before. He was surprised that she looked so much worse than the last time he'd seen her.

Geoffrey's pause must have been longer than he'd realized because Melody buried her face in his neck as she tried to fight back tears. "I know. She's bad, maybe the worst she's ever been."

Melody needed to be comforted, but Geoffrey didn't know what to say or do. He had no recollection of ever being comforted by anyone himself, so he didn't know where to start with helping Melody.

Unsure what else to do, Geoffrey stood there holding Melody and letting her cry until the tears slowed to a trickle and she asked him to carry her close enough to check a host of readouts that didn't make any sense to him.

Once Melody was satisfied with the information the medical equipment was reporting, Geoffrey helped her into the kitchen where she pulled a medical bag that contained a sugar and saline solution out of the refrigerator.

The next twenty minutes were some of the hardest Geoffrey could remember. It was obvious that Melody was running on nothing but willpower. He was trying to help, but she was the one with the knowledge of what needed done and how it needed to be accomplished. All he could really do was to be there for her to lean on.

Melody collapsed as she finished taking care of her mom, but Geoffrey caught her before she could damage any of the monitoring machines surrounding the poor woman.

"You've done everything you can for her. She'll be fine. You need to take care of yourself now, or you won't be able to take care of her later."

The lights came back on about the time Geoffrey got Melody back to her bed and working her way through the bread he'd found. Reasonably sure that both Melody and her mom would be okay, the vampire found his thoughts wandering through the things he'd learned when he was inside Melody's mind hours before.

"It isn't your fault, you know."

Melody looked up questioningly and for a second Geoffrey almost couldn't make himself continue.

"Your dad's death, your mom's sickness; neither came about because of anything you did."

Melody looked for a second like she wanted to be angry and tell Geoffrey it was none of his business, but after a few seconds she nodded. "I know in my head that's true, but sometimes the rest of me doesn't believe it, especially the part about Mom. After Dad died I was so angry, and she was busy trying to be strong for both of us. I said a lot of hurtful things that mostly centered around me wishing she was gone too so I could live my life how I wanted."

Brown eyes looked away from Geoffrey for a minute, and when they returned they were full of unshed tears. "Sometimes I think about how much easier my life would be if my mom was just dead so that I didn't have to take care of her all of the time."

Geoffrey waited until Melody had put the remnants of her meal on the nightstand and then reached over and hugged her. "I can help with that if you want. I could make it so you know it wasn't your fault, I might even be able to take away the memory of ever wishing she wasn't here."

"By going inside my mind like you did before?"

"Only if you want me to."

"No, the wounds are almost gone, and that's part of who I am. If you took that away, I might not be as careful about what I said or thought in the future. Thank you for offering though."

The pair remained next to each other on the bed while Melody cried herself out again, and for the first time since he'd been injured Geoffrey was once again conscious of how attractive Melody was. There was something there between the two of them now. He'd felt it inside her mind, but the feelings he'd read there still had too many elements of a childish crush.

Melody wiped her eyes and snuggled closer to Geoffrey. "You still haven't asked me what I see when you're inside my mind. Did you find out the last time we were together?"

Geoffrey shook his head and then realized in the darkness that she probably couldn't see. "No, I figured that was your secret to tell or keep as you saw fit."

There was a pause; it was like Melody wasn't sure she really wanted to tell now that she'd arrived at the moment of decision. "I saw a being of light and goodness, but with an overlay of darkness trying to extinguish the light."

Melody's revelation was so unexpected that Geoffrey was having a hard time processing it. "What do you mean?"

"You've done terrible things, but you're essentially good and wholesome. There are deep scars that the black has seeped into, which chains you away from your potential, but the good is fighting back trying to cast the bad out."

All of sudden Melody hugged Geoffrey fiercely. "I'm worried though, the darkness and light inside your mind were both stronger this time than I remember them being last time, and I think as the war grows stronger it's killing you inside."

Chapter 21

Geoffrey was incredibly nervous the entire trip home, but even that wasn't enough to distract his thoughts away from Melody. As much as he would have loved to stay there with her for another day, Melody had needed to get back to school. It was for the best though; he still needed to figure out what to do next about the attack that had nearly killed him.

Thinking about the attack made Geoffrey remember that there was a chance Imastious would order his death. He'd just have to cross that bridge if it came to that. An outcome where he died would probably be best for everyone involved, but he found that now, more than ever, he wanted to live.

When Geoffrey finally arrived and opened up the tired-looking door to his apartment, he found Venice pacing back and forth.

"Where the hell have you been?"

Trying to remain ready for a battle while not appearing to be ready for a battle was a losing proposition, so Geoffrey pulled out his katana and pretended to be inspecting it. "I got jumped the night before last by some red-headed pyromancer and a couple of other guys. I killed them all, but got pretty beat up in the process, so I holed up somewhere other than my apartment, which I thought might have been compromised."

Venice's eyes got big for a moment and then she looked at Geoffrey's weapon and smiled. "You can put that away for now; Imastious is the one who'll make the decision as to whether or not you have to be eliminated. You've got some time before you need to worry about him sending someone to collect your scalp."

"You think you'll be the one he assigns to do it?" The words came out colder than Geoffrey had intended, but it was too late to take them back.

The slender vampire looked at Geoffrey appraisingly and then shrugged. "You mean will I do it if he tells me to?"

"Maybe. Why don't you answer that one too while you're at it."

Venice frowned. "I've told you before, love. I won't come out in open defiance against him no matter how I feel about you. That's a losing proposition, and will be for quite some time. Right now even the two of us aren't strong enough to take him on and have a chance of winning. So yes, if he commands me to kill you I'll give it my absolute best. I don't want to suffer a gruesome death any more than you would in my place."

A chill ran down his spine at her words. They felt more significant than he could explain but he tried to chalk the feeling up to exhaustion. He didn't think Venice was right about how far he'd be willing to go to avoid Imastious' wrath, but more and more he believed that she wasn't lying about what she would do to stay alive.

Venice walked over and gently pulled Geoffrey's sword away before leading him over to a chair and then sitting down on his lap. "Why are you taking this out on me, love? I've told you my boundaries, but I'm going to do everything I can to help you short of that--short of actually defying Imastious."

Letting Venice sit on his lap felt natural and right at the same time that it felt like a betrayal of Melody. "I didn't know that there was really any other option once they found me."

Venice shook her head and smiled. "When you get all forceful and angry like that I have a hard time remembering you aren't the Geoffrey I fell in love with so long ago. Then I forget that you don't have his knowledge of our ways. I'm currently serving as your handler, just like you used to serve as mine."

The blonde vampire stretched, showing off her stomach in a display that Geoffrey suspected was staged but which nevertheless pulled his eyes towards the expanse of skin revealed by her pale peasant top.

"The handler/operative setup is pretty standard among vampires in this city. It helps protect the Elders from being attacked if one of their operatives is compromised. In our case things aren't quite like they are supposed to be, since you know who I report to, but at least you don't know how to find Imastious and me, so in theory we're still somewhat protected."

Geoffrey fought off a spate of anger at Venice's tone. He needed her help if he was going to get out of this alive, and he needed to survive so that he could help Melody and her mom.

"In certain cases, that chain of cutouts is compromised without the vampires in it being killed. Once that happens, the operatives aren't any good for the covert actions that tend to make up the majority of the conflict between vampire Elders, but they can still be used to clean up things that everyone expects the Elder in question to get involved in."

"Like hunting down the executioner of a known asset," breathed Geoffrey.

Venice flashed one of her winning smiles. "Exactly. I don't know if Imastious knew Eculdes was that councilman's patron or not, but the fact that Burnout got assigned to track you down pretty much confirmed the fact. Luckily it is pretty common knowledge that Burnout reported to a telekinetic named Rogers, who in turn reports to a mentalist who goes by the handle of Gothic. It's pretty certain that Burnout passed whatever he knew up to Rogers, and it is likely that once he decides Burnout is dead, Rogers will pass what he knows up to Gothic. That still gives you a chance though. If you can take Rogers and Gothic out before Gothic reports in to Eculdes, you should be pretty safe. We'll just need to move you to a different part of the city."

Geoffrey raised an eyebrow. "Pretty safe?"

Venice shrugged. "If you manage to eliminate both of Eculdes' men, he'll take one of two actions. He'll either decide that they got too close to someone more powerful than he wants to piss off right now, or he'll decide that maintaining his power and influence requires that he take down whoever just clipped his people. In the first case, you're pretty much home free. In the second case, you'll have to try and keep a low profile until the search dies down and they get caught up trying to solve some other problem."

Nodding, Geoffrey sighed. "How do I find these two?"

It was hard for Geoffrey to believe that Rogers could walk around so unconcernedly considering that by now he had to know that Burnout was dead. Then again, Rogers had essentially had a target on his back ever since he and Burnout were compromised years ago. The fact that Eculdes would avenge his death had always been enough to save him in the past, so he probably continued to think it would serve as an adequate shield.

Geoffrey carefully checked the handgun he'd taken from the gang member who'd assaulted him weeks ago, and wished once again that he'd had a chance to practice with it. There just hadn't been a time or place to do that, though, inside the city. Rather, there probably were such places, but he couldn't get access to them on such short notice.

Venice had exploded when Geoffrey had told her he wanted to use a firearm to attack Rogers. The strength of the response still wasn't something that he fully understood. Geoffrey wasn't keen on losing his hand to a pyromancer, but from everything she'd told him, Rogers was older and more powerful than he was. If Geoffrey didn't bring some kind of equalizer to the fight he wouldn't stand a chance of winning. Even attacking from an ambush wouldn't equalize those kinds of odds without something else in the mix.

Rogers was expected to mingle with the rest of vampire society so that he could serve as a conduit for people wanting to get information back to Eculdes, but he was still careful about making sure he wasn't tailed back to his apartment. Geoffrey had decided against trying to follow his usual plan of attacking his target once they were at home and their guard started to come down. Instead he'd spent the last two days waiting around one of the seedier clubs that Rogers was known to frequent. The plan gave him a chance of ambushing Rogers, but Geoffrey had been starting to worry that it wouldn't happen. When he wasn't worrying about that, he worried that he would succeed in ambushing Rogers, but not before Rogers reported in to Gothic. Fortunately, it looked like the gamble was just about to pay off.

Geoffrey had fed again since Burnout had attacked him. He currently felt as though he radiated strength and power, so much so that he had to keep reminding himself that Rogers could easily turn the ambush around on him if he wasn't careful.

Once the other vampire passed Geoffrey's hiding place, he brought the Beretta up and after checking the sights to ensure he was on target, pulled the trigger.

It was too dark to see where the bullets were impacting, so Geoffrey emptied the handgun as quickly as he could and then sprang from hiding, his katana drawn as his thoughts snaked over to the other vampire's mind.

Rogers was fast, a hair more so than Geoffrey, and his blows, despite being executed with a duelist's weapon, left Geoffrey's palms tingling from the impact. Fortunately, one or more of the nine-millimeter bullets must have hit because the older vampire didn't seem to have the concentration to be able to use his telekinetic powers.

In the first few seconds Geoffrey was nearly stabbed twice, but then his frantic efforts to hammer through Rogers' mental shield succeeded and he suddenly knew exactly what the other vampire was about to do.

The slender blade that had been giving Geoffrey such problems executed a slash towards his neck, but this time he knew it was a feint. Geoffrey stepped to the side as he brought his weapon around to parry the true attack, a lunging stab to his chest.

Rogers' emotionless gray eyes had a split second to grow alarmed as he realized what had happened and then Geoffrey's right foot smashed into the older vampire's knee, destroying the joint and dropping him to the ground.

A second later the fight was over and Geoffrey was wiping his blade on Rogers' clothes. It was time to leave before the police arrived or another vampire happened by.

Chapter 22

Geoffrey had been flush with success after his fight with Rogers, but things had gone rapidly downhill since then. He should have known that things were going too well. Geoffrey had even managed to avoid the nagging guilt he'd expected to experience. He'd seen enough of Rogers' crimes while he'd been inside the other vampire's mind to know he was as deserving of execution as anyone could be.

Things had been perfect. Now if he could just find Gothic...

Venice had left a note in Geoffrey's new apartment reluctantly congratulating him on succeeding. Apparently word had gotten around regarding the unorthodox nature of the hit on Rogers, and as a result the city's vampires were more unsettled than Venice had led him to expect.

Venice had anticipated his astonishment and reiterated that these kinds of things were done in a certain way. As a general rule, firearms were only used in fights between vampires in their first few decades. Popular opinion seemed to be split on whether some neonate had just gotten lucky, or whether there was a much more powerful vampire who was trying to lay some kind of false trail.

The note had also included a time and meeting place, with strict instructions to make sure he wasn't followed. The order had been even more frustrating than normal. He needed to be hunting for Gothic rather than jumping from one subway to another in an attempt to make sure that one of Eculdes' other goons didn't follow him to the meet and endanger Venice's lovely skin.

Realizing how bitter he sounded, Geoffrey tried to run through some of the relaxation exercises Venice had taught him. If he were going to be honest with himself, the order probably smarted less than the fact that he had absolutely no chance of taking Gothic down even if he did manage to find him.

Geoffrey left the subway and headed towards Central Park certain that there was no way that he could have been followed, but still unable to escape the feeling that he was once again being watched.

Walking along a path he'd taken the last time he'd gone running, Geoffrey wondered if the leaves on the trees were still as vibrantly green as he'd imagined them, or if they'd started to change colors as fall approached. It was funny that you couldn't actually see color in the dark, just black and white.

A few minutes later the vampire came around a curve in the path and saw Venice standing uneasily before him.

"Are you positive you weren't followed?"

Geoffrey nodded. "Why the sudden concern?"

Venice slowly turned around in a circle, scanning their surroundings. "I'm not sure. It doesn't make any sense, but up until a few seconds ago I felt like someone was watching me."

Turning to complete a similar sweep of the park, Geoffrey saw an entire block go dark as it lost power for some reason before flickering back on a few seconds later. Geoffrey idly wondered what could cause just a single block to go down like that. Just one block and just for a short time.

Geoffrey shivered as he realized that he was trying to distract himself from the creepy sense that they were indeed being watched. The vampire thought about saying something to Venice, but knew admitting to the same feeling after having been told to make sure he wasn't followed would result in trouble.

When no response was forthcoming, Venice shrugged and gestured for Geoffrey to follow her. "Imastious is already here and waiting."

The shiver from a second before was nothing in comparison to what moved down Geoffrey's back now. A hundred questions flashed through his head, but he didn't bother asking any of them. He already knew that Venice wouldn't betray the slightest hint of what was about to happen. She wouldn't want Imastious any more suspicious of her than he already was.

Venice led Geoffrey down a little-used path that ended at one of the maintenance buildings. Inside, the pair found Imastious impatiently standing in a corner.

A feather-light touch brushed against his defenses, but before he could steel himself for the attack he thought was imminent, Imastious' probe moved on.

"It appears you were both successful in ensuring that you weren't followed. I detect no human or vampire minds in close proximity." Imastious broke off for a second and for the first time Geoffrey was able to recall looked unsettled. "There was something unusual out there though. It almost seemed to pull my thoughts towards it, but it is gone now."

Shaking himself a little, Imastious turned his dead eyes on Geoffrey. "You are indeed full of surprises, aren't you?"

Remembering Imastious' proclivity towards violence, and still unsure whether he'd been brought here to be executed, Geoffrey licked his lips, trying to buy himself time before answering. "I'm sorry, Master, I'm not sure that I understand your question."

Imastious' face took on an expression that was, if anything, even less pleased than the one he'd worn when Geoffrey entered the building. "Stupid child, of course you know what I mean. Your attack on Eculdes' pawn did not go unanswered, but instead of whining about how it wasn't your fault, you actually worked with Venice to avoid that fate which would have otherwise been yours. I still expected you to be trying to avoid adding to the blood already on your hands; instead you've actually gone after Eculdes' minions in a proactive manner."

Geoffrey bowed his head appearing to acknowledge Imastious' comments while trying to sort out the implications of what had just been said.

Luckily, true to form Imastious didn't appear to want much, if any, response from his subordinates once he got started.

"I should have said that you worked with Venice to try and avoid the fate you fear, because it is by no means certain that I won't still be forced to have you killed before this is over."

Geoffrey once again wished he could really trust Venice. She had obviously told Imastious about their plan to stop information from getting back to Eculdes. It was possible that she had really been trying to help him, but it was more likely that she'd been trying to protect herself if he failed to kill Gothic.

"I believe that the information you fear has been passed on to Gothic, and as a result one of you must be disposed of."

Geoffrey had been preparing for a statement like that for days now, but it was still terrifying to hear it said with such cool indifference. Imastious truly couldn't care less about the possibility that he might have to kill Geoffrey just to cover his own tracks.

Imastious seemed pleased that Geoffrey didn't respond to the acknowledgment that he was under a sentence of death, and continued. "The worst possible result of all of this would be for you to kill Gothic after he's had a chance to pass what he knows on to Eculdes. I've taken steps to ensure Eculdes' attention will be directed elsewhere for the next few days. Gothic's allegiance is well known, and Eculdes has accrued enough powerful enemies over the years that he must be very careful in arranging any communication between the two of them, so relatively little effort or risk was involved."

Imastious paused, maybe just for dramatic effect, but if so his aim was accomplished. His next words sent a third and final chill down Geoffrey's spine. "You have three days."

THE GREATER DARKNESS

Exhaustion pulled at Geoffrey, but he refused to give way to the despair that loomed larger and larger inside him with every passing hour. There still hadn't been any sign of Gothic, and he was down to his last twenty-four hours of purchased time.

Everything Venice had told Geoffrey indicated that Gothic very much enjoyed being out and about in vampire society, but ever since Burnout had been killed there hadn't been a single sighting of the mentalist that Venice had been able to track down. Geoffrey was well aware that there was a limit to the questions that Venice could ask without getting pegged as belonging to the faction that killed Rogers. Even so, to hear her tell it, Gothic usually made such a big splash that it would be all but impossible for her not to hear about his activities if he wasn't lying extremely low right now.

The sense of being followed hadn't gone away, but Geoffrey had finally decided his paranoia was just taking on a life of its own and begun to discount the feeling. Still, he'd double-checked regardless before heading to Melody's again. The last thing he wanted was for some murderous vampire to track him back to Melody and her mother.

Looking up at Melody's building, highlighted as it was by the first rays of the sun, Geoffrey considered his options and then just decided to knock on the door like a normal person.

Melody sleepily answered the door in a faded tank top and the shorts she always wore to bed, and then threw herself at Geoffrey, barely suppressing a squeal of delight. "Where have you been? I've been so worried."

Geoffrey wrapped Melody up in a hug and then half carried her back into her apartment. "Sorry, I just don't want your neighbors to talk."

Releasing Geoffrey for a second, Melody grimaced. "Almost everyone here has nothing better to do than gossip. They've never even tried to get to know us, but they wouldn't be above telling Anna something to get me in trouble."

Geoffrey hesitantly returned Melody's hug once again as she latched onto him for a second time. "I missed you too. I'm not a very safe person to be around right now though, so I thought I'd better stay away as much as possible."

"What's going on?"

Geoffrey shrugged uncomfortably as he tried to decide how much to tell Melody. "Friends of the vampire who stabbed me may know enough to track me down."

"So they'll try to kill you too?"

"Maybe. It depends on a lot of things, but if they do find me, they'll at least torture me. They might even invade my mind so they can find out who I've been working for. Imastious, my master, doesn't want that to happen. If I can't find the friends and kill them before they report back to their master, Imastious will probably kill me himself."

Melody's eyes got very big, and Geoffrey feared for a moment that she was going to faint.

"What are you going to do?"

"I'm not sure. I'm trying to kill the last friend, but I can't find him. Even if I do, he's much stronger than me. If Venice was willing to help we might have a chance, but Imastious seems to be treating this as a test that I have to pass on my own, so she won't really get involved."

Geoffrey watched as Melody's eyes became ever so slightly guarded, and felt like something inside him was tearing. "You killed some of the friends already then?"

The vampire nodded. "Just one, he was really bad. I was inside his mind, and he'd done terrible things to so many people."

Melody gave Geoffrey a tremulous smile, looking all the while like she might break into tears. "I'm glad he wasn't an innocent, but what would you have done if he had been? Killed him anyways?"

The tearing inside was worse now. The exhaustion of the last two days combined with the level of emotion in the room to almost have Geoffrey in tears too. "What do you want me to do? I've thought about letting them just kill me, but there's more than just me involved now. These people can get inside my mind and find out about you. If that happens they'll kill you, your mom, and maybe Anna too, all just because you were important to me."

Melody pulled Geoffrey down onto the threadbare couch next to her. "I don't want that. More than anything I don't want you to die; I'm just worried about what all of this killing will do to you."

Geoffrey wanted to tell Melody he was worried too, wanted to say any number of things, but there was a distance between them that hadn't been there the last time they'd been together. He just couldn't bring himself to say any of the things that needed to be said. "I came to try and convince you to leave the city. That's the only way to make sure that no matter what happens they won't be able to find you. I can give you money; I have about ten thousand dollars."

Melody smiled again, but this time it was touched with a sadness that didn't seem fair on someone so young. "Geoffrey, if they can read your mind, how is our moving going to help? They can still track us down. The only way that would work is if we just leave without telling you where we are going, and I won't do that. You need me too much and I won't abandon you. Besides, I've talked a little with Anna about moving, and ten thousand dollars won't be enough—not to move Mom. Even if it was, Anna wouldn't be there to help me take care of her. The welfare people would give us someone else, but Anna is here much more than she's paid to be."

Geoffrey closed his eyes for a second trying to come up with an argument that would compel Melody to leave, trying to find a way that it would all be possible, but he'd somehow known all along he wouldn't be able to convince her to leave.

There wasn't anything else to do but kill Gothic or at least do his best to make sure that Imastious killed Geoffrey without invading his mind first.

The vampire rose to leave, but Melody grabbed his hand. "Geoffrey, *you* could leave. That would be plenty of money to get you out of the city and to somewhere safe."

Geoffrey shook his head, shivering as he remembered his one attempt at running away. "I tried to leave once before and it didn't work. Somehow Imastious knew where I went. He let me stew for a couple of days and then came and collected me. You can't imagine the things he did to punish me."

As Geoffrey departed Melody pulled his head down so she could whisper into his ear. "I'll pray for you, I still have faith that you'll do the right thing."

It wasn't until the vampire had made it back down to the street that he started wondering about that last comment. There were so many people who'd suffered so much less than she had and yet didn't believe in God. With all that she'd been through, how could she still believe?

Chapter 23

The exhaustion Geoffrey had felt before at Melody's had impossibly grown even worse in the last twenty-four hours. He hadn't really had a chance of killing Gothic in a fair fight before. As tired as he was now, there was no hope of him winning, even if he did somehow manage to find the other vampire. The best he could hope for now was that if he did manage to find Gothic, that the older vampire would at least kill him out of hand rather than trying to search his mind like Imastious more than likely would.

Geoffrey was tempted to stay out and watch for Gothic despite the rising sun, but the light was starting to hurt his eyes. Besides, he was virtually positive that Gothic wasn't going to be moving around during the day.

There didn't seem to be anything left to do but return home and prepare. He would need to try and goad Imastious into killing him quickly.

If he didn't then Imastious would break him to see what little tidbits he might have managed to keep to himself.

The trip back home should have been filled with despair, but Geoffrey found that he was curiously calm. He wasn't okay with how things had turned out, but he was prepared to do what had to be done to try and protect Melody. It was possible that this was what the priest had been talking about all along. Maybe death wasn't so bad, even for one like him, doomed to go straight to hell, assuming such a place really existed.

When Geoffrey finally arrived back home, Venice was waiting for him. "I was starting to wonder if you'd made a run for it."

Geoffrey shrugged, being very careful to keep his hands free. "I thought about it a couple of times, but I didn't figure I'd be able to get away with it."

Venice pretended to pout. "What, you didn't decide to stay because you love me?"

The exhaustion was still nipping at Geoffrey, making him irritable and unwilling to play along tonight. "So, is this it? Imastious decided to just have you clip me rather than seeing to it himself?"

Shaking her head, Venice pointed to the bed. "Sit down, love. I'm not here to take you out, although based on the way you're swaying it wouldn't be much of a challenge tonight."

"Why should I trust you? We both know if you've been instructed to take me down it's entirely possible this is how you'd play it."

Judging by the fire in the slender vampire's eyes, it looked as though Venice was starting to get angry, but she flashed Geoffrey another smile and slid out of her stylish jacket. The black halter top obviously left nowhere to conceal a weapon. "Look, nothing up my sleeves. All of my hardware is in my purse, so sit down and shut up while I tell you about the latest set of developments."

There wasn't anything stopping her from using her powers to call her weapons to her at need, but Geoffrey felt like she was telling the truth. That, or maybe he was just too tired to care.

Geoffrey stumbled over to the bed and collapsed into a more or less sitting posture. "Sorry if I'm a bit testy tonight. Having people deliver ultimatums and threatening to kill me tends to bring that out."

Venice shrugged. "I understand. It would tend to do the same to me, but you have to believe after all we've shared that I'm on your side as much as I can be."

Geoffrey suppressed a biting response and settled for looking at the blonde expectantly.

"Okay, essentially you're off the hook. It turns out something extremely nasty got a hold of Gothic already. He was found a few hours ago, literally torn to shreds. Imastious is confident no information was passed on to Eculdes."

Tension that Geoffrey hadn't even realized he'd been carrying drained from him, and his mind blanked for a moment as he realized that he wasn't about to die. When he finally came back he found Venice had continued talking.

"...like the old man is furious, but he probably isn't going to do anything about it. He figures his people essentially stumbled into something that was vitally important to one of the other Elders, and that the master in question personally took Gothic down to ensure that the proper message was passed along."

Venice looked at Geoffrey and cocked her head to the side. "You going to be okay there, love?"

It was all Geoffrey could do right now to keep his eyes open, but he strung together a response. "Yeah, I'll be okay. I'm just exhausted; it's been a rough week."

The giggle Geoffrey received in response seemed entirely appropriate. "Now that's an understatement if I've ever heard one."

Scooting over to the bed, Venice sprawled out suggestively. "Imastious wants to see us tonight, but we have plenty of time still. Now that we have everything else out of the way, do you feel like doing a little celebrating?" The slender vampire watched Geoffrey tense up and then sighed. "I hadn't offered for a long time, I thought maybe things had changed."

Geoffrey shook his head. "If events had occurred slightly differently with Gothic you would have killed me tonight. How can you expect me to just put that from my mind so quickly?"

Venice shrugged. "That's part and parcel of who we are, you told me so yourself a hundred times before you lost your memory. Any relationship between vampires is pursued under the tacit understanding that whatever your feelings for the other person may develop into, you're still always running risks. You may find something out about them, they may find out something about you, or some Elder's pursuit of power may come between you both. You have to go into things knowing that you may eventually have to cut them down to protect yourself. You get used to it. Eventually it's all part of the spice that helps keep things interesting."

Geoffrey shook his head as pictures of Melody flashed through his mind. "I'm just too exhausted to think this through tonight."

Venice rolled off of the bed and gathered up her jacket and purse. "Whatever. Just remember I'm not going to keep offering indefinitely. What we had was good, and I know you're developing feelings for me, but sooner or later I'll stop waiting and get on with my life."

THE GREATER DARKNESS

Imastious motioned Geoffrey and Venice over to a pair of chairs set before him. "Venice has some inkling of why you were both called here, but even she doesn't fully understand the ramifications of what's happening."

Turning dead eyes on Geoffrey, the ancient vampire continued. "There has been a statistically significant jump in vampire deaths this last month."

At Geoffrey's blank look, a dry, mocking chuckle escaped Imastious. "I won't bore you with all of the painful details of how one arrives at the determination that something is statistically significant, but suffice it to say that based on the marked increase in deaths among our kind this month, there's a ninety-six percent chance that there's been some kind of change to the existing power balance."

Venice seemed to be understanding, and at a nod from Imastious she tried to help explain. "A few vampires get killed every month, typically because they get involved in something they shouldn't, or because one of the Elders figures out who they work for and eliminates them to weaken a particular rival."

Geoffrey nodded as he started to get an idea where things were headed. Venice bestowed a smile on him and continued. "The fact that we had so many extra vampires killed this month probably means a large number of Elders are starting to make major power plays, meaning that things could get nasty out there before all is said and done."

Imastious nodded impatiently. "It could also mean that there is some kind of new power out making its presence known, but there hasn't been the kind of influx of new vampires into the city that would be required if a master from another city were trying to move his base of operations here."

Pacing now, Imastious continued. "From everything Venice has reported, the various meeting places of our kind are starting to be characterized by a nervousness and tension that tells me a significant number of the Elders weren't expecting this sudden outbreak of murders. Obviously the ones who were prepared for these events are trying to blend in, to convey a sense of nervousness to all but their most trusted lieutenants, so we can't divine who is responsible that way."

An unpleasant thought crossed Geoffrey's mind as Imastious paused.

"Master, is it possible that the jump in deaths is somehow linked to the outbreak of rabies?"

Imastious' face went blank for a moment. "I'd forgotten about the disease. That's an interesting hypothesis. The rabid animals do seek us out, but you yourself had no problem dispatching two rabid beasts. While the outbreak represents a very real danger, it would take large numbers of infected animals to account for the death of even some of the weaker of our kind. The humans seem to have the outbreak under control."

Shaking his head, Imastious resumed pacing. "No, that seems unlikely. We must proceed under the assumption that this is driven by an attempt to upset the current balance of power, and do what we can to capitalize on the situation."

The rest of the meeting had dragged on well past the time when Imastious would usually have dismissed them. By the end, Geoffrey was wondering if the uptick in deaths had the older vampire more worried than he was letting on.

Ultimately it didn't matter one way or the other. Geoffrey had his orders and for once it involved protecting humans instead of killing them.

Imastious had indicated that there was one particular Elder who had been hit hardest in the recent violence. Apparently Imastious was hoping to use this rival Elder as a foil for the other Elders to wear themselves out against. Geoffrey was responsible for easing some of the pressure. The first item of business was to stop a bank robbery.

Once Imastious was able to point Geoffrey towards the vampire-sponsored gang responsible for conducting the robbery, it had been a simple matter for the younger vampire to use his mentalist abilities to find out exactly when the robbery was to go down. All of which led to Geoffrey standing in line in front of a teller as six hooded figures burst into the bank yelling and waving guns.

Extending his thoughts as far as they would go, Geoffrey began his assault.

The closest pair never even realized they were under attack before the bitter edge of Geoffrey's blade had beheaded the first and pierced the second through the heart.

Geoffrey's thoughts hammered away at the remaining four, confusing them and slowing their responses as he disarmed the next closest opponent. The disarm required shattering the kid's elbow, but that was fine with Geoffrey. He'd decided beforehand that this one hadn't done anything worthy of death yet, and the pain from the ruined joint would prove an effective neutralizer.

Sensing that the remaining robbers were shaking off the effects of his mental assault, Geoffrey dived and rolled as shots went cracking over his head. His movement had put the leader of the group between him and the other two, and he ruthlessly forced the gang member to serve as a shield while he used his captured handgun to down the farthest enemy. A quick push sent Geoffrey's captive into the remaining opponent. The two of them were easy pickings as they went down in a tangle of limbs.

THE GREATER DARKNESS

People were still screaming and dropping to the ground as Geoffrey calmly pocketed the empty gun, sheathed his weapon and then walked out of the bank.

The police response to the bank was faster than Geoffrey expected, but he made it safely into the subways as he heard the first sirens, and once there he knew that he'd be able to lose himself in the tunnels.

The feeling that he was being watched had returned again, but Geoffrey wasn't headed anywhere important, so he simply ignored it. Imastious hadn't been kidding when he'd implied that things were going to get nasty.

Most of the covert warfare between the vampire Elders had remained below the threshold of awareness of the general populace, but people were becoming increasingly nervous when faced with a sudden spike in drive-by shootings, robberies, and violence in general. Venice and Imastious had limited their communications to instructions regarding who he was to kill or protect, so Geoffrey had been forced to turn to the human media in an effort to stay abreast of the war.

It wasn't doing him much good though. He didn't know enough about the various players to separate out which incidents were the result of some kind of vampire directive and which ones were just caused by two-bit crooks trying to take advantage of the rising tide of violence.

Even so, he could tell that things were starting to get really bad. The mayor was talking about imposing a curfew and asking the Governor to send in the National Guard in an effort to take some pressure off of the police. It still might not be enough to avoid the riot that Geoffrey was pretty sure was developing.

Sometime in the last two weeks Geoffrey had lost track of how many missions he'd run. He'd quickly realized that high-profile actions like he'd taken at the bank would eventually get him killed or arrested, so he'd stretched his creativity in an effort to influence events in a more subtle manner. One set of bodyguards had been mentally prepped over the course of a couple hours, so that when the assassin assigned to kill a prominent businessman finally showed up, they were ready and waiting, unconsciously in a state of high alert. The assassin had only managed to get off a single, poorly-aimed shot before being mowed down.

A second bank robbery had been foiled when conditioning that Geoffrey had spent an entire exhausting night on had prompted two of the robbers to cut down their companions in the early stages of the holdup. Geoffrey was pleased with his efforts, but couldn't avoid recognizing that once again, even in the little corner he was responsible for, it was the humans who were bearing the brunt of the vampires' conflict.

Geoffrey continued to hold out some hope he'd get a chance to help take out some of the vampires responsible for the ongoing conflict, but so far Imastious hadn't obliged him.

As frustrating as that was, at least Geoffrey wasn't being assigned to kill innocents. Those kinds of missions seemed to be going exclusively to Venice, who so far wasn't showing any qualms about completing them. Geoffrey's mental jury was still out on whether his reprieve meant that Imastious was worried about pushing him too far, or whether it just meant that Imastious didn't have the spare time right now to punish Geoffrey severely enough if the missions weren't completed to schedule. Every mission seemed very time sensitive given the way that the vampires had abandoned their normal, measured pace of operating.

This was actually the first night in ages that Geoffrey hadn't had some kind of mission to either execute or set up for later. It either meant that the conflict was starting to die out, or that Imastious was coming to the end of his intelligence and was therefore running out of targets that he could positively confirm as belonging to a specific rival. Geoffrey was cautiously optimistic it was the former. He was pretty sure that once Imastious did run out of known rival assets, he'd just start eliminating people on the basis that if they didn't belong to him he'd be better off if they weren't in play any longer.

Either way, it was nice to have a night free. Geoffrey knew he should probably be inside trying to recuperate, but something pulled him out into the darkness and frankly, he was happy to have some time to just walk through the city, even with the risk involved in being outside.

The night had started out very pleasant, well-lit as it was by a full moon, with plenty of other people out and about on the streets. As it had gotten closer to midnight though, foot traffic had diminished until there wasn't anyone else in sight. The drop-off in pedestrians wasn't surprising. You couldn't blame people for wanting to be safe at home given the number of 'crazies' who had come out of the woodwork lately.

Geoffrey suddenly noticed the lights across the street fading in and out. It was too localized to be a brownout, but Geoffrey couldn't think of anything that would cause that kind of fluctuation in the power grid.

A chill ran down his spine, but he felt oddly compelled to investigate the alley. Surely he could get just a little closer and execute a quick mental sweep without exposing himself to undue risk.

Exhaling a couple of times to help him relax, Geoffrey cast his thoughts free of his physical being and probed the darkness, only to reel back in alarm as he brushed up against a mind that was alien and harsh. The vampire tried to pull his probes back, but something pulled at them, exerting a strange force that made it difficult to break contact.

As Geoffrey finally succeeded in severing the tendrils of thought, a shambling figure, clad in nothing more than rags, came out of the darkness and sprang at him. Geoffrey had a brief second to register he was fighting a familiar-looking woman and then she reached him and carried the both of them to the ground.

Geoffrey rolled with the force of the impact, placing a foot in the woman's stomach and kicking her free so her momentum carried her away as he came back to his feet and turned to face her again.

The intermittent light from nearby shops revealed that the figure Geoffrey had expected to see had been replaced by something bigger. The creature facing Geoffrey now was more than seven feet tall, with a thick coat of fur, and muscles that made a professional bodybuilder seem small and effeminate.

Geoffrey just had time to draw his katana before the beast charged him with jerky motions that were deceptively quick. The vampire somehow knew that allowing the beast to close with him would be a deadly mistake, so he sprang away at the last second, earning a wicked set of slashes across his chest. He'd almost waited too long. The beast's arms were longer, proportionally, than a human's would have been.

That, plus the fact that it was taller than Geoffrey, meant that the reach advantage his katana normally would have provided had essentially been nullified.

The gashes in Geoffrey's chest immediately began to bleed, but he forced away what little pain made it past the surging adrenaline in his system, and prepared for the next rush as the creature spun around and charged again.

Geoffrey waited until his opponent was almost on him and then feinted to the right before whipping his weapon through a short, vicious arc that intersected with a clawed hand which would have torn his head off had he continued the feint.

The blow would have easily sheared completely through the torso of a large man, but only barely managed to cut through the creature's arm. The impact almost wrenched the katana from Geoffrey's hands.

Palms smarting from the force of the strike, Geoffrey tried to move to the left to avoid the creature, but he'd lost too much momentum as a result of the blow and was only partially successful.

The creature clipped him with a shoulder as it went past, sending Geoffrey sprawling as it howled in rage and pain from trying to spin around without using its missing right paw.

Whether due to his wound, the efforts of the past two weeks, or some special property of the creature, Geoffrey's strength was quickly fading away. He had to finish the fight quickly before some exhaustion-induced mistake allowed the creature to close with him.

Taking a step back to give himself more room to react, Geoffrey bumped up against the outside wall of a building and cursed the distraction that had prevented him from realizing the creature had been maneuvering him.

The creature was approaching again, but it was moving more slowly now, seeming to have decided its previous tactics hadn't been effective.

Geoffrey watched the three-inch claws on the beast's left hand as they slowly circled back and forth. As the creature reached the outer limits of the vampire's reach, he brought his katana around in a slash designed to deprive it of its remaining hand.

The blow from the bloody stump was completely unexpected and launched Geoffrey to the side with bone-breaking force.

Before the vampire had even landed, the beast charged. Acting on instinct, Geoffrey placed the handle of his weapon against the building at his back and guided its tip towards where he thought the beast's heart would sit.

The walls protected Geoffrey from the deadly claws that otherwise would have beheaded him, but suffered incredible damage as four deep grooves were torn through the brick.

As the point of his weapon entered the creature, Geoffrey tried to drop out of the way to avoid being crushed. Once again the right angle of the walls at his back helped protect him as the creature's broad shoulders impacted the unyielding masonry before the rest of its bulk could crush the vampire.

Even after colliding with the walls, the creature's momentum was sufficient to severely bruise Geoffrey. More importantly, the force served to drive the tip of his sword through its unyielding flesh.

Geoffrey momentarily blacked out as his head bounced off the building. When he regained his senses, he found not the creature he expected, but the woman who'd initially attacked him. She'd somehow changed forms, but that still didn't explain the nagging familiarity. He had to have seen her somewhere before, but the setting had been different and that was making it difficult to put the pieces together. He thought there was something about the clothes that was throwing him off, but couldn't be sure.

Realizing that it was only a matter of time before police were summoned to investigate the fight, Geoffrey pulled himself to his feet. The first sirens were already approaching, but Geoffrey disappeared effortlessly into the pools of shadows created by the interplay of streetlights and neon signs. Even limited to no more than a slow hobble, it should be a small matter to avoid being detained.

Chapter 24

Venice paced back and forth, seemingly unwilling to believe what Geoffrey was telling her. "How can that be possible? How could centuries pass without anyone figuring this out?"

Geoffrey shook his head in exhaustion, and tried not to move. It was hard to hold still, but he didn't want to break any of his wounds open. Once he'd realized why the woman had seemed so familiar, he'd known there was going to be far too little time for rest and healing.

The last time he'd seen her, she'd been dressed in an expensive dress suit and scared out of her mind by the rabid dogs attacking them. That bit of information was critical, but it still didn't give Geoffrey anything even approaching real answers as to what was going on.

"I don't know for sure why this is happening now, but I think this isn't the first time. This all fits too well with the legends and the outbreak of rabies for it to permit any other explanation."

The slender vampire momentarily looked like she was going to argue with him some more, but then she closed her eyes and seemed to deflate slightly. "Then the legends are true. The human ones about people changing under the light of the full moon into beasts, *and* the tales passed from vampire to vampire about something that preys upon vampires like we prey upon humans."

Geoffrey slumped a little and nodded. "I'm sure that the myths have all changed somewhat over the centuries. There are probably aspects of the legends which are misleading, or blatantly incorrect, just like the legends about vampires, but the core of truth is there. What we would call werewolves do indeed exist, and the mechanism that seems to transfer the disease is what we've previously called rabies. There's already a mountain of evidence indicating that animals exposed to rabies are predisposed to respond very aggressively to vampires."

Venice sighed and collapsed onto Geoffrey's bed. "Okay, run me through what we know about the werewolf again, and then I'll take it to Imastious. He'll probably want to talk to you later, but for now I'll have to be the point gal."

Geoffrey nodded, but he wasn't convinced. He suspected that Venice didn't have much better access to Imastious than he did. Imastious wouldn't have trusted her with the location of his home, which meant that she would just be waiting for Imastious to contact her or wander by one of the message drops they'd no doubt arranged.

Geoffrey kept his thoughts to himself and just nodded. "We've essentially gone over everything. Once she'd changed, she was bigger, faster, and stronger than me. Also, she seemed to absorb my probes almost like a black hole sucking energy from me."

Venice stood as if to go and then cocked her head slightly to the side. "I know you, and the fact that you don't like to put forth anything that you're not sure of, but if you have any suspicions, now would be the time to share them too."

Geoffrey looked down uncomfortably. "I'm not sure. Like I said, something about her was playing havoc with my mental abilities, but it seemed as though what I brushed up against wasn't quite sane. Also, the mind I touched was too full. Maybe like there were too many memories in it, that or possibly multiple personalities."

It turned out that Imastious did visit Venice first, but as soon as the beautiful vampire had finished relaying Geoffrey's story, the Elder had brought her straight to Geoffrey's so that he could hear the tale again.

Geoffrey had noticed Imastious looking at him with what appeared to be a touch of uneasiness on several occasions while the story was told, but he'd been unable to pin down a reason why the older, more powerful vampire would be worried about someone so obviously at his mercy.

Instead of continuing to worry at it, Geoffrey decided to just be glad that Imastious hadn't accused him of lying outright or decided that he'd somehow made a mistake in the way that the conflict was handled. Of course Imastious' vaunted information sources had probably already told him about the fight, so Geoffrey's fears had probably been unfounded from the beginning.

Geoffrey hadn't anticipated that Imastious would want to see the site of the battle. Previously Imastious had always had enough external information that a trip like that, at least one with Geoffrey, would have been redundant.

Geoffrey looked at the long furrows in the brick before him and shuddered. It was still hard to believe that the werewolf had been so fast. He was still shocked that he'd managed to survive the attack.

Imastious finished examining the damaged walls and then turned and pointed out claw marks on the pavement. "You didn't notice these last night?"

The younger vampire shook his head, suddenly nervous about being overheard by someone who would carry the tale to the police stationed nearby. "No, everything was happening so quickly. It would help explain how she was able to change direction so suddenly though."

Hopefully Imastious would deal with the police. He wouldn't want to be associated with someone who was a suspected murderer, so it was probably safe to assume that he'd blank the minds of both of the cops before the three of them left the site.

The Elder nodded and then turned and walked away, apparently expecting Venice and Geoffrey to follow.

Geoffrey suppressed questions about where they were headed and followed Venice to Imastious' private car. The trio soon arrived at what looked to be one of the more exclusive condominiums in the city.

The doorman tried to refuse Imastious entrance, only to assume a blank, compliant expression as Imastious gestured him away. Geoffrey wondered momentarily if he'd ever have such easy power, but he wasn't entirely sure he wanted it. That kind of power couldn't help but be seductive.

Inside the elevator Imastious spoke again. "The Elder known as Byington owned the three top floors of this building. He used the top and bottom-most floors as a buffer and lived in the middle floor."

It wasn't clear from the way that Imastious had said 'owned' whether Byington was now dead, or whether Imastious had taken over the floors. From what Venice had indicated, it was almost unheard of for vampire Elders to meet face to face. There was just too much chance that they'd try to assassinate each other. Given that, it seemed very unlikely that Imastious was taking them to meet with Byington.

Venice volunteered information for the first time all evening. "It was primarily Byington's assets that we've been protecting for the last couple of weeks."

Another tidbit of knowledge there, but it was hard for Geoffrey to place it in context. Venice had indicated that Imastious was using the Elder as a foil, bolstering him so that other vampires would be forced to expend more resources in their quest to destroy him, but maybe there was more to the relationship then he'd been led to believe.

The other logical possibility was that Imastious had simply compromised Byington's organization so severely that he figured he could eliminate Byington at any point. Once you knew where someone lived there was always a way to get inside and take them out if you wanted it badly enough.

The elevator came to a stop and Geoffrey looked forward as the doors slowly opened, only to feel his breath catch as the sheer scope of the destruction he was seeing registered.

THE GREATER DARKNESS

Imastious exited the elevator, seemingly unconcerned by his surroundings. "Byington apparently felt more than a little threatened. It looks as though he'd gathered at least four of his more powerful subordinates here to serve as a personal bodyguard. They are all dead, as is he."

Just based on what Geoffrey could see in this first room, it looked like there were probably pieces of them scattered throughout the floor. It actually surprised him that Imastious had been able to estimate that there had been five people here to start out with.

Byington had either been nothing at all like Imastious, or he'd been scared out of his mind. It was hard to imagine any situation in which Imastious would have trusted any of his subordinates with the location of his home.

"I have of course formed my own opinion of what happened here, but the two of you will examine the evidence and share your thoughts with me."

Geoffrey waded through the wreckage of what had once been an opulently-furnished dwelling, and did his very best not to become sick. He'd killed people before, but tearing them apart like this added an additional level of depravity to the act.

When the trio met at the elevator again, Venice was the first to speak up. "The remains all seem to be from Byington's vampires, so either none of the attackers were killed or they were carried out by their comrades."

Imastious nodded. "You are of course omitting the fact that there are claw marks on the wall which closely match the ones from the scene of Geoffrey's most recent conflict simply because it is so obvious it needs no mention."

It looked as though Venice was on the cusp of delivering the kind of scathing retort she sometimes inflicted on Geoffrey when he was exceptionally slow picking up on the finer points of unarmed combat, but she quickly regained her self-control, and Imastious turned to Geoffrey.

"What did you notice?"

Geoffrey couldn't escape the feeling that the test being presented to him was more important than it appeared on the surface, and he took a deep breath before answering. "Based on the general level of destruction throughout the apartment, it appears that there were one or more very powerful telekinetics involved here."

A cruel smile made its way onto Imastious' face. "Byington was a pyromancer and his chief lieutenants were all mentalists. There may have been one or two telekinetics here, but none of his people were particularly powerful in that regard."

Confusion filled Geoffrey as he reviewed the destruction he'd just looked at. "Master, there was limited evidence of fire in the apartment, but nothing on the scale one would expect from an Elder who was fighting for his life."

Imastious nodded, apparently satisfied at last. "Geoffrey has unwittingly stumbled upon the key observation regarding this conflict. The claw marks would tend to support his story of what we will call werewolves for lack of a better term. Venice is correct that no attackers can be found, either in their bestial forms, or in the human shape that Geoffrey reported his opponent returning to once dead. I think not because the dead were carried away, but because none of the attackers were mortally injured."

Geoffrey's mind was spinning at a frantic pace. He arrived at the idea Imastious was headed to a split second before the older vampire verbalized it. "The reason none of the attackers were killed was not just that they exhibited strength and speed equal to or in excess of what is common among our kind, but also because the defenders' abilities apparently were unable to work against their attackers."

Imastious' eyes turned to Geoffrey, and although they still looked inhuman and cold, there was now also a trace of something that, in another person, Geoffrey would have called fear.

Chapter 25

The full moon was only a couple of nights past, but the last forty-eight hours felt like they'd taken a week to roll by. Geoffrey had expected as much, but that didn't make the sheer terror any easier to handle.

The autopsy report on the woman Geoffrey had killed came back late last night and confirmed that she appeared to have been infected with an unusual strain of rabies. Imastious must have done something to ensure that she was tested for the disease because Geoffrey was pretty sure that wasn't part of a normal police autopsy.

However Imastious had affected the test, it had combined with the recent, high-profile vampire deaths to provide him with the evidence he'd needed to mobilize the other Elders. Venice had indicated that none of the other Elders seemed to know where the information had come from, and nobody was cooperating on any kind of large-scale basis, but the shadow war that had been in high gear had pretty much died out overnight. Geoffrey hadn't seen any of them yet, but supposedly there were large numbers of patrols out all over the city looking for evidence of other werewolves.

Venice tapped Geoffrey on the shoulder and he realized he'd been woolgathering. At least all of the recent developments meant that he didn't have to go out and face all of this by himself.

Casting his thoughts out as widely as he was able, the vampire searched for any trace of werewolves. In theory, if they were out there it should be easy to find them. Their very ability to absorb his power should make them stand out, but so far he hadn't been able to find the slightest indication that there was anyone out there other than Venice, him and a few humans.

Apparently most people still weren't convinced that the dramatic reduction of violence was there to stay. In some ways they were right. The authorities were telling people that things were back to normal, but that wasn't the full story. Human deaths seemed to be down considerably from what they'd been a week ago, but missing person reports had increased dramatically.

It appeared that the werewolves were either eating people or doing such a good job hiding the corpses that nobody was finding them. Even the humans' current wariness was aimed in the wrong direction, but it should at least help ensure that there weren't quite as many witnesses to deal with if they did encounter a werewolf.

Shrugging to indicate he hadn't found anything, Geoffrey picked a direction at random and started walking. One way was as good as another considering that he didn't know where they should be headed.

Venice slipped her arm through his before the pair had made more than a couple of steps, presenting the illusion of a happy couple exploring the city despite the cold of the night. Geoffrey thought about untangling his arm from hers, but decided the effort wasn't worth the ill will it would generate. He was finding that he really enjoyed working with her now that he didn't have to worry about whether she was going to try to kill him on short notice. If she hadn't been pushing for more than just friendship, things would have been nearly perfect.

Geoffrey sent his thoughts out and once again found no hint of the alien presence he'd fought previously. Thirty seconds later a terrible howl split the night, and Venice and Geoffrey broke into a sprint as he cast his thoughts ahead and found a werewolf where seconds before there hadn't been one.

Three blocks later, the pair rounded a corner and found four vampires engaged against a beast that was even bigger than the one Geoffrey had fought. The humanoid combatants moved back and forth with speed and grace that was impressive, if slightly less than what Venice or Geoffrey was capable of. The werewolf, on the other hand, moved with the same jerky motions as the smaller woman Geoffrey had fought, but with even greater speed.

Normally vampires reporting to different Elders, and even sometimes those working for the same master, wouldn't help each other, but Geoffrey and Venice didn't hesitate as they crossed the remaining distance to the conflict.

Reflex took over and Geoffrey sent out questing thoughts in an effort to learn his opponent's plans, only to find that the absorption of his tendrils was weaker than he'd expected. He could almost sense the beast's thoughts, alien though they were.

One of the other vampires went down from a lightning-fast swipe, and the power fighting Geoffrey's probes suddenly strengthened dramatically.

"Use your powers," cried Geoffrey in a panting, breathless voice, and suddenly the force holding him away from the werewolf's mind was overwhelmed.

The five vampires surrounded the werewolf and succeeded in forcing it into a more defensive stance, but its raw speed and power made it difficult to bring down and Geoffrey's allies seemed to be tiring. They needed to do something quickly or it would eventually succeed in bringing one of them down. Once that happened, the rest would fall in short order.

Geoffrey's blade licked out and impacted on the werewolf's upper thigh, but did little more than scratch the abnormally hard flesh. It wasn't good enough.

The alien thoughts before Geoffrey suddenly seemed to morph and change into something nearly understandable, and without thinking about it the vampire responded to the course of action he thought the werewolf was about to take.

The beast lunged at Geoffrey, flailing with both hands, and then pulled up in astonishment as the vampire wasn't where he was supposed to be. Geoffrey completed his dive between the creature's legs and rolled to his feet in time to launch the most powerful blow he was capable of to the same spot he'd struck previously.

As in his last confrontation, Geoffrey's weapon was nearly ripped from his hands, but he managed to hamstring his opponent, after which the vampires were able to finish the creature quickly.

Looking around at the other vampires, Geoffrey made an effort to stand up straight and control his breathing. This wasn't the time to appear weak. He and Venice were outnumbered three to two and there wasn't yet any proof that this informal truce would hold.

The biggest of the vampires checked his fallen companion and then shook his head. "He's dead, that thing ripped him completely open. It would have gotten all of us if you two hadn't shown up when you did."

The vampire cocked his head and then extended his hand. "I don't know that I'd have risked my neck like that, but I'm glad that you did. My name is Alexander."

Geoffrey shook the offered hand, trying not to be surprised at the humanity of the gesture and then released Alexander's hand so that Venice could shake it.

He suppressed the urge to tell Alexander that he'd faced a werewolf previously. There wasn't any reason to give away any information that he didn't have to. The other vampire might seem friendly, but underneath that exterior it was very probable that he wasn't any different from Imastious.

One of the other living vampires, the smallest one, finished inspecting the dead werewolf, which now had the appearance of a human male. Looking up with something that was a close cousin to fear, the bearded vampire looked from Alexander to Geoffrey and back again.

"Do you think that was the only one?"

Geoffrey shook his head. "No, as powerful as that was, it couldn't have killed Byington and his men by itself. Either there are several more of them, or there's one even stronger and faster still running around."

Alexander looked at Geoffrey appraisingly and then nodded. "Well then, things are probably going to get much uglier before this is all over."

Chapter 26

Geoffrey couldn't escape the thought that after such a vicious battle he should be sore and tender regardless of whatever superior regenerative abilities he might have. The first time he'd faced one of the werewolves it had all but killed him, and he'd just finished healing from that when they'd fought the second wolf.

The vampire mentally shrugged and then checked his back trail one more time in an effort to satisfy himself that he wasn't being followed. He couldn't shake the feeling that someone was watching him. Geoffrey almost turned around and went home without finishing his trip, but he was certain that this would be his last chance to visit Melody for quite some time. Based on the debrief the night before with Imastious, it seemed that Geoffrey and Venice would be on the front lines of the hunt. If that was really going to be the case, he'd be lucky to get adequate sleep over the next several weeks. Sneaking away for another visit would be practically impossible.

His mind made up, Geoffrey crossed the last few blocks to Melody's building, wrinkling his nose at the smell. There'd been another brief rainstorm during the day. That usually cleared out the smell of garbage for a little while, but either it hadn't made any difference, or the smell was already back. This really was a depressing place to live.

The climb up the graffiti-covered stairwell went quickly, and then Geoffrey scanned the apartment to make sure that Anna wasn't around. She never stayed this late that he was aware of, but it was a good habit to get into if he was going to avoid causing Melody awkward questions at some point.

Satisfied that Melody was alone with her mother, Geoffrey knocked gently on the door. As always, the peephole in the door darkened for a moment, and then there was the sound of multiple locks being opened.

This time Melody was crying before she even managed to hug him, and Geoffrey felt a stab of guilt. The last time he'd been able to stop by he'd told Melody that the odds were good he'd be killed in a few short days.

"I thought you were dead. Why didn't you let me know you were okay? I kept thinking that someone was watching me, and I didn't know if it was you trying to protect me, or someone coming to kill me."

The vampire hugged the slender teenager to him and guided her inside. "I'm so sorry, but things have been happening, big things that I haven't had any control over. I haven't had the time or freedom to get away so that I could come talk. Nobody's traced me back to you; it was just your imagination."

Melody's surface thoughts were full of relief, anger, and a few other equally conflicting emotions, but she nodded and then pulled him in to see her mom. "Is there anything you can do? Anna says that the disease hasn't taken a turn for the worse, it's as stable as ever, but she's getting weaker. I think maybe she's stopped wanting to live."

Thinking of the struggle he'd faced that last time he tried to plumb Debbie's mind, Geoffrey wanted to tell Melody that there wasn't anything he could do, but looking into expectant brown eyes, he knew he couldn't lie to her of all people.

"I can try, Melody, but I can't guarantee anything."

Even as he was telling her he would try, his insides tightened up at the thought of how likely he was to fail. Then again, he'd just picked up Melody's surface thoughts without meaning to. It was possible that his powers were growing faster than he'd realized.

THE GREATER DARKNESS

Melody nodded her understanding, and then pulled up a chair for Geoffrey to sit in while he worked.

Closing his eyes, Geoffrey rested a hand on Debbie's forehead and then sent probes into the raging mind below his palm. He did a mental double-take as he saw how much things had changed. The whirlpool was gone. The thoughts weren't much different, the medications were still eating away at her reason, but everything was calmer.

Rather than wasting time in the shallower parts of Debbie's mind, Geoffrey immediately started pushing his way to the center. As his strength ebbed, Geoffrey worried that this time he wouldn't be strong enough to make it, but he knew the fear for the irrational thing that it was, and pushed on. He'd made it all the way down before, he could do it again.

It seemed to take ages to arrive at the natural, flexible barrier protecting the center of Debbie's mind, but it still happened much faster than Geoffrey had feared. Matching his thoughts to the barrier, the vampire slid through it and felt a shock of astonishment lance through his being.

His constructs had worked. They'd eaten away at the mental pain and guilt to the point where she was almost completely free of them. That had to be the reason why her surface thoughts were so much less tumultuous. Without the self-loathing in her core, there wasn't anything to reinforce the maelstrom, and it had mostly died out.

Geoffrey's elation evaporated as he tasted the rest of the feelings in Debbie's center. Now that her hate was gone, she was at peace with the idea of death. The hope that he'd tried to leave when he was there last had morphed to a hope for salvation in the afterlife. Ultimately she'd lost the will to live.

Parts of Geoffrey wanted to skitter from place to place, examining the change that had happened more fully, but the larger, overwhelming part of him worried about Melody. Not just the question of what to tell her, but the more important question of how she'd cope with what he'd tell her.

It was possible that this was just the natural course her mother's mind would have taken if the disease had happened independent of all of the other tragedies in her life, but Geoffrey couldn't escape the suspicion that he'd just ruined the life of the person that was most important to Melody. His attempt to help stop an endless round of self-punishment would ultimately just bring more pain to the person he wanted to help above all others.

Geoffrey debated possible solutions that might grant Melody a chance of more lasting happiness, but in the end he didn't do anything other than create a construct that would temporarily block some of the pain so that

Debbie wouldn't have to be as heavily medicated. With a bit of luck it might be enough to help. Maybe then they could cut back the pain medication enough to let her regain consciousness and talk to her daughter. Maybe that conversation would be enough to rekindle her desire to live.

As much as Geoffrey wanted to help Melody, to protect her, he couldn't force her mother back into a pain-filled existence, not when the pain was so severe, not if it wasn't what her mother wanted.

Exhausted by his efforts, Geoffrey let his thoughts snap back to his physical body and looked up at Melody. Fresh tears had filled the slender teen's eyes, as if she somehow knew what Geoffrey was about to tell her.

"She doesn't want to stay anymore, does she?"

Geoffrey shook his head. "It isn't that she doesn't love you, she's just ready to move on."

Shaking her head violently, Melody denied his words. "Make her stay! You can make her stay, I know you can."

Emotion rose inside him, but Geoffrey managed to maintain his control. "I could, but doing so would be counter to what she wants. It would only be a matter of time until it caused some kind of problem."

Geoffrey pulled Melody to him and hugged her. "I blocked some of her pain. You can step down the painkillers for the next few days. I think that might be enough for her to wake up and be coherent for a while. Maybe that will spark a desire to stay."

The hope that flashed through Melody's eyes tore at Geoffrey's heart. It was so strong that he didn't even have to stretch his abilities to feel it.

"I can't guarantee anything, and if she doesn't you shouldn't blame yourself. She's lived with unimaginable amounts of pain for years now. It may just be her time to go."

The hope guttered, nearly dying out, but amazingly none of that crossed her face as Melody nodded. "I understand, thank you for trying."

It seemed impossible that someone still so young could possess so much willpower.

Taking Geoffrey's hand, Melody pulled him back into the living room. Once the pair was seated on the old green sofa, Geoffrey explained events of the last few weeks. By the time the vampire finished, Melody's eyes were wide.

"It was hard enough to believe that vampires existed, and I have you as proof. To think that werewolves are out there too is amazing. Amazing and scary."

Geoffrey nodded. "Scary is right, they are faster and stronger than anything I've ever encountered. The more I examine my memory of the thoughts I touched last night, the more I'm positive that they will kill humans too. They seem predisposed to kill vampires, but I think anything that walks on two legs is an acceptable target to them."

The brown eyes that looked into Geoffrey's eyes were momentarily ancient and wise beyond anything he would have expected from Melody. "So you've found your cause. You'll hunt them down, and in so doing protect innocents from being torn apart and killed."

Geoffrey hadn't thought things through as clearly as that, but as Melody said it he realized she was right. "I guess so. Someone has to help stop them or they'll destroy the city."

Melody wrapped her arms around her knees and shivered. "I don't feel very good about all of this. Run away, Geoffrey. Get out of the city. You can fight these things still, but do it once you are out from under Imastious."

A sudden spark of anger flared up inside Geoffrey. "Haven't you been listening to me? I can't beat these things by myself, they're too strong. If I don't have the help of other vampires I don't stand a chance. Why are you so anxious for me to leave, when you aren't willing to do so yourself?"

Hurt blossomed in Melody's eyes. "I'm just worried about you. You don't understand what it's like to wonder if you're dead. How much it hurts when I try to sleep but can't because I'm worried that you've done something that you can't come back from. I constantly worry that the next time I see you the darkness will have grown, will have killed off the light."

Geoffrey was suddenly exhausted, not physically, but emotionally. "I'm sorry, I shouldn't have snapped. I just feel like things are the best they've been, and you're not even happy for me."

The tears were back, but Melody refused to let them escape this time. "I'm happy that you've found a purpose, I'm just worried it will be twisted by Imastious and Venice to something darker than you would have chosen for yourself."

"You don't understand. Even if that's so, I'll still be doing good. I'll still be protecting people from the werewolves."

Melody reached out and captured Geoffrey's hand. "I do want to leave the city, just as much as I want you to leave. I just can't do that while I have to take care of my mom." Melody's hand tightened inside of Geoffrey's as her breath caught. "If that ever changes, I'll leave the city like you want me to, but only if you come with me. You've been inside my mind. You know how I feel about you, just like I know what you feel for me."

Chapter 27

Geoffrey shifted slightly, trying not to make noise or let his companions know that he was starting to get antsy. He hadn't really believed that Alexander was serious about teaming up with him and Venice, but this was the second night that the trio of other vampires had come hunting with them.

The big, dark-skinned vampire sat motionless in the darkness, a respectably-sized ax balanced across his knees. Alexander appeared to be from Middle Eastern stock, and something about his manner made Geoffrey think that he'd been born to a culture from that area of the world. It begged the obvious questions of how he'd become a vampire, and how he'd reconciled his existence—and the things he'd done—against whatever value system he'd grown up with.

Next to Alexander sat Brit, which Geoffrey assumed was a shortened version of her name rather than a nickname resulting from the homely blonde being British. In fact, if anything, Brit seemed to despise Europeans in general and the British particularly. If she'd been older, Geoffrey might have suspected her of having been around back when the American colonies were being oppressed, but he was pretty sure that wasn't the cause of her dislike.

The other vampire from Alexander's group had disappeared from sight, but Geoffrey had come to expect as much from Mouse. It was becoming clear that the slight vampire was doing so less out of a desire to set up for some dark betrayal and more because he wasn't comfortable around so many people. Especially when he didn't know two of them very well.

Another hour passed, and Brit began to fidget. Finally looking up with challenge in her eyes, she hissed a question. "Why are we sitting here instead of hunting them down?"

Venice responded, venom dripping from her voice, before Geoffrey could open his mouth. "Geoffrey has more experience killing these things than anyone else in the city. If he says we wait and let them stumble onto us, then we wait."

It was hard to tell how much of the heat in Venice's response was due to her desire to protect Geoffrey's position of leadership in the group, and how much of it was simply a dislike of Brit. It couldn't have been lost on Venice the way that Brit looked at Geoffrey. More than once there had been a clear invitation in her gaze.

Alexander shot Brit a commanding look that killed her response before it made it out of her mouth, and then nodded. "Venice is right. Geoffrey is the most experienced of us in this area. Not only that, it's possible his hunches are the result of things he saw in that beast's mind, but didn't consciously recognize. We'll stay here as long as he feels it necessary."

Relieved that the building conflict had at least been momentarily defused, Geoffrey relaxed once more and sent his thoughts ranging out in an effort to find one of the alien presences that they were hunting. He knew the odds were against him finding one of the werewolves using his mentalist powers. It appeared that they could turn their absorption power off at will, that or maybe that it wasn't active until they changed forms. Either way, he was pretty sure that they could sense vampires, and both times he'd encountered them the beasts had been stalking the vampires, not the other way around.

When the attack finally happened, it was only luck that gave the vampires any warning at all. Geoffrey had just sent his mental probes out looking for werewolves when he'd felt the alien presence he'd been waiting for suddenly appear nearby.

"Incoming!"

The vampires had all just managed to get to their feet when the werewolf was upon them. Geoffrey's muscles tensed as he took in its sheer size. It was even bigger than the last one they'd fought.

The vampires spread out and tried to encircle the beast in the unsteady light, but it was so fast that they were having a hard time pinning it in one place long enough to do so. "Slow it down!" screamed Geoffrey as he dived to the side to avoid a lethal swipe of the creature's claws, receiving a shallow set of gashes despite his efforts.

Rolling back to his feet, Geoffrey tried to push his thoughts into the werewolf's mind. It was simply too strong—the five of them weren't going to be able to overwhelm its absorption abilities.

As Geoffrey charged in to try and score a blow on the creature, Mouse suddenly appeared out of the shadows behind the creature and stabbed it with his twin short swords.

Roaring in pain, the beast backhanded the smaller vampire, knocking him into a wall with bone-crushing force. Now it was only four to one, but they'd backed it into a wall.

The werewolf moved so fast it seemed to flicker from one place to another, not bothering to cross the intervening distance between points as it parried attack after attack from all four vampires.

Geoffrey pushed himself, reaching new levels of speed in an effort to get through the creature's defenses. For four or five seconds it made no difference, and then the vampires felt a slight change in the werewolf's parries; they were the tiniest fraction of a second slow, possessed of the barest feeling of being hurried. Geoffrey's weapon slashed out in a lightning fast blow to the creatures arm, and amazingly enough succeeded in scoring a shallow cut.

The creature whirled around faster than Geoffrey could follow, and leaped over him as it howled its rage to the waning crescent of the moon. Geoffrey had been struck in passing by one of the beast's feet, the force of which was enough to knock him to the ground. Springing to his feet, the vampire suddenly felt his blood run cold as he realized the second howl he'd heard hadn't come from the werewolf they were fighting.

There'd been no guarantee that the four of them were going to be able to defeat the first werewolf. If a second joined the fray, Geoffrey and the others would be torn apart.

A brief glance at Alexander revealed that the massive vampire was fully aware of the implications of what he'd just heard, but no trace of fear clouded his face as he roared back at the werewolf and charged in swinging his heavy ax. It was the right answer, the only answer. If they could press the first werewolf hard enough to kill it before the second arrived, there was a chance that they'd still be able to fight off the second before succumbing to exhaustion.

Again and again the monster tried to disembowel one or another of the vampires, and each time its target escaped with little or no damage, but the vampires hadn't managed to score even light wounds in return.

Several seconds passed before Geoffrey realized that the sound hammering away at the back of his mind was that of a police siren. It was one more thing to worry about, but there wasn't anything he could do about it now. They'd just have to deal with the police after the fight, assuming they survived the fight.

Almost drowned out by the siren, the sound of running feet made their way to Geoffrey's ears just before five figures came sprinting around the corner. More vampires, but there wasn't any telling whether they'd help or hinder.

The unvoiced question was answered as the second group surrounded the werewolf and began cutting. Geoffrey had a brief second of relief, and then a heavy impact behind him caused reflexes to take over and send him diving out of the way.

The vampire knew without looking that a second werewolf had arrived, jumping down from a building, and he felt hope beginning to die again as one of the recently arrived vampires went down in a spray of blood.

The arrival of the second werewolf had completed the blackout that the first hadn't quite had the power to accomplish. The battle progressed in inky darkness relieved only by the weak light of the moon.

In theory, the eight remaining vampires should have been fairly evenly matched against the two werewolves, but the arrival of the second opponent seemed to have resulted in a greater shift than Geoffrey would have predicted. It was like the two beasts were more comfortable fighting in the disorganized melee they'd created than the vampires were. The werewolves took blows of opportunity on whichever target happened to be nearby, while the vampires tended to focus on one opponent at a time.

Dodging another slash, Geoffrey slipped in a side-thrust kick to his opponent's knee, but the blow left his foot numb. It was just like he'd kicked a tree.

Despair seemed to be manifesting on every vampire face to one degree or another, but none of the combatants broke and ran. Geoffrey's questing thoughts picked up a sliver of intention, and he threw himself to the side, bringing up his katana to block an attack that would have killed the vampire to his left.

The force of the block knocked Geoffrey to the ground, but a coordinated offensive by three of the other vampires forced the smaller werewolf back so that it couldn't take advantage of Geoffrey's immobility.

Once again footsteps sounded behind Geoffrey, but he'd forgotten about the sirens, so he was surprised when a voice yelled. "Police, don't move."

Without thinking, Geoffrey reached into the two minds behind him and nudged thoughts already headed the direction he wished, giving both officers the certainty that the two large forms before them must be stopped.

Geoffrey rejoined the fight just as the first shots cracked overhead impacting the werewolves more often than not, and causing the pair to scream in pain. Hardly pausing, one of the werewolves ripped a parking meter free from the concrete it was embedded in and hurled it towards the two policemen.

A sickening thud announced that the blow had struck flesh, and the decreased volume of fire indicated that one of the officers was down or dead, but the bullets had combined with the myriad of lesser wounds that the vampires had inflicted to start bleeding the werewolves out, and they were slowing.

Alexander connected with a mighty blow from his ax, and the smaller of the werewolves went down momentarily stunned. The beast never got a chance to get back up as a trio of vampires swarmed over it, cutting and slashing.

The larger werewolf suddenly sprang away from the battle, landing halfway up the wall of a building, where his claws were able to sink into the brickwork and find enough purchase to climb up and disappear into the night.

Exhaustion robbed Geoffrey's limbs of strength, but he somehow managed to remain on his feet as he tried to figure out what to do about the police now that the werewolves were gone.

"Nobody move!"

Geoffrey had forgotten about the policeman behind him, but he reached out with his thoughts to calm the man down, only to have his mind overwhelmed with incredible waves of pain as a series of sharp cracks were followed by a scream.

Turning, the vampire saw a figure wreathed in fire try to drop to the ground and roll to put the flames out. It was the right response, but the effort was futile. The fire was just too hot to be put out.

Reeling from having been inside the man's mind when he died, Geoffrey looked back at the new vampires. One of them was wearing a satisfied smile and blowing on his finger as if to clear the smoke from a gun.

Rage washed through Geoffrey. He never even paused to consider his actions as he walked over and backhanded the pyromancer into a nearby wall. The other vampire probably would have seen the blow coming and dodged it, but Geoffrey had simultaneously attacked him with multiple blows of pure mental force.

His opponent had impressive mental shields, ones that under normal circumstances Geoffrey wouldn't have contemplated trying to crack, but fueled as he was by anger, Geoffrey's assault on the other vampire's mind was relentless, and in less than a second succeeded in acquiring the access his blood cried for.

Recoiling slightly from the sick satisfaction that spidered through the other vampire's thoughts at having killed the police officer, Geoffrey considered his options briefly and then started creating a construct that he thought would accomplish what he desired.

Partway through his efforts, no more than a couple of seconds after he'd assaulted the other vampire, Geoffrey heard motion behind him. There was no choice but to ignore it, to hope that Venice would warn him if he was about to be attacked.

The entire process took less than twenty seconds, and then Geoffrey looked up to find that Alexander, Brit, and Venice had all surrounded him with drawn weapons, each having squared off against one of the other vampires in an effort to protect him.

Geoffrey picked up the now-unconscious pyromancer and threw him to one of his companions. Eyeing the dark-skinned vampire who seemed to be the nominal leader of the group, Geoffrey pointed to the unconscious form and tried to phrase his words in a way that someone as morally dead as Imastious might believe.

"He destroyed an asset that could have potentially been useful in the fight against those things."

THE GREATER DARKNESS

The other vampire opened his mouth to respond, but Geoffrey cut him off. "The Elders declared truce solely to avoid squandering resources and men that could otherwise be used to defeat creatures that want nothing more than to rip our hearts from our chests. As far as I'm concerned, that truce extends to humans that can be used to help us win this war."

Alexander stepped up next to Geoffrey and nodded. "The mentalist speaks the truth. Without those humans we would have died."

All seven remaining vampires stood poised and ready for conflict, but finally Geoffrey received a nod from the leader of the other group. "You've made an enemy here tonight, but that's his business to pursue once he awakes. We've no wish to die on your blades."

Geoffrey watched the three vampires carry their unconscious companion out of sight, and then he followed Alexander the other direction as the lights came back on. It was chilling to consider that the lights being off probably meant that the werewolf had been watching them from the darkness the entire time they'd been at each other's throats.

Once the quartet was far enough away from the scene of the fight to feel safe, Alexander turned to Geoffrey. "You did make an enemy there, no doubt about that, but you also just demonstrated the will required to enforce this treaty, a will that most of us 'peasants' haven't been sure our masters truly possessed."

Holding out his over-sized hand once again, Alexander smiled. "You'll have to watch your back somewhat, but I think you've made a fine start to this business."

Chapter 28

Geoffrey had spent the last two days worrying about how Imastious would respond to the fact that he'd assaulted another vampire for what most would consider no good reason.

There was a chance that Geoffrey would be able to convince Imastious that he'd been motivated by the kind of thing Alexander had keyed into. It was true that someone needed to demonstrate the willingness and ability to enforce the truce, but Imastious believing that his actions had been motivated by something other than concern for a 'mere' human seemed like a long shot.

He'd tried, but Geoffrey had found it nearly impossible to get the image of that burning police officer out of his mind. Almost as bad was the way that he couldn't seem to get the memory of Melody's words to leave him alone. He was only a few steps down the path he'd chosen and already his efforts seemed to be turning out in ways he hadn't wanted them to. He could only hope now that his attempt to right a small part of that wasn't going to cost him everything.

It appeared, however, that Imastious wasn't going to threaten him with death—at least not over what he'd done to the pyromancer.

Examining the younger vampire with cold eyes, Imastious sighed in resignation. "I examined your work on Scorch. While I don't for a second believe you pursued that course of action out of anything other than rage that he'd killed a human, I've decided it is useful for other vampires to look at you with more than a normal amount of respect and fear."

Relief nearly made Geoffrey's knees sag, but he forced himself to pay attention to what Imastious said next. "To that end, I made a quick trip to Scorch's residence, and strengthened the construct you built inside his mind. What you created was potent and inventive, but wouldn't have lasted more than a week or so. It will now last for a month, possibly two."

Geoffrey felt a brief pulse of satisfaction to know that anytime Scorch derived sadistic enjoyment from something over the next month that he'd be overcome by an intense bout of pain and sickness. His relief didn't stop Geoffrey from understanding Imastious' other message.

Geoffrey had proven stronger than Scorch, but Imastious was more powerful still. What

Geoffrey could do, Imastious could better by a factor of eight. Still, once word got out that Scorch hadn't recovered after a few days, people would start granting Geoffrey the kind of respect that would ensure no further violations of the truce, and that respect would only grow with each day that Scorch's punishment remained in effect.

Imastious studied Geoffrey for several seconds until he seemed to be satisfied that the message he'd delivered had indeed been understood and then pointed at a folder on the table before Geoffrey. Inside was a stack of photos displaying all of the carnage and destruction that they'd both come to associate with a werewolf attack.

"Another Elder?"

Geoffrey thought for a moment that Imastious was going to take exception to the casual way in which he'd just referred to the assassination, but the older vampire settled for letting his piercing gaze rest on his minion for several seconds. "Yes, it was. In this case Eculdes, along with a respectable number of his servants."

Geoffrey almost thought he detected a trace of fear in Imastious' voice, but he knew better than to let that thought make its way to his face. "Did they manage to kill any of their attackers?"

Imastious pointed to one of the pictures. "That man isn't a known vampire, and he was left relatively intact, so my suspicion is that he represents the first werewolf to be killed in an attack on an Elder."

Imastious recaptured Geoffrey's gaze. "I don't think you understand the worry these attacks are generating. There is extreme alarm at the highest levels of vampire society. Eculdes was surrounded by no less than eight men that we've identified so far, and he *may* have taken one of them with him."

Imastious gestured at the heavy concrete bunker walls surrounding them. "Most of the Elders are currently hiding below ground trying to avoid being killed. Every vampire knows there is a chance he'll be assassinated by a rival, but the Elders are unaccustomed to death befalling their number in such a sudden, seemingly unstoppable manner. They are getting to the point where they will do almost anything to guarantee their safety."

Geoffrey nodded, still unsure what this had to do with him. All he could come up with was that his efforts hadn't been good enough and Imastious was going to threaten to kill him after all.

"You personally have been involved in killing three of these creatures. You probably are unaware of this fact, but those three, and the one that Eculdes may have accounted for, represent the only confirmed kills I'm aware of in the entire city."

It seemed impossible. There were supposedly dozens of patrols out in the city and Geoffrey couldn't believe that none of them had encountered a werewolf.

Imastious lifted a sheaf of papers from the table next to him and tossed it to Geoffrey. "That isn't to say that nobody has come up against the beasts. That is a list of the patrols that have been out this last week, and the results of their efforts. As you'll see, one patrol claims to have encountered a werewolf. They apparently had it on the ropes when it bowled one of them over and escaped. Some of them have wounds which would tend to confirm that they at least ran into a werewolf. Two of their number were killed in the battle. Three other patrols of varying sizes have been destroyed and their members were found dead with wounds consistent with those inflicted by werewolves."

Geoffrey was surprised to see Imastious rise and begin pacing. "You, on the other hand, especially after what you did to Scorch, are starting to look like some kind of miracle worker. You've touched the werewolves' minds and seem to have come away with an understanding of them that, while admittedly limited, is vastly superior to what anyone else can boast of at this point. As a result, the other Elders are starting to press for you to become our general in this little war. Obviously the presumption is that I can command you to give this effort your very best, and you'll do so in the name of self-interest."

Imastious' eyes came to rest on Geoffrey and he could feel the intensity of the Elder's gaze. "We both know that isn't necessarily the case. You have motivations and taboos which most of them don't begin to understand. Consequently, I'd like to offer you something that will motivate you to give this conflict your full attention."

Geoffrey's heart skipped a beat.

"If you are able to wage a successful campaign, I will grant you your freedom. I will also provide you with suitable resources with which to set yourself up as an Elder in this city, or continue your life elsewhere. I give you my word on it."

The negotiation process had taken several hours, and even after addressing every point Geoffrey could think of, he still felt as though there were hidden loopholes he hadn't covered, but he'd left with a spring in his step that hadn't been there a short time previously.

He now essentially had carte blanche with regards to waging the conflict with the werewolves. Imastious had committed his talents and resources to make sure that Geoffrey was given sufficient vampires to work with. If Imastious didn't manage to deliver the agreed-upon troops and Geoffrey failed as a result, he'd still been promised his freedom. Assuming he survived.

The difficult part now would be finding a way to defeat the werewolves.

Venice shifted slightly next to him as she adjusted the black, button-up shirt she'd worn out hunting that night.

"The Elders must be incredibly worried for Imastious to make you a deal like that."

Geoffrey nodded. "I suppose so, but I'm no closer to figuring out a strategy tonight than I was last night when we made the deal."

Picking up the folder Imastious had given Geoffrey from the table, Venice sighed. "I don't suppose that this is much help. There is almost too much here to make sense out of it. Any underlying pattern is drowned out by all of the rest of the information."

Leaning back against the sofa, Geoffrey closed his eyes and tried to force his mind to come up with the insights he needed. "Have there been any new developments since this was compiled?"

Venice leaned back and rested her head on Geoffrey's shoulder. If she was surprised that for once he didn't move away, she hid her feelings very well.

The slender vampire turned her head towards Geoffrey and whispered. "I love you."

When Geoffrey opened his mouth to respond, Venice put a finger to his lips. "You don't need to say anything. I know you worry the darkness inside me will keep us apart, but I also know you're starting to love me too. We'll just have to see what happens, and I'm fine with that."

Having said what she needed to say, Venice leaned back against the sofa once again and took a deep breath before continuing. As she started talking, Geoffrey wished for the hundredth time that things were easier. Everything would be so much clearer if Venice always behaved as the villain he'd first thought her to be, or if Melody never questioned what he had to do.

"There have been a few vampires killed recently who were either by themselves in their homes, or were serving as couriers for their masters."

Geoffrey shrugged. "That doesn't bode well for our continued survival, but it's simply the expected progression of what has been happening prior to this."

Venice nodded and then continued. "Indications are that there is a contingent of vampires and Elders who aren't satisfied with waiting while you come up with a plan. They are setting a trap which they hope to use to start thinning out the werewolf population."

It was actually a very good response to the situation. They'd never been able find the enemy, so the conflicts were always at a time and a place of the werewolves' choosing. The one that had attacked Geoffrey had overmatched him and he'd only survived because he'd been very lucky.

THE GREATER DARKNESS

Venice had to know that Geoffrey was on to something by the way his body had tensed up, but she remained silent, allowing him to follow whatever chain of thoughts he was pursuing to its conclusion rather than interrupting him.

Geoffrey continued to run through the fights so far. The werewolf that had attacked Alexander's people had overmatched them as well. If Venice and Geoffrey hadn't happened onto the fight when they had, there would have just been one more instance in Imastious' reports of a patrol being wiped out.

That was the pattern that he and Venice had been looking for. Every time the wolves had been beaten it had been because of an unexpected force that had been waiting in the wings to help. Every time there hadn't been some unexpected help, or a great deal of luck, the vampires had lost.

Geoffrey looked over at Venice with a new fire in his eyes. "Tell me about this trap."

"You're not going to like it."

Chapter 29

Venice had been right; Geoffrey didn't like the trap that had been laid at all.

The vampires had placed their trap in one of the nearly-abandoned areas at the edge of the island. That would help ensure that they weren't bothered by humans while waiting for werewolves to stumble into its jaws.

That didn't, however, explain the five people chained together where you'd expect to find the bait. Even when Venice had told Geoffrey that there'd been talk of doing exactly this, he hadn't wanted to believe her. Taking humans and biting them to infect them with the virus was terrible. Gambling so many lives on the slim chance that the fledgling vampires might serve as bait fit with the other kinds of things these people had already done, but it still seemed to Geoffrey as though they'd managed to descend to a new level of evil.

THE GREATER DARKNESS

As horrific as their idea of bait was, Geoffrey couldn't do anything about that right now. Instead he forced himself to focus on dealing with the larger issues. He needed to find the jaws to the trap.

Standing next to the bait had the desired effect. A pair of vampires quickly appeared out of the shadows with the obvious intent of forcing Geoffrey to leave. In hindsight, maybe he should have taken Venice's advice and brought some backup, but he hadn't wanted to force a confrontation.

Scorch looked at Geoffrey with hatred in his eyes, but it was the second vampire, an emaciated, dark-haired male, who did the initial speaking.

"Ah, Geoffrey, while we are of course pleased that you would come down and bless our effort with the aura of your legitimacy, we have to ask that you come with us. It's vital that the bait be left unattended so as to not give away the trap."

Bile burned the back of Geoffrey's throat at the barely hidden venom behind the other's tone, but he reminded himself that he had a job to do. "Due to some unexplained oversight, I was not provided the details of your plan, and I've consequently come by to ratify its design. I can't have it resulting in a needless loss of vampires who could otherwise be used to combat the creatures."

Scorch broke in now, all but hissing with rage. "You have no power here, and no right to stick your nose in this. Some of the masters may have fallen in line with the idea of you as some kind of martial hero, but there are enough who don't feel that way for us to carry this out without having to go to you with hat in hands for additional warriors."

Geoffrey opened his mouth to respond, but the second vampire shook his head while fondling the hilt of his weapon. "I really think it would be best if you just left."

A hundred different responses flowed through Geoffrey's mind, but none of them would buy him anything, so he simply backed away, turning and walking quickly once he was out of sight. There wasn't anything he could have done to save them without forcing some kind of violent confrontation.

Geoffrey was no more than a block and a half away when the city lights to the left of him dimmed and flickered. It looked like nearly three blocks had died, which made the situation even more dire than he'd expected. It would take more than just two or three werewolves to drive that kind of blackout. They must have sensed the vampires waiting in ambush, as well as the bait.

Terror clawed at Geoffrey's mind as he realized he might be close enough for them to sense him, but he forced it down and broke into a run.

A host of questions clawed at Geoffrey's mind. Would three blocks be enough? Four blocks? What would happen after they killed the vampires hiding in ambush? Would they stay to rend and celebrate or would they disperse back into the night? Most important of all, what were their chances of finding him before he made it somewhere safe?

Geoffrey considered running to a subway entrance, but discarded the option as he realized that a blackout like what he'd just seen would bring the whole system to a halt. A taxi might be an option if he saw one around this late, but it was a long shot. He'd have to plan as though he'd be escaping entirely on foot.

Five minutes passed as Geoffrey forced himself to push on through exhaustion which was inspired as much by terror as it was by exertion. Just as the vampire began to think that he might be able to slow his pace to something he could sustain longer, he heard a howl behind him and turned to see lights flickering ominously several blocks back.

It had taken less than five minutes for the werewolves to find the vampires, kill them and then pick up his trail.

Geoffrey felt a growing pressure on his left. The lights in that direction were turning unsteady, so he veered to the right and kept running. At this point his best bet was just to hope that he stumbled into one of the other vampire patrols.

The chase continued for two more miles, by which time Geoffrey had a strong suspicion he was being herded. He just didn't know why.

The werewolves hadn't ever demonstrated that kind of intelligence before. It didn't make sense for them to want him in one particular place when they killed him. It was always possible that they were just enjoying the chase, but if it were as simple as that, why would it matter where he went?

Casting about for what lay in the path the werewolves seemed to want him to take, the vampire felt his blood run cold as he realized he was headed almost straight to Melody's. The recurring feeling of being watched hadn't been vampires. That was why the power went out while he was at her apartment. They knew about her.

Frantic with worry for Melody, Geoffrey tried a number of times to escape the werewolves. The last mile to Melody's building was a thing of nightmare as each of the vampire's attempts was frustrated.

The creatures weren't particularly skilled in their efforts to drive Geoffrey before them. Several times it seemed as though one or more of the beasts were going to either abandon the chase, or attack Geoffrey before they got to Melody's, but always at the last second, a werewolf appeared at the appropriate place to keep the vampire from escaping.

Turning onto Melody's block, Geoffrey felt his heart sink. The top few floors were dark; there was only one possible conclusion. There was already one of them up at the top of the building.

Sprinting up the stairs through an eerie, half-alive darkness, the vampire heard a scream just before he burst into the hallway. The door to Melody's apartment, locks and all, was torn off of its hinges by a single, desperation-fueled kick, and then Geoffrey was inside looking at a scene from his nightmares.

The werewolf holding Melody's still, bloodied body turned towards Geoffrey and looked at him with an intelligence he'd never seen in any of the other creatures he'd fought. Waving the limp body before him like a shield, the werewolf paused to howl its challenge before leaping out the remnants of the window it had used to force its way in. Geoffrey stumbled to the window, but the beast had already disappeared, still carrying its grisly burden, and Geoffrey numbly collapsed to the floor.

Chapter 30

Something inside Geoffrey hurt, but he ignored it as he bowed to Imastious and respectfully waited for the Elder to initiate conversation. The pain wasn't physical. There wasn't anything he could do about it. Nothing except avenge Melody and her mother by killing as many of the beasts as possible.

"Allowing those opposed to your leadership to design that failed trap was a true masterstroke, my child. In a single move you allowed those beasts to eliminate our opposition. All indications are that no fewer than twenty vampires were killed when the werewolves attacked the northern prong of the trap rather than pursuing the bait they'd placed in the center."

Geoffrey knew that he should be worrying about the loss of fighting effectiveness those vampires represented, but he couldn't seem to conjure any sort of feeling right now. He couldn't afford to break down, couldn't afford to let himself feel anything until this was all over.

Imastious seemed to take Geoffrey's lack of emotion as a positive sign and smiled. No doubt he figured it for proof that Geoffrey had started to leave behind his troublesome worries about the right or wrong of things.

"Casualties among those involved in the trap would have been even higher, but apparently after the surviving vampires scattered, five or six of the creatures abandoned the pursuit for some reason."

Geoffrey pulled out a set of diagrams which he hoped adequately described his plan and passed them to Imastious. "Although their plan didn't work, I believe that a trap is the correct method to try and break our opponents."

Imastious looked the plan over for several minutes and then looked up with what appeared to be eagerness. "Very good. By positioning small groups along the periphery of the trap, you've created the perfect bait."

Nodding, Geoffrey pointed at the four perimeter groups. "The werewolves appear to have the advantage in that they choose the time of any attacks, and they have been quite careful to make sure they only attack in numbers sufficient to kill whatever concentration of vampires they encounter. Whether this is an instinctive response or effected by some level of intelligence shouldn't really matter for our purposes."

Withered hands turned to the next sketch. "Once engaged, you'll have them pull back towards the main body of vampires, which should be beyond the beast's ability to initially sense."

Indicating groups positioned between the main force and the perimeter groups, Geoffrey nodded again. "The other thing that struck me about these creatures is that they don't appear to view humans as a legitimate threat, so these intermediate groups will consist of humans who shouldn't serve to scare away the werewolves, but who can change the balance of force relatively quickly once the engagement starts."

Imastious stacked the diagrams and turned his gaze back to Geoffrey. "What do you view as being the biggest risk with this plan?"

The younger vampire remained silent for a moment and then pointed to the main reserve still showing on the top sketch. "This represents your reserve against unexpected numbers of werewolves. If we misjudge the distance at which they can sense us, if they're actually smarter than we think, or if there just happens to be too many werewolves in a close proximity, the defenders might be swamped, resulting in substantial casualties."

Imastious shrugged. "That is a very real chance, but we can offset the latter risk, at least, by including most of the surviving Elders in that main group. They will dramatically increase the strength of the reserve. Convincing them will prove difficult, but should be doable if they are provided sufficient assurances against treachery."

Pausing for a moment in thought, Imastious looked at the top diagram again. "Do you have any set plans regarding which vampires are to be placed where?"

The shock and numbness had started to give way, and a black rage had settled over Geoffrey in the two days that had been required to make all of the arrangements for the trap. Venice had tried multiple times to convince Geoffrey to open up, but he didn't dare tell her the cause of his increased hatred towards the werewolves.

His mood wasn't helped by the way that even Venice seemed more than half convinced that he had indeed allowed Scorch's people to be butchered as some kind of Machiavellian plot. It had further cemented his hold over Alexander and the other vampires, who'd started looking at him like he was some kind of hero general. Alexander had actually looked at him with more respect rather than less once he'd had a chance to fully process the implications of what had happened.

Geoffrey had spent the early hours of the night wandering the industrial park, going from station to station ensuring that the various vampires or heavily-armed humans waiting at each were fully briefed on their various roles.

Everyone had seemed more or less up to speed, but Geoffrey was more and more convinced that he shouldn't have let Imastious convince him to put the vampires who'd been involved in the failed trap out on the perimeter. There was an undercurrent of something in those groups that he didn't like.

Putting the most battle-hardened veterans out on the edge had seemed smart at the time, but they all seemed convinced that Geoffrey had left them out there to die.

Venice, Alexander, and Brit had all followed Geoffrey, serving as bodyguards and a tangible sign of his authority over the various groups. Thankfully they'd all sensed enough of his mood to leave him more or less alone with his demons.

Somewhere along the way in the last forty-eight hours, it had been suggested that the humans be given crossbows rather than firearms, a suggestion Geoffrey had wholeheartedly approved. He'd picked the most deserted area of the city that anyone had been able to suggest and then Imastious had paid hefty bribes to make sure there would be a substantial delay to any police response. Changing the humans over to crossbows meant that there shouldn't be any gunshots to draw the kind of attention that would result in the dispatch being called in the first place.

Training the bruisers the vampires had turned up had been more difficult than Geoffrey had expected it to be. None of them had been particularly excited to learn how to use the ancient weapons but hopefully they would prove the equalizer his plan needed to succeed.

Once Geoffrey was satisfied with all the arrangements, he'd returned to the main group and tried to relax, but the presence of the Elders made that impossible. The host of cold, emotionless, dead eyes staring at him was almost enough to drive him back out to the perimeter, but that was one thing he couldn't do.

He couldn't let them think they'd run him off or the whole plan might come crashing down. In many ways it was built on the bluff that he was nearly an Elder in power and ability, one who had no real history of rivalry with anyone present. If that were to be taken away there was a very real risk that some of the Elders would quietly start defecting.

Geoffrey had just about decided that nothing was going to happen when the lights to the east started flickering. The vampires and humans around Geoffrey sprang to their feet and looked to Imastious who was currently assigned to run mental overwatch. The Elder's cold eyes swept the group and then nodded. "They're coming."

Waving everyone forward, Geoffrey broke into a trot that would quickly eat up the four blocks to the perimeter group without leaving him exhausted once he got there. A few seconds later, the group rounded a corner and was welcomed by a vista that made it seem as though hell had temporarily annexed the intersection.

He'd never in his worst dreams thought there might be so many werewolves in the city.

Werewolves seemed to be rushing in from everywhere, appearing as if from magic in the looming shadows cast by lights far enough away not to be disabled by such a large gathering of the creatures. Geoffrey had a split second to hope none of the humans or vampires would run, and then the battle caught him up.

Luckily, Venice, Alexander, and Brit had followed Geoffrey, or the first beast he encountered would have killed him. It was that much faster than any of the others they'd encountered so far. The werewolf charged Venice, who rolled out of the way taking a minor wound. Brit connected with a shallow slash as it went past.

An incredible sense of heat and the crackling of flames told Geoffrey that some team of vampires working with a pyromancer had managed to overcome the werewolf's ability to absorb their attack, and that he no longer had to worry about it attacking him from behind.

The next creature stopped to engage Geoffrey's team, and for several seconds it was all the vampires could do to avoid being torn apart by the beast. It was simply too powerful for them to overload its abilities.

A vicious hissing filled the air and a flight of crossbow quarrels sprouted from the beast at the same time that its absorption collapsed under pressure from another team of vampires, or possibly a single Elder.

Geoffrey's thoughts slipped into the werewolf's mind, and he acted on barely understood whispers of thought to score a number of strikes on its arms and legs.

Brit and Venice had their powers in play, and the creature moved slower now as it turned to concentrate on Geoffrey, who'd hurt it severely in just a matter of seconds.

Even being able to half sense the creature's plans, it was all Geoffrey could do to survive its full attention while Venice and Brit harassed it from the sides.

A backhand knocked Geoffrey to the ground and for a heartbeat he thought he was dead. Just before the killing blow landed, the creature collapsed to the ground, roaring in pain with Alexander's ax jutting out of the center of its back.

All of the werewolves seemed to be engaged by teams of vampires now. Many of them were falling to the beasts' superior speed and power, only to be replaced by the surviving members of teams that had managed to kill their original opponents.

As Geoffrey and the others ran to aid another team, a werewolf that had just managed to dispatch its opponents burst into flame, burning with the white-hot intensity of a blast furnace. It was welcome evidence that at least some of the Elders had survived the initial rush.

Here and there, flights of quarrels sliced through the night. The humans weren't skilled with the archaic weapons, but there were enough of them that a respectable number of hits were being accomplished with the needle-tipped projectiles that had been designed hundreds of years before to pierce armor. The sheer size of the werewolves served to protect their vitals as much as their amazingly durable flesh, but a few of them had fallen to the deadly weapons, and even when the humans didn't manage to kill a werewolf outright, the wounds helped slow the beasts.

The next werewolf Geoffrey's team faced off against had killed all but two of its vampire opponents. It managed to kill another before the five of them drove it back to a defensive stance.

It couldn't have taken more than another minute before the cumulative effect of all the small wounds the vampires were inflicting finally slowed the creature enough for Venice to hamstring it, but the nightmarish combination of dodging blows that could easily kill him, alternated with desperate strikes to score only slight wounds made the battle seem to stretch on for hours.

When the second werewolf was dispatched, Geoffrey looked up and realized the significance of the new set of flickering lights moving their way. For a second time Geoffrey was shocked. He'd been sure they must have the entire force of werewolves in the entire city engaged already, but instead there was a second force headed towards them.

The Elders were in the center of the melee now, presumably to reduce the range at which they had to use their powers. The fight shifted and surged around them, and occasionally the dark figures had to use physical force to defend themselves. Even so, they remained a cohesive group, and each time the leading figure pointed at a werewolf, it would suddenly burst into flame, or slow drastically enough for vengeful vampires to swarm it under.

It appeared, even with their considerable losses, that the vampires were in firm control of the battle until the second wave of werewolves arrived.

Geoffrey's team went from one opponent to the next, often gaining a member or two, only to lose them or others to the razor-sharp claws that struck home with increasing frequently as exhaustion slowed the vampires. As Geoffrey's physical body became more and more tired, he pushed his mind harder in an attempt to make up for his weakness. Alien thoughts began to make more sense, and in one instance he was even able to momentarily overwhelm the mind of the creature before him, causing a brief pause that was all his companions needed to mortally wound the confused werewolf.

Brit, slowed by exhaustion, was struck down by their next opponent just before her remaining teammates were able to bring the beast down.

Their number reduced to four once again, Alexander proceeded to take insane risks in an effort to take out the next werewolf that attacked them. The massive vampire darted in and out with a speed that seemed to defy belief, providing the rest of the group with opportunity after opportunity to wound their adversary.

The odds finally caught up with Alexander, and as he sank his ax into the creature's arm, it brought its other hand around and slashed him across the chest. The rage which had given way to exhaustion flared again inside Geoffrey and he poured his hatred and anger into one alien mind after another, slowing the werewolves as he burned up what remained of his strength. When Geoffrey finally came back to himself, he saw that a knot of vampires surrounded the last two werewolves, which were quickly cut down.

Exhaustion nearly robbed him of his ability to stand, but Geoffrey maintained his feet, mindful of the need to appear strong. A terrible scene of death and wreckage surrounded him, but Geoffrey forced it from his mind as he walked towards the knot of Elders.

A mind stressed beyond its capabilities was more than capable of hallucinating, of seeing things that were nothing less than impossible. For a split second, Geoffrey was convinced his mind had snapped. It wasn't his senses, though, that were doing the betraying, and he watched in astonishment as two-thirds of the dark figures turned on some unknown signal and cut the other masters down without warning.

Some of the minions of the fallen masters looked as though they might protest the treachery that had just occurred, but their numbers, already reduced by the failed trap from a few days before, had been further decimated in the battle. They quickly threw down their weapons and fell to their knees.

Geoffrey's mind seemed to shut down in disbelief, but his feet carried him the rest of the way to the surviving Elders, to Imastious, whom he somehow knew had orchestrated the betrayal.

Imastious looked Geoffrey over with the same cold eyes that had promised to release him a few days previously. "It looks as though your plan was a complete success. We've eliminated the backbone of the beasts."

As simply as that he'd delivered a powerful message. Imastious had promised to release Geoffrey just like he'd promised a truce between all of the Elders. Geoffrey was smart enough to know that Imastious had just told him precisely how far he could trust the promise he'd been given.

The dead gaze left Geoffrey for a second. "Well, General, I suppose you should probably see to our troops, don't you think?"

Chapter 31

Geoffrey packed the last of his meager possessions into a duffel bag he'd used when he'd changed apartments weeks ago, and then his heartbeat soared nervously as the locks on his door rattled. He turned just in time to see them rotate open, seemingly moving of their own accord.

The vampire wasn't sure if he was relieved it was Venice who had discovered his flight, rather than Imastious. It made no sense, but he almost would have preferred Imastious.

"Changing apartments?" Venice's tone was casual, but the glitter in her eyes revealed she was completely aware of what Geoffrey had in mind.

"You know that isn't the case."

The slender vampire nodded and then folded her arms over her snow-white blouse. "I figured that you'd be contemplating something like this.

Good thing I arrived in time to talk you out of it before you pissed away the goodwill you've just accrued with Imastious. He's really quite ecstatic about the coup he pulled off."

"You knew that his promise to let me go was worthless?"

Anger made Venice's pale cheeks flush for the first time Geoffrey could remember. "Of course I did. You would have known too if you'd stopped to think for half a second about what kind of a person he is. I thought about telling you, but you were focused on exactly what you needed to be focused on. We couldn't risk distracting you when it could mean the destruction of us all."

"Alexander knew too?"

Venice started pacing, apparently frustrated with his naivety. "Not all the details, but he saw the change come over you. We both knew anything less than your best effort might not be sufficient to save everyone."

Geoffrey was still glad Alexander's wounds hadn't been severe enough to kill him, but somehow it hurt as much as anything that the stocky vampire hadn't told him. He'd known the other man was a vampire and therefore subject to all of the normal darkness inside each of them, but he'd almost thought they were friends.

Shrugging, Geoffrey zipped up the duffel bag. "None of that matters now; you all did what you felt you had to, now it's my turn to do the same. I'm leaving."

Shaking her head, Venice positioned herself in front of the door. "Geoffrey, Imastious owns you. Haven't you wondered about your memory loss? He did it to you. He destroyed or suppressed everything to stop you from plotting to take his position. While he was in there, he conditioned you to make sure he could maintain control. How do you think we knew to find you in the church? It was a programmed response to your trying to run away. You can't trust your impulses; they'll just lead you back to him again and again."

It made perfect sense now that it had been pointed out to him. He idly wondered if his lack of ability to see it himself was also part of the conditioning.

Seeing that her words had hit Geoffrey with an almost physical impact, Venice continued on. "If Imastious knew that I'd told you that he'd kill me, but there's another way. Alexander is the key. You and I aren't strong enough to take Imastious by ourselves, but now you're stronger even than you were before he wiped your memories. With Alexander's help I think we can do it."

Geoffrey shook his head, but Venice didn't give him a chance. "I know. Alexander could sell us out to Imastious, but he won't. After last week he all but worships the ground you walk on. Think about it, Geoffrey, we'd be free. No more Imastious to make you do things you don't want to do."

THE GREATER DARKNESS

"How long would it be until another Elder pulled us into his snare? Or until Alexander needed our help with something that was wrong? No, Melody was right. Fighting evil in the service of evil is still evil. The only true way to achieve good is to do it when you aren't under evil's thrall."

Venice's eyes became unreadable. "Who is…never mind, it isn't important. I can't let you go. He'll kill me for not trying to stop you."

"He doesn't have to know."

"He'll know. For something like this he'll drag me in and rape my mind. I won't be subject to that again. There's too much at risk now."

Tears started to gather in Geoffrey's eyes. "You could run away too."

Venice's laugh was a bitter thing. "You won't let me come with you, I can see that in your eyes, and I can't make it on my own. I don't have your ability to alter people's thoughts and memories to protect myself."

She was right. If he let her accompany him eventually he'd be party to another murder. The darkness inside her was just too strong to allow any other outcome.

Geoffrey had come to the realization Venice had known all along. Eyes bright with unshed tears, she drew her katana from the sheath hidden by her leather trench coat.

"There has to be another way."

"No, Geoffrey, there isn't any other way."

Part of Geoffrey wanted to argue, wanted to find a way that didn't involve someone dying, but the rest of him seemed to act of its own accord. Before he knew it, his weapon was unsheathed and ready, his thoughts trickling out to probe Venice's defenses.

Venice might have attacked first, or maybe Geoffrey had wormed a probe far enough past her defenses to preempt her action. In the end it wasn't important. The battle whirled by in a flurry of flashing metal, with neither side gaining the advantage. Geoffrey's limbs soon moved with wooden slowness, executing techniques with nothing resembling his normal ability as exhaustion and Venice's gift robbed him of grace.

The only thing saving Geoffrey was the crack he'd created in Venice's mental defenses. Now a flood of memories poured into him from Venice. For a second he thought it was an unusual defense meant to overwhelm him and limit his ability to predict her actions.

His sense of self had nearly vanished under the assault, but he managed to hold onto his identity and even counter her attacks. The flood slowed to a trickle, picking up in vibrancy what it lost in volume. Pictures of a dark, brooding figure flashed across the link as Geoffrey parried a high attack and shuffled back out of the way.

Somehow they'd begun the practice pattern Venice had begun Geoffrey's training with.

THE GREATER DARKNESS

Weapons flashed with increasing quickness through the set techniques as the feelings and thoughts of the young woman that Venice had been when she was turned to a vampire settled into his mind.

The incredible loneliness and fear that her cruel master inspired had been offset to some extent by the aloof fellow slave's actions. If those actions had been sometimes tinged with malice and oftentimes been unpredictable and hurtful, they still represented the greatest kindness shown to Venice in her entire life.

The exchange of blows had reached the third practice pattern now, each technique coming without conscious thought, as Venice shared the events that led her from the innocent she had been to the hardened killer she'd become, and then suddenly her blade wasn't where it was supposed to be. Geoffrey's stab caught Venice in the chest, parting soft flesh in an action that couldn't be taken back.

The scream that burst from Geoffrey as Venice's weapon fell to the ground was something made terrible by the loss of innocence he'd just witnessed, and he caught her as she crumpled to the ground.

"It was for you." The words came out as the barest shadow of a whisper, but they bubbled to the surface of Venice's mind where Geoffrey could see them, so it didn't matter. "It was all for you."

"I know, I know it was."

"You and..."

The tears that Geoffrey had somehow been storing since the day that Venice had been turned spilled out in a hot flow, and he held her until long after eyes that had regained some of the innocence they had lost long ago, dimmed.

The train was just like any other headed west. The passengers were eminently normal, all restless to be done with the endless series of transfers, all wishing they'd already covered the countless miles to their destination. There was one passenger with the faintest aura of *different* about him, but he went unnoticed as he moved about his fellows, stopping for a while here and there before moving to the next car with feet that seemed to grow heavier as his journey progressed.

Despite the remarkable company, the trip was something from a storybook. Passenger after passenger found tears in their eyes as they remembered old friends they'd lost touch with. Others contemplated estranged family members, and remembered all the things they'd personally done to contribute to the hatred now walling them away from their loved ones. In another time and place, surrounded by strangers, it might have seemed odd to make the call required to apologize and reconcile. Today that somehow didn't seem important; maybe because those same strangers were in the middle of patching marriages that had been on the verge of collapse. Watching relationships come alive once again with shared purpose and mutual respect, it seemed only natural to heal their own flagging friendships.

The barriers that we all create to shelter our vulnerable parts from each other came down that day, and strangers became fast friends.

Nobody noticed when a weary figure stumbled off the train at a routine stop, but they all felt a change. It was universally dismissed out of habit, but the nagging feeling that something important had just happened wasn't quite so easily forgotten.

Author's Note

I'm glad that you made it all of the way to the end, and I very much hope that you've enjoyed the first installation of Geoffrey's story. Eldon Murphy is actually an 'open' pen name for Dean Murray. I chose to release The Greater Darkness under a pen name because it is a tad darker than the stuff that I usually write under the Dean Murray name. Think PG-13 still, but more PG-13 'heavy' than PG-13 'light.' The Greater Darkness is actually one of the very first novels I ever wrote and I set it in what I'm calling my 'Reflections' universe, basically a modern-day world with vampires, werewolves, shape shifters and other assorted supernatural elements.

I've already got the material mapped out in my head for at least a couple more novels including Geoffrey in some form or fashion, but before I ever got started on them I got sucked into two other universes. The Guadel Chronicles is epic fantasy, and may or may not be the kind of thing that you're interested in trying out, but the other series so far features different characters but is also set in my Reflections universe. I will match the two of the universes up (have the characters meet and interact) at some point in the future, and in fact I've start laying some of the more obvious groundwork for that in a short story called *Intrusion*, and in the new Reflections novel that I'll be releasing around Christmas time in 2012.

I'm very excited at the trip that all of these characters are going to go on over the next few years, so I hope that you'll go check out *Torn, Broken, Splintered* and the rest of the Reflections novels (written by Dean Murray) so that you can join in the ride. I'll put a short description of each of them a little further down after the acknowledgements.

You may want to check out my blog, deanwrites.com. I've got a reading order for the Reflections Universe (there are currently three different 'start' points for the series) posted there along with semi-regular updates on when to expect new releases and a link that will sign you up for my mailing list (so you get a reminder when a new book is released).

Thanks for giving *The Greater Darkness* a try—I hope you'll tell your friends and family how much you enjoyed it and if you've got a minute, please consider leaving a review to help others decide whether or not Geoffrey's story might be something that they'd be interested in.

About the Author

Eldon Murphy is an open pen name for Dean Murray, a prolific author with dozens of titles across multiple pen names and more than half a million copies of his work currently in circulation.

Dean started reading seriously in the second grade due to a competition and has spent most of the subsequent three decades lost in other people's worlds.

Things worsened, or improved depending on your point of view, when he first started experimenting with writing while finishing up his accounting degree. These days Dean has a wonderful wife and two lovely daughters to keep him more grounded than he used to be, but the idea of bringing others along with him as he meets interesting new people in universes nobody else has ever seen drags him back to his computer on a regular basis.

Keep up to speed on Eldon's/Dean's latest projects at deanwrites.com.

Acknowledgements

I want to express a big helping of thanks to Dana Marchenko, RJ Locksley and Amy Jirsa-Smith for editing and proofing help, and my advance readers (Mom and Dad, Shalese, Matthew, Mark, Mimi, Kim, Jenine, Janelle, Mei and Heather) for some great finds. Any errors you might have found are probably a case of me being stubborn and ignoring their advice.

I also greatly appreciate Katie Jane's work on the cover. I'm tickled pink with how it turned out and can't wait to get more books done so that I can see what else she cooks up.

Lastly, I need to say a final word of thanks to my wife and daughters who let me jump into this writing thing with both feet and then put up with me being locked away in my office for long hours instead of spending as much time playing with them.

The Darkness Mirrored

Warrior, werewolf killer, slave, lover... vampire...murderer. Geoffrey was all of those things.

He killed hundreds—possibly even thousands—of people without a single regret, but that's only part of the truth.

For one person, Geoffrey was more than just a murderer—he was a father.

More than just an orphan Geoffrey took in off the streets, Lucy became the woman Geoffrey sacrificed everything for.

This is Lucy's story.

Torn

Shape shifter Alec Graves has spent nearly a decade trying to keep his family from being drawn into open warfare with a larger pack. The new girl at school shouldn't matter, but the more he gets to know her, the more mysterious she becomes. Worse, she seems to know things she shouldn't about his shadowy world.

Is she an unfortunate victim or bait designed to draw him into a fatal misstep? If she's a victim, then he's running out of time to save her. If she's bait, then his attraction to her will pull him into a fight that'll cost him everything.

Reborn

True love never dies.

A new arrival at Selene's high school is about to turn her entire world upside down. She's never met anyone so attractive—or so mysterious—before this, but Jace's unyielding insistence that they've known each other for decades can't be denied—not given how familiar he feels to her.

In the hidden world of gods and fairies what you don't know can get you killed faster than anything else and only those you love have any chance of saving you.

The Society

People need to be monitored, or they'll repeat the mistakes of the Desolation, a centuries-old war that killed billions of people and destroyed civilization.

Skye is part of the Society, the hi-tech, nanite-endowed group responsible for making sure that the millions of surviving people—grubbers—are confined to the ancient, decaying cities where they can be watched to ensure they aren't redeveloping the weapons technology that came so close to extinguishing life on the planet.

When the Society's monitoring programs pick up troubling developments in one of the grubber cities, Skye is ordered in to deal with the man responsible, but what—and who—she finds once she arrives will change everything.

Frozen Prospects

The invitation to join the secretive Guadel should have been the fulfillment of dreams Va'del didn't even realize he had. When his sponsors are killed in an ambush a short time later, he instead finds his probationary status revoked, and becomes a pawn between various factions inside the Guadel ruling body.

Jain's never known any life but that of a Guadel in training. She'd thought herself reconciled to the idea of a loveless marriage for the good of her people, but meeting Va'del changes everything. Their growing attraction flies against hundreds of years of precedent, but as wide-spread attacks threaten their world, the Guadel have no choice but to use even Jain and Va'del in their fight for survival.